# TEMPT ME

# TEMPT ME

The Wolf Hotel #1

K.A.TUCKER

ISBN 978-1-990105-04-3 (ebook)
ISBN 978-1-777202-75-0 (KDP paperback)
ISBN 978-1-990105-36-4 (Ingram Paperback)

Editing by Hot Tree Editing

Cover design by Shanoff Designs

Published by K.A. Tucker Books Ltd.

# *one*

**F***ebruary*

"I didn't mean for it to happen, Abigail. I swear!"

"You didn't mean for it to happen! You didn't mean to put your..." My words fall apart with my sobs. I can barely see Jed's face through my tears. Tears that haven't stopped since I ran for my dorm room earlier today. Tears that have left my skin raw and tight. And every time I think I'm all cried out, the image of Jed and *her* flashes inside my head and a fresh wave hits.

I wipe my dripping nose against my sweatshirt sleeve. I'm far past the point of caring what I look like. "Who is she, anyway?"

"Nobody important." He brushes his own tears away with his palm and then reaches for my face, cupping my cheeks. "You are my whole life. You've *always* been my whole life. Always! You know that, right? Tell me you know that!"

I swallow against the sharp knot lodged in my throat but

it doesn't budge. I *knew* that. Up until today. "Then why would you break my heart?"

His handsome face flinches as if I'd slapped him. Something I wish I had the nerve to do. "You weren't supposed to find out."

*Oh my God!* "That makes it better?"

"No, that's not what I'm saying." He hangs his head for a moment. "Look, we're getting married next year and then it's just you and me. It's been just you and me for *all* these years. And," he swallows, hesitates, "this is something I've been thinking about. A lot, lately."

"About cheating on me?"

"No! About, you know..." He winces. "Sex."

*That's* what this is all about? "Why didn't you tell me? I would have—"

"No, Abigail." Jed's face is suddenly stern. "You and me, we're doin' it the right way by waiting until we're man and wife. You're so innocent. So pure." He leans forward, pressing his forehead against mine. "It means everything to me that you'll give that to me on our wedding night. But"—a sheepish look overtakes his face—"I'm a guy. It's different for me."

"How is it different?" Who is this person sitting in front of me?

"Because we're weak! This is something I need to do. I need to get this out of my system, or I'm afraid I'll make a mistake down the road, when it *really* matters. Trust me on this one. You don't want me straying later on, when we have kids, do you?"

I'm listening, but I'm not believing these words coming out of Jed's mouth. "So we're breaking up?"

"No." He frowns. "Not exactly. We're taking a little breather, okay? Just until I can get my head on straight. But we're meant to be, you and me." He brushes strands of hair off my face, like he's done a thousand times. "I'll come back to you. I promise."

I'm so angry and hurt, I can't even face him anymore, so I fix my eyes on the small gumball machine promise ring he gave me on my sixteenth birthday, my sobs drowning out the rest of his words.

~

*April*

"Look directly into the camera when you answer the questions," the woman commands, her cold blue irises piercing behind a pair of trendy horn-rimmed glasses. Between those, her honey-blonde bun, the fitted black business suit and four-inch heels, she could pass for one of those librarian/strippers instead of a corporate recruiter.

I adjust my practical gold-wire-framed round spectacles. "Okay."

She readies the iPhone sitting in the stand for taping while I fidget on my stool, tucking wayward strands of my ginger hair behind my ear and smoothing the wrinkles from my shirt. I didn't come dressed for a videotaped interview. I figured this job fair would be like any other; I'd wander by some basic booths, collect a few pamphlets, and talk to representatives who want to be anywhere but a Chicago library on a Saturday.

For the most part, that's what it is. But the booth for Wolf Hotels is different. It's three times the size of the others, with sharply-dressed recruiters and an on-site interviewing station behind a screen, to help speed up the hiring process for those who meet the basic criteria.

And the only reason I made the basic criteria is because

I lied on the paper application that I filled out twenty minutes ago. Now I'm petrified of getting caught.

"Full name, please."

I've always hated being on camera. I clear my throat nervously. "Abigail Mitchell. But I go by Abbi," I'm quick to add. My mama calls me Abigail, and everyone else from my hometown calls me Abigail because of my mama. I've never liked it.

The interviewer is stone-faced. She doesn't care what I go by. "The role that you're applying for?"

"Outdoor Maintenance and Landscaping?" I think that was the official title on the application form.

"And please describe your experience that will be invaluable to us, Abigail."

"It's Abbi." I force my biggest smile and hope my annoyance doesn't show on video when they play it back later. "Sure. Well, first off, I love the outdoors. I grew up on a farm and have spent years baling hay, throwing bags of grain, and hauling buckets of water for the animals. So don't worry, I'm plenty strong." People don't believe that I am. My slim five-foot-five stature is deceiving, but one look at my body in shorts and a tank will attest that I'm feminine but honed with muscle from long days on the Mitchell farm.

I've already provided all of this information on the handwritten application form, but I guess they want the live version as well. "I've run my own landscaping company for five years, operating out of Greenbank, Pennsylvania, maintaining commercial properties with excellence." I've been pulling dandelions and cutting grass around my podunk town every summer since I was fourteen. To call what I do "landscaping" is a farce. But if it gets me this job, far the hell away from my life, I'll say anything.

"Were any of these properties hotels?"

"Yes." Never say "no" in an interview. Always find a way to spin it into a yes.

"Please tell me about these hotels."

*Crap*. And there it is. I've never been a good liar. "It was just one, actually. It's called the Inn. It's...an upscale bed-and-breakfast." Three rooms in an old Victorian house, run by Perry and Wendy Rhodes. I hear one of the rooms is decorated with a cat theme. Cat wallpaper, cat pillows. Cats, everywhere.

By the way the woman's painted red lips are pressed together, I'm pretty sure my answer is not the one she was looking for. "Okay. Thank you. I also see here that you worked weekends serving customers at a place called the Pearl for several years."

"Yes. That's my aunt's restaurant. I'd help her out during the busy season." I hesitated about using Aunt May as a reference. I can't be sure she'll give me a glowing recommendation if it means I won't be coming back to Greenbank for the summer. Mama would have her skin if she ever found out she helped make that happen.

"What type of establishment is it?"

"A family restaurant."

"So, not fine dining?"

I sigh. "No. I wouldn't call it that." Slapping together hot turkey sandwiches and pouring Cokes from a fountain does not make for fine dining.

"And have you ever cleaned houses professionally... No," she says, seeing me shake my head fervently, my face twisting with disdain at even the suggestion. That means dealing with fitted sheets all day long, and that sounds like torture to me.

"I see you've also done receptionist work."

Finally, something I can answer truthfully and positively.

"Yes. I've worked part-time in my church's office for years. I still do, when I go home for the summer."

"What exactly did you do for them?"

"Answer phones and schedule appointments for the Reverend. I also balance the church's books and organize the annual Corn Roast weekend charity BBQ for our parish." Something I can't bring myself to do again this summer, but will be guilted into doing by my mama and the reverend, should I go back to Greenbank.

She scans my application. "I see you're in school right now." She pauses, and I realize that I'm supposed to answer her.

"Yes. I have one more year in a Bachelor of Arts degree." The right side of my face is burning from the heat of the lamp. I imagine this is what an interrogation feels like. How much longer is this going to take?

"Are you able to commit to the four-month contract, from May through August?"

"North Gate College starts in September and exams finish at the end of this month, so that won't be a problem."

She smiles. "Good. And what are your plans for after college, Abbi?"

My face falls before I'm able to control my expression. That question catches me off guard. She's talking about next summer, and all I can focus on is getting through today, tomorrow, and this summer. Ideally in Alaska.

Is this where I'm supposed to lie and say that I aspire for a career with Wolf Hotels? I debate my answer for a few heartbeats, and finally decide on the truth. "Honestly, I'm not sure anymore. I was supposed to get married and help run the family farm, but my fiancé and I are—" I stop myself with a deep breath and then an embarrassed little smile. So inappropriate for an interview. "My personal situation is in limbo," I say instead, my voice growing husky, my eyes burning with the threat of tears. It's all still too fresh, too raw. "I'll probably go back home. My family's there."

"And help run the farm?" Her eyes graze over me—over my thick braid that I can't help but toy with when I'm nervous, over my favorite royal-blue button-down that's probably been washed one too many times, over my generic jeans, and down to my Converse—and I know she's judging me. I sit up straighter, feeling more self-conscious than I already do being in front of a camera.

I look nothing like her, or any of the other recruiters here. They're all put together, with smooth, richly colored hair and perfectly painted faces. I don't wear much makeup; just a little lip gloss and, on occasion, shimmery pink nail polish. I don't use hairspray and not a drop of dye has ever touched my hair for fear that it'll make the color worse than it already is.

"Yes." That has always been the plan. But now I feel like I need to defend myself. I'm not just another farm girl, getting ready to bake pies and pop out little farm babies. "I started a side business making soaps, moisturizers, and essential oils a few years back. It's called Sage Oils. I'm going to focus on expanding that." Sage, after my favorite herb, though my products involve everything from mint to lavender to lemon. Up until this point, the bulk of my sales have been thanks to the annual Christmas bazaar and summer fair. I can't complain though; that money will pay for my flight to Homer, should Wolf hire me.

"My, you're quite the enterprising young woman. And so busy. Landscaping and soapmaking businesses, college, farming..." I can't read the woman's tone to tell if she's genuinely impressed. "And what do you do for enjoyment, Abbi?"

I bite my bottom lip to stop myself from saying "Umm" while I think. Wolf Hotels is one of the most posh lines of hotels in the world. I need to sound smart if I have a hope in hell of getting this job. "As you have noted, I'm quite busy with work and school. When I have free time, I spend it with my family, and with my church, solidifying my faith." Which is in some dicey water as of late. "I also volunteer at the local animal shelter, both here in Chicago as well as at home."

"So you like animals?"

"Yes!" I nod emphatically. "I'm excited to see Alaska's wilderness."

She offers me a tight smile. "Right. Last question. Why should we hire you to work at Wolf Cove in Alaska?"

I look down at the pamphlet in my hand—pictures of white-capped mountains, vast wilderness, and glacier valleys.

Thousands of miles of serenity, of nothingness.

Thousands of miles from my current life.

They don't want to listen to my sob story, and it's sure as hell not going to get me hired. I struggle to smile as I stare into the camera, silently pleading with my eyes to whoever is making the hiring decisions. "Because I'm smart, hard-working, diligent, and ethical. I respect people and I love a challenge. Plus, I've always wanted to visit Alaska, and this looks like an incredible once-in-a-lifetime opportunity." I clear my throat. "I have nothing to distract my focus. I will give Wolf Cove *everything* I have to offer this summer."

She presses a button and steps around. "Great. Thank you. We'll be in touch."

"When will you be making your decisions?" It's the beginning of April; I'd be flying out in four weeks if I get hired.

"Shortly. We've already filled many of the positions from our pool of current Wolf employees who are interested in the Alaska location. We're just plugging some last-minute holes with outside recruitment." She sticks my application into a red file folder. Is that the reject file?

"Do I have a chance? Honestly." I can't believe I asked that, but I have nothing left to lose.

"We tend to hire people who already have luxury hotel chain experience. But we'll be in touch." She stands there with her arm leading the way to the exit.

My shoulders sag. I force myself to leave before I beg her to put in a good word for me.

There's no way I'm getting this job.

# two

May

I inhale deeply, reveling in the crisp ocean air as land approaches ahead. Chicago was in the seventies when I left this morning. Two layovers, a flight delay, and fifteen hours later, the fifty-five degree day's high has dipped to low forties and I had to dig my winter jacket out of my suitcase.

"Have you ever been to Alaska before?" the captain, a soft-spoken white-haired man named John asks, his hands resting easily on the ferry's wheel.

I shake my head, my gaze drifting over the sea of evergreen and rock as far as the eye can see. We left the dock in Homer thirty minutes ago. It didn't seem like it would take that long to cross, but Kachemak Bay is vast and wide and unlike anything I've ever seen.

And on the other side of it is my home for the next four months.

I'm so glad I remembered to pop an Antivert an hour before boarding. I'd be puking over the rails by now had I not. Boats and I have never coexisted well.

"So, what made you come?" I can tell John likes to talk, as much for conversation as to assess the foreigners coming to his homeland.

"A brochure," I answer simply, honestly.

He chuckles. "Yeah, it'll do that, all right. Lures plenty of folk our way."

I smile, though his words resonate deep inside. It "lured" me. Yes, that's exactly what it did.

Frankly, the brochure didn't need to work too hard.

When things take an ugly turn, people are always saying they're going to pick up and move far away. Australia, France, anywhere that puts an ocean between them and their problems. Most don't ever act on that. I certainly had no intention of doing so.

And then I went to that job fair in the city library, more than a little panicked about what I was going to do this summer. Recruiters were peddling administrative and counselor positions, trade internships, day care. Nothing I was interested in. Plus, they were all local Chicago-based positions. The last thing I wanted to do was stay in Chicago for the summer. I needed to separate myself from it and its bitter memories, if for only a few months until school started again in the fall.

But the idea of going back to Pennsylvania, where everyone including the cows had heard the nitty-gritty details about my breakup with Jed, was even more unappealing.

That's what happens when you grow up in a small town and then go away to college with your high school sweetheart, who's also the reverend's son, who you were supposed to marry the summer after you both graduate college.

Who you've been saving yourself for.

Who you caught with his pants down and thrusting into some raven-haired jezebel.

And, while in the depths of despair, though you know better, you tell your upstanding, churchgoing mama, who is known around town as much for her raspberry pie as for her big mouth.

That scandal sure gave the folks of Greenbank something to talk about during Pennsylvania's long, cold winter. It's been months since D-Day, or what I like to call Dick Day, when I caught him. February 2, to be exact.

I'm sure tongues were wagging across pews during church service. When I visited over Easter weekend though, I got nothing but sympathetic nods and pats. Jed, sitting in the pew directly across from us, earned more than a few glowers. Not everyone shared those feelings, though. His father, Reverend Enderbey, decided that giving a sermon on man's weakness for carnal flesh and the need for forgiveness and understanding would be more appropriate than discussing the resurrection of Christ that day.

Much like Jed promised me, Reverend Enderbey has promised my parents that this is just a momentary blip in Jed's faith; that he's feeling confused and needs to sort out his priorities. He'll come back to me, after he's done sowing his wild oats.

Why do they all think I'll want to take him back?

He broke my heart that day, and has continued breaking it daily, every time I see him walking hand in hand around campus with *her*.

He's not just sowing wild oats. They're *dating* now.

So when I passed by the Wolf Hotels booth at the job fair a month ago and spotted the pamphlet with a beautiful vista of snow-capped mountains and forest, I immediately stopped and started asking questions, and within ten minutes I knew that Wolf Cove was my ticket away from sadness, temporarily at least. I just needed to get myself to Homer, Alaska. They'd provide transportation to the hotel, subsidized accommodations and meals onsite, and weekly transport to Homer, if needed, and in turn I'd work like a dog and keep my mind occupied.

The best part? It was almost 3,800 miles from everything I know.

It sounded perfect. And unattainable. I walked out of that interview feeling hopeless, assuming that there was no way I'd get the job.

And yet I'm standing here today. I call that divine intervention. God knew I needed this miracle.

It came in the form of a phone call a week after the interview, with an official offer for a position in the Landscaping and Maintenance crew. I screamed. I even shed a few happy tears, which was a nice change from all the sad tears I've spilled since February. Knowing that I could avoid Greenbank, Jed, and my family, that I would be leaving my dorm room the day after my last exam and hopping onto a plane... that's the only reason I've held it together this long.

The ferry turns left to run along the coastline, farther into the bay.

"What are those places, over there? Do people live out here?" I point toward the little huts speckling the shore, camouflaged within the trees.

"Nah. They're mostly lodges and cabin rentals."

I study the structures, like yurts on stilts overlooking the water. "They're nice. Rustic."

"They are, indeed."

"Not like Wolf Cove, though."

John chuckles softly, shaking his head. "Not quite."

If the pictures in the pamphlet are at all accurate. My

mama's convinced that it's all computer generated, that nothing that luxurious would exist up in Alaska. That I'll end up contracting West Nile from the thick fog of mosquitoes, or I'll wake up in the rickety shack that I'm sleeping in to find a bear gnawing on my leg.

To say Bernadette Mitchell is unhappy about this Alaska job is an understatement. At first she flat-out told me that I wasn't allowed to go. I hung up the phone on her that night, the first time I'd ever done that. Probably the first time *anyone's* ever had the nerve to hang up on a woman like her. I half expected her to drive the nine hours and slap me upside the head.

Two days later, after she'd cooled off, she called and tried to persuade me. I was making a grave mistake, leaving Greenbank and Jed. We'd be away from the chaos of Chicago and the temptations that made Jed stray. We'd have each other, day in and day out, and I could remind him of why we're so perfect together.

I know it's not going to be that simple.

So I dug my heels in. I've been "good girl Abbi" all my life, sitting next to my parents at church service every Sunday, keeping company with like-minded people, staying away from the "bad kids" who drank and smoked pot and had sex. Always listening to Mama.

Maybe if I'd just spread my legs for Jed, my heart wouldn't have been smashed into a thousand pieces.

While she's my mama and I know she wants what's best for me, she, too, thinks that Jed and I belong together, and that our reunion is inevitable, once he gets "the devil" out of his system. I had to bite my tongue before I pointed out to her that the girl currently sucking Jed's dick is a significant obstacle in this imminent reconciliation of ours.

I scan the approaching buildings, my excitement triumphing over my exhaustion. "Where is it?"

"Wolf Cove is just around the bend."

Wolf Cove Hotel in Wolf Cove, Alaska. "How do you go about renaming a cove, anyway?"

John chuckles softly again. He's such a pleasant man. "The cove has been Wolf Cove for hundreds of years now. The Wolf family has a lot of history up here, with the gold mines. That's where they made their first fortune. Though I'm sure they could afford to have it renamed, if it came to that. They're a successful lot. Generous, too."

Man, to be a part of that family. They must have a lot of money, to risk opening a location like this all the way up here, and set their employees up the way they're doing for us, and all the benefits. "Hey, thanks for coming back for me. I didn't want to stay in a motel." It's just John and me on the ferry, and a deck full of crates and supplies. He was kind enough to make another trip across the bay and pick me up after my flight delay. Apparently he carted a full load of college-aged employees over hours ago.

"We didn't want to leave you stranded. 'Specially on the first day. I woulda had to come back for the supplies first thing in the morning, anyway."

I glance at my watch with dismay. "I've missed the orientation session." It started at seven, almost an hour ago. The skies are deceptively light for this time of evening. "I can't believe how bright it still is."

"Wait 'til June."

"Less than five hours of darkness on the equinox, right?"

He grins. "Someone's been doin' her homework."

"I like to be prepared." The day I applied for the job, I ran home and researched Alaska late into the night instead of studying for my exams. The further I dug, the more excited I became, and the harder I prayed that I'd get the job.

"Well, I'm sure one of the ladies will be kind enough to fill you in on what you missed. They seemed like a nice group. Polite youngsters like yourself, for the most part anyway."

At twenty-one, it feels strange to be referred to as a "youngster," but I guess next to John, who's got to be pushing seventy, that's exactly what I am.

The ferry rounds the crop of small islands and turns toward the cove. John points to the massive building ahead. "And there's Wolf Cove Hotel."

My eyes widen. "Whoa. The brochure pictures weren't fake." And they don't do this place justice.

John chuckles again. "No, they certainly weren't."

I stare at it quietly, mesmerized. The main lodge towers over the water. Even from this distance, I can see that the lodge is grandiose in its design and massive in size. I can't make out the details to appreciate it yet, but there's no doubt it's something to be admired.

"They just made the finishing touches two weeks ago. Been working on it for almost three years, now."

"Is it still opening on Sunday?" Belinda, the woman who called to formally hire me, said that these first few days would be focused on training and last-minute preparations.

"I'll be ferrying in the first guests at noon. I've been bringin' employees in by the boatload over the last two days. There are a lot of you. A high staff-to-guest ratio, I heard someone say."

"How is the Wolf family going to make any money?"

"I'm guessing the twelve-hundred-dollar-a-night price tag will help."

My mouth drops open. "Who can afford that?" I barely

scraped together the eleven hundred I needed for my plane ticket here.

"What's that famous line from that movie? Oh, shucks. You may be too young to remember. The one with the baseball and all those cornfields. 'If you build it...'"

I smile. It's only my dad's favorite movie.

He winks.

We fall into a comfortable silence as we approach, and I realize that I've been rolling my promise ring around my finger unconsciously this entire time. It's been three months since Jed and I broke up and I haven't been able to bring myself to remove it. Now, I slip it off, letting the cheap metal rest in the palm of my hand. A part of me—the hurt, angry part—wants to toss it into the water and be done with it. A symbol of my faith in Jed.

But I can't bring myself to do it just yet. So, I slip the ring into my pocket and try to focus on the months to come.

# three

The farther into Wolf Cove Hotel I venture, the more enchanted I become.

Standing at the shoreline, the main lodge serves as a centerpiece, an enormous rustic building constructed of thick timbers and stone, but adorned with balconies and chandeliers, and entire walls made of glass, giving it an opulent feel. Crushed granite paths lit with coach lights lead guests past the boat docks and water sports equipment—more kayaks and canoes and paddle boats than I've ever seen. On the left side of the lodge are three cabins modeled after the main building, each one set high up on the rocks, shrouded by trees and adorned with balconies overlooking the water. John said those are the penthouse suites.

On the right are gardens to sit and ponder in, and beyond them are signs leading to Wolf Cove's own hiking trails. Miles of Alaskan wilderness to explore, according to the pamphlet.

I push through a heavy set of glass doors and revel in the warmth and smell of cedar in the grand lobby, offering a young woman who passes by me a nod and a smile. She returns it, zipping up her jacket before heading outside.

I've never been one to have a lot of friends. Just a few, really, mainly through church groups and study groups. The problem is they've all been "our" friends and now that Jed and I aren't together, I'm acutely aware of something missing when I see them.

So I've isolated myself from them over the past few months, staying in my dorm room, focusing on my studies. Most of them don't even know that I'm up here.

I'll make new friends here, I assure myself. Ones who know nothing about me, about my life back home. It's kind of refreshing, getting to be whoever I want to be. That's what I told myself this summer would be about. Answering to no one, including Mama. Not concerning myself with what people will think, or what they'll say, or weighing all my words and thoughts and decisions based on what would be considered appropriate by Jesus, the Reverend Enderbey, and my mama.

I've spent far too much time worrying about those things. Look where it has gotten me? Alone, while the guy I've loved for years is having, I'm sure, copious amounts of sex.

It's past nine in the evening now, and a few people mill around. The e-mail sent out last week says that I'm supposed to report to the main lodge check-in upon arrival, so I head toward the expansive and chic rustic desk, made of timber logs. A woman stands behind it, her eyes glued to the computer screen in front of her.

Not until I've approached do I see her name badge. It's Belinda, the woman I spoke with on the phone.

I smile. "Hi, Belinda." My mama taught me to always use a person's name when you can.

She looks up, her sharp gaze peering out from behind stylish red-framed glasses. I wish I had the guts to buy a pair of glasses like those. "Name, please?"

I remind myself that she probably spoke to hundreds of employees. She's not going to remember me. "Abbi Mitchell."

"Oh. Yes." She does a quick once-over of my bulky coat and what I'm sure is wild hair—wind and braids never play nice—before settling on my face. What is that I see flicker across her expression? Annoyance? Dislike? It vanishes too quickly for me to identify it. "You left me a message about missing the orientation session, didn't you?"

"Yes, that was me. My flight was delayed."

"Okay. Give me a minute." I use my shirt sleeve to clean the mist from my glasses as she pulls my file up, her nails tapping against the keyboard. "Okay, here we go. Abigail Mitchell."

"It's Abbi."

She flashes me a tight smile, such a contradiction to her soft, seductive voice. She's stunningly beautiful—her makeup flawless, her blonde hair cascading over her shoulder in movie-star smooth waves—but she's dressed inappropriately, in a tight black dress that barely covers her butt, her fingernails blood red and clawlike. My mama would turn her nose up at associating with this woman, and remind me never to dress like this if I want any respect. "Right. Welcome to Wolf Cove, Abbi."

I grin. "Thank you. It's beautiful here."

"Uh huh. So, Abbi, I see here that you were hired for Housekeeping and Guest Services."

"What?" I blurt. "No. Outdoor," I correct her.

"Well, it doesn't say that here. See?" She taps the screen with her nail. All of my information—my home address, social security number, even my picture—is there, as well as a line that, sure enough, reads position applied for "Housekeeping and Guest Services."

"That's got to be a mistake. When we spoke on the phone, you confirmed Outdoor." I can't spend the summer cleaning toilets. And bed sheets! I'll go crazy.

She frowns. At least, I think she frowns. Her forehead doesn't actually wrinkle. "A mistake like that would be a first for us."

"Well, can you fix it?" I'm mildly panicked now.

"I'll look into it." She doesn't sound at all concerned. "For now, please stand over there so we can take your picture."

I stifle my groan as I follow her direction and stand in front of a digital camera with a white screen set behind me.

"Smile," she says as the flash goes off, catching me off guard, taking what I'm sure is a horrible image. "Okay, here's your orientation package. Training begins tomorrow morning at 8:00 a.m. in the grand ballroom." She reaches behind the desk and hands me a canvas tote bag. "Inside you'll find all kinds of useful things like our employee guidelines handbook, information about the hotel and what our guests will expect of service; a complimentary bottle of bug spray, though the main guest areas are equipped with magnets to deal with them. A pocket-sized flashlight and a can of bear spray." She must see the flash of panic on my face because she quickly adds, "Don't worry; you won't need that within the main gates. The perimeter's wired with electric fencing. We want our guests to enjoy Alaska's wildlife through guided tours, not find it waiting for them as they step out the lodge doors."

I give a nervous laugh. "Okay. Good." I know the state

has plenty of black and brown bears, but I didn't think I'd have to worry about them here.

"And here." Her fingers are clicking furiously on her screen again and then, with a jangle of her key chain, she's unlocking a drawer and handing me an iPad and headset. "There's an orientation video loaded up on here. It has everything on it that you missed tonight. You can return the iPad to me here, tomorrow."

"Thank you."

"And if you hurry, you can still grab a bite to eat in the staff lodge. Go out these doors," her hand gestures to the left, "and follow the signs for the village."

"Great. Is that where I can make calls home?" I sent a quick text from Homer to let my parents know I landed, but my mama will be calling the front desk if I don't send exact coordinates for where she can find me should she need to.

"Yes. The bandwidth isn't enough for streaming videos, but you'll be able to do basic things like send e-mails and messages, check Facebook, that sort of thing." Belinda pulls the freshly printed card out of the printer and, after swiping it across a machine, sets it on the counter along with a lanyard and two other cards. "You need to wear your employee card at all times. This card is for the cafeteria." She taps the blue one. "Food is greatly subsidized for staff, and it's a no-cash system, so you can load money onto it or ask that a portion of your salary be garnered for it."

"Just like campus."

"Yup. And this other card gets you into your cabin. You're in cabin seven. The others are already here."

"How many others are there?"

"Six per cabin."

I let that news sink in. I haven't had a roommate since my first week of freshman year. That was a short-lived disaster. When I phoned my mama to tell her that the girl locked me out so she could smoke pot and have sex with her boyfriend, Mama quickly forked over another two thousand dollars and I snagged one of the last available private rooms. We're not poor, but my parents like to live frugally.

Either way, neither Mama nor her bank account will fix a problem with a shitty roommate here.

Or five shitty roommates, potentially.

I smile wide, another trick I've learned. The worse the situation, the bigger my smile needs to be. My face hurts from all the smiling I've done these past few months. "Okay, great. Thank you so much."

"I'm the hotel manager. You will be reporting in to Paige Warhill for the housekeeping department. But, if there's anything I can do to help, please let me know." That doesn't sound genuine.

Slinging my hiker's backpack over my shoulders, I remind her, "You'll look into my position, right?"

She's already typing away on the computer, her eyes on the screen. "Yes. Definitely."

~

"Jed came home today."

"That's great." No matter how hard I try to remove him from my daily—heck, hourly—thoughts, Mama's always good for reminding me. She was probably watching for his arrival since noon. We can see the Enderbeys's front porch from our kitchen window.

"Have you talked to him lately?"

"No." Not for nearly two months. For a while there, we kept in regular contact. That's what he wanted, to stay close friends. Ever since he started dating her though, we've been incommunicado.

"Well, he brought that trollop along with him. Can you believe that? I don't understand what he sees in her."

"What?" The word comes out like a hiss, the news a swift kick to my stomach, even all the way up in Alaska. I hadn't expected it so soon. Jed has officially brought *her* into our world. Into the place of our childhood, where we'd lie in the grass and decide what the clouds were shaped like, where we nursed an abandoned kitten back to health. We've lived next to Jed and his family for as long as I can remember. Jed and I used to swing on the tire tied to the oak tree and catch toads in the pond between our properties when we were little.

"But let's not worry too much. Reverend Enderbey thinks that a few days with his family and her together will prove to him that she doesn't belong in our lives."

*Our* lives.

I squeeze my eyes shut and will this nauseating churn in my stomach to go away. I don't want to talk, or think, or cry over Jed anymore. "I'm in cabin seven, if there's an emergency. I already sent you all the other information. Remember, I won't be carrying my cell phone around with me. It doesn't work well here, anyway."

"I don't like not being able to get hold of you when I need to, Abigail," she says in her typical stern voice. There is no other tone with her, even when she's happy. Right now, I'm guessing she's sitting at the harvest table in our kitchen, her floral robe stretched over her hefty frame, enjoying her coffee. The woman drinks coffee late into the night and then complains that she can't fall asleep.

"I'm going to be fine." *As long as you stop giving me updates about my ex and his new girlfriend.*

"Are you safe there?"

"Yes. They have security and cameras and, honestly, I don't think anyone is going to pay twelve hundred dollars a night to commit crimes."

"Rich people make for immoral people."

I roll my eyes, but only because she can't see me. She'd wallop me if she knew. For someone so forgiving of Jed, she sure is judgmental of everyone else.

"Do they have plumbing, at least?"

I gaze around the place and burst out with laughter. It's a log building with a cafeteria-style dining section on one side and several sectional couches on the other, with a mammoth two-sided stone fireplace situated in the center, the fire burning within giving off considerable heat. Beyond swinging doors in the back, I can hear dishes and cutlery clattering, and the occasional laugh. While there aren't crystal chandeliers, it's beyond simply "nice." "Yes, they have plumbing."

"Don't you be laughing at my concern for you," Mama scolds. "Are they feeding you well?"

I push the pan-seared chicken around on my plate. I'm not sure what the sauce is but it's delicious, as are the mashed potatoes and string beans. Then again, I'm not picky when it comes to food and I have a healthy appetite. Thank God I also have my father's high metabolism, otherwise I'd likely be waddling out of here by August. "I'm going to eat better here than all year on campus. I've gotta go now. I haven't even made it to my cabin yet."

"Are there a lot of people working there?" she asks, ignoring my attempt at a dismissal.

"Yes. Quite a few." The staff lodge looks like it could accommodate a hundred people. According to the video I just watched, Wolf Cove Hotel—an adults-only getaway—

has fifty guest rooms and three penthouse cabins available, so it's not nearly as big as a typical Wolf hotel. Apparently the one down in LA can accommodate 1,500 guests.

"What kind of people are there? Do any of them look like good Christians?"

"Yeah, they look like Jed."

"Abigail Margaret Mitchell. Are you gettin' smart with me?"

I sigh. "It feels like being at school. Everyone's young." And attractive, from what I've seen so far. I guess that makes sense though. A high-end hotel that's focused on aesthetics would extend that focus to what their staff looks like, right or wrong. "Mostly female."

"That's good." I hear the relief in her voice. I know what she's thinking. An all-female staff would be the best way to preserve Abbi's virtue for marriage. I don't know how many uncomfortable birds and bees and "wait until you're married" and "you'll get pregnant if he touches you" lectures I've had from my mama. The only reason she allowed me to go away to school is because it's a Christian college, Jed was going, and the Reverend's son can do no wrong in my parents' eyes.

Even though my eyes saw exactly the wrong he can do, firsthand.

"Okay." She sighs. "Remember that your father and I love you, and..." There's a long pause. "If this trip is what you need, then we support you."

I can almost hear her teeth grinding as she forces those words out. But I don't call her on it. I don't tell her that I'm old enough to make my own decisions without her approval. If giving it helps her sleep at night, so be it.

"Just don't forget who you are, and how you've been

raised. And no alcohol. Look what happened when Jed got mixed up in that stuff."

That's one of their excuses for what happened. Alcohol. Parties.

A.k.a. the devil.

"It's late. You best be goin' to bed now. And text Jed. Let him know you're safe. I'm sure he'd like to hear from you."

I have no intention of texting him now, knowing that *she's* there. "Right. Gotta go. Love you, Mama." I hang up and sigh.

"People been doin' that all day long," a voice says beside me.

I look over. A guy with dark skin and a cropped haircut wipes the table behind me, the chain that dangles from his pocket slapping against the wood. "Doing what? Telling their parents that they love them?"

"Sighing with relief as soon as they hang up. Though the 'I love you' is sweet."

I chuckle. "If their mamas are like my mama, then I believe it about the sighing."

He works on a spot of ketchup, his tattoos prominently displayed on his forearm. "Name's Miguel."

I offer him a polite smile. "I'm Abbi."

"Where you from, Abbi?"

"Pennsylvania, originally. Going to school in Chicago."

He takes a break from wiping to stand up straight. His chocolate eyes wander over the area. "Another beautiful college girl."

I blush at the compliment, though I don't know how valid it is. While I don't think I'm a complete troll, I've spent many years wishing away my dull ginger hair for blonde, my owlish hazel eyes for blue, and natural D-sized breasts for Bs, so it doesn't hurt so much when I run.

They say every girl battles self-doubt, feeling ugly or fat or undesirable. I never really did, because I always knew I was desirable to Jed. He told me so regularly.

But everything has changed. I'm becoming more and more self-conscious, more unsatisfied with myself.

"Where do you live, Miguel?"

"San Jose."

"Wow. That's a long way to travel for a job."

"And it's damn cold up here, too." He emphasizes the temperature change by shuddering, making me laugh.

"What made you come here to work then?"

"Me and my cousin are line cooks for the Wolf San Diego. This job came up and we were lookin' for something new. An experience, you know?"

"Yeah, I know." I stack my dishes onto my tray.

"And you can't beat the money. But," he chuckles as he continues wiping, "not sure this Mexican can handle remote wilderness and lack of basic communication with the outside world. It's a good thing they got me working the staff lodge where the Wi-Fi is. I may go loco otherwise." He collects my dirty plates for me. "Listen, anything you want, my sweet Abbi, you call my name and I'll hook you up."

"Thanks, Miguel."

He winks and then leaves with a slight swagger, the rag over his shoulder, humming to himself. He's obviously flirting with me, but it's the kind of casual flirting that I'll bet he's done with every female he's come across so far today. I'll bet there are plenty of sweet Saras and sweet Jennifers.

He's a good-looking guy, though too wiry and short for my taste, and I don't much care for tattoos. Still, it feels good, the attention, given where my confidence has sunk to over the past few months.

I like the classic tall, dark, and handsome. Jed fit that

mold, in my eyes, anyway. And I had his eyes without fail, too. They were glued to me. To my face, to my chest, to my ass. Just because we were choosing the parent-approved route of saving ourselves for marriage didn't mean we didn't suffer from normal teenager hormones.

He's palmed my breasts more times than I can count, playing with my erect nipples until they were sore. I wrapped my fist around his erection plenty, too. Only, it was always through his clothes. That was our rule—pants stayed on at all times. He came up with that rule. He said he wouldn't be able to control himself otherwise, and honestly I wasn't sure I would be able to either.

You can do a lot of things with clothes on. I loved teasing him, and I used to do so mercilessly, up until last summer when I teased him so much that he got mad and decided to teach me a lesson. That's why, in the barn behind my house, he held me down by my wrists, pressed himself between my legs and ground against me until I was begging him to take my pants off and touch me.

The perfect time for my father and the farmhand to walk in.

That Sunday at church, Jed's father gave a full-hour sermon on the sins of the flesh. Mama began prepping for a shotgun wedding, assuming I'd be delivering news of a future grandchild any day, even though I've been on birth control to help alleviate terrible menstrual cramps since I was seventeen. Boy, was getting her to agree to me on birth control a battle. My cries of pain were what finally softened her resolution.

Since last summer, we were both more considerate of each other, and maybe a little more careful, realizing exactly how wound up we could get. How easy it would be to ignore everything we've been taught to value and give in to human desires.

Jed ended up throwing it away anyway, only with someone else.

It's not until a tear lands on the iPad screen that I realize I'm sitting here in the staff lodge in Alaska, still crying over Jed. I give my eyes an angry rub and then, collecting my backpack and tote bag, head for cabin seven.

# *four*

The staff accommodations remind me of summer camp, with small rectangular cabins lined up in rows and narrow pathways weaving among them. There are at least fifteen, from what I can see.

I make my way toward cabin seven, where a faint glow of light fills the windows. Laughter explodes the moment I open the door.

"Hey!" The closest woman comes forward with a grin. She reaches for my tote bag with her free hand. Her other one is gripping a silver flask. "Someone's late to the party!"

I feel my face growing red, never one for overt attention. "My plane was delayed."

She grins wide, showing me a beautiful set of white teeth. She's extremely pretty, her pixie-cut hair framing her delicate features nicely. "No worries. I'm Autumn. You and I are bunkmates. Hope you don't mind being on the bottom."

"Not at all. I'm Abbi."

"You're going to get to know us all *really* well, and *really* fast."

"I see that." I do a quick scan of the cabin. Three sets of

twin bunkbeds, one on each wall, and a tiny powder room opposite me. I'm not sure how six women are going to handle being in here together, but I guess we'll manage.

Autumn waves a hand around the space. "Abbi, everyone. Everyone, Abbi."

I nervously make the rounds as the others take turns introducing themselves to me. All of them look to be in their midtwenties. In the bunkbed kitty-corner to us are Rachel and Katie—two giggly bottle-blondes from Tampa. Across from us, a brunette named Lorraine from Oregon is lying on the top with a magazine in hand. A stunning redhead from Atlanta named Tillie sits on the bottom. Her hair is a vibrant, deep orangey red instead of my flat, boring shade; a color I've wished for since I was twelve. And her voice... I could listen to her accent all day long.

"We have to share a dresser. We each get two drawers and can split the middle one with our unmentionables. I took the top because I'm so tall. I hope you don't mind," Autumn says with a sheepish smile. She's sweet. And she *is* tall. She must have at least five inches on me.

"I don't mind at all." I toss my backpack onto the floor, glad to have finally reached my bed. "What's this?" I ask, reaching for the thick black material hanging against the wall.

"Privacy curtains." Autumn yanks on it and the curtain flies across the track, around the bunkbed, closing us off from the others.

"Like a hospital." I guess some privacy is better than none.

"Yeah. Sort of." She giggles, tucking strands of cinnamon hair behind her ear. She throws the curtain back, until we're a part of the group again. "The toilet's there, and the showers are three buildings over, to the left. Thank God, because at five in the morning, it's a cold walk." She shudders. "At least they gave us robes."

"Any guesses on what Autumn was hired for?" Lorraine asks.

"Wilderness guide?" I guess, and everyone laughs.

"Close. Concierge. Trust me, you don't want me as a wilderness guide. Everyone would get eaten."

"Well, I for one am not leaving the confines of this beautiful property, so no one's gonna be eatin' this southern girl," Tillie purrs.

"Except maybe the big bad wolf," Autumn mocks, and they all explode with laughter. It must be an inside joke. Great. A few hours late and I'm already an outsider.

Autumn reaches out to grab my arm. "Have you seen him yet?"

I frown, confused. "Who? The big bad wolf?"

She laughs. "Henry Wolf, the owner."

*Oh.* I chuckle and shake my head.

Her eyes widen knowingly. "Just you wait. There isn't a warm-blooded female here who wouldn't spread her legs for that man's tongue."

My cheeks flush. Not that I haven't wondered what it would feel like to have a man—Jed—go down on me. I don't understand how I'll ever psych myself up to allowing it. I can't even touch myself without knowing that I'll feel sinful once my climax has come and gone. I clear my throat. "So the owner's here?" I never bothered to read up on the Wolf family, more interested in Alaska and the hotel itself.

"I saw him step out of his helicopter yesterday morning."

"You *think* you saw him," Rachel corrects.

"Oh, believe me, there's no mistaking that man." Autumn takes a swig from her flask. "He spoke at my grad ceremony two years ago. I guarantee you every woman's panties were soaked through by the end of it. Maybe a few men's, too."

Another round of laughter. I can feel my face turning red at the crassness of their conversation. Not that I don't think these things, or feel these things. I've just been taught never to discuss them openly like this. And my circle of friends at school doesn't talk like that either.

But if I'm going to be living and working with these ladies for the next few months, I probably should start getting used to this now.

I keep my hands busy and my eyes down as I unpack my backpack, filling the two bottom drawers with clothes for both warm and cold weather, while the girls discuss the owner.

"The exposé on him in Forbes says he made his first million when he was sixteen, on some stock investment."

"That's a crock. He was already born a millionaire. His grandparents owned an Alaskan gold mine."

"Yeah, but he didn't earn that. It was handed to him."

"I heard this property was given to him."

"And his brother."

"No, apparently it was all willed to him! Can you imagine the family feud over that?"

"It's not like his brother hasn't gotten enough. Well, maybe not yet. Their dad is still alive so he still technically owns this hotel."

"Do you know who he's dating? That Victoria's Secret model. What is her name? The one on the cover of the holiday edition."

"No. They broke up. She caught him in bed with two of her friends."

"So that means he's fair game."

"I heard he's super rigid and law-abiding, like his father. Honorable to a fault."

"No way. Word around the Wolf is that he's an arrogant, controlling prick who fucks women and then ditches them."

"A guy like that must go through women like underwear."

"I'll gladly be his underwear."

I listen to the back-and-forth chatter as I line my few basic toiletries up on top of the dresser. I unwrap the picture I brought of Mama and Dad and set it on the dresser, too. It's my favorite one of them, back when they were in high school, and she was trim enough that Dad could easily wrap his arms around her waist. They got married as soon as she finished high school, my mama graduating two years after my dad. I came along almost nine months to the day after their wedding.

I leave the picture of Jed and me in the bottom of my duffel bag. The one that I've thrown into the trash and then fished out at least a dozen times, the pathetic, emotional part of me unable to let go. We're sitting back-to-back on a bale of hay during the parade at the festival last summer, both smiling wide at the camera, happy as can be.

The only things I have left to put away are my bras, panties, and socks. They'll have to go in our shared drawer. I hope Autumn doesn't mind.

I slide open the drawer and stifle a gasp.

"I used a piece of cardboard to separate the space. You know, so we don't end up wearing each other's panties," Autumn says.

"Great. Thanks," I force out, my face burning as I study the long green dildo tucked into the side. When is she planning on using that? I could never bring myself to buy one, let alone bring it into a cabin with five other women!

I quickly empty the rest of my things out and slide the drawer shut, in case she forgot to hide it.

"So, is everyone getting together in the staff lodge tonight?" Tillie asks, watching herself in the mirror as she drags a scarlet lipstick over her bottom lip. I tried red lipstick on once, while getting dressed for Halloween, only to scrub it off minutes later. I looked like a clown. Tillie doesn't, though. She looks sultry.

"Yeah. May as well enjoy the fun now before they work us to the bone." Lorraine slides off her bunk and exchanges her magazine for a flask from the top drawer. I guess I missed the flask memo.

"Oh, please. I heard the massage therapists work six-hour shifts, max," Tillie scolds.

Lorraine wiggles her hands in the air. "My precious hands need rest."

"Those precious hands of yours better be giving my body a deep tissue massage after a long day of answering rich people's stupid questions," Autumn says, topping up her flask from a bottle of vodka. How much has she had? Is she always this friendly, or is she drunk? "Hey, Abbi, where'll you be working?"

"I'm supposed to be doing Outdoor, but they put me in Housekeeping."

"Oh, that's where I am! We can go to the training session tomorrow morning together. Us redheads need to stick together." Tillie's obviously happy about this. I hate to burst her bubble and tell her that I'm being transferred as soon as Belinda sorts things out, so I keep quiet and simply smile.

"That Outdoor crew is a bunch of male pervs, anyway. They all stood behind the yoga team this morning and watched them walk through their sessions," Rachel warns, peeling her shirt off. Katie follows suit. "We're gonna grab a quick shower. We'll meet you there, okay?"

"Sure thing. Hey, Abbi. You're coming, right?" Autumn zips up her vest.

I'm exhausted. I've barely slept in the last two weeks, thanks to finals and nervousness over this trip. Fear of the unknown. Normally, I'd curl up in bed with a good book and read until I drift off. I even loaded my e-reader with about fifty novels to get me through four months of summer nights and off-work hours.

They're all drinking, obviously, and not bothering to hide it. Back at college, people would have get-togethers, but they were tame and kept undercover as compared to what I've heard happens on other campuses.

This is all new to me.

But I want to have fun. Plus, it's the best way to keep my mind off Jed and *her* in Greenbank.

"Sure. Yes." They're the kind of girls I never hung out with in school, though sometimes I wondered what it'd be like, to be their friends; to be a part of the "in crowd."

"Great! The alcohol in the lodge is the only thing not subsidized, and it's super expensive, so you'll want to bring your own," Autumn warns, adding, "Unless you're made of money."

I bite my tongue before I admit to them that I don't drink. That I've never been drunk before in my life.

"Here. We can share until you can get to Homer to stock up next week." Tillie thrusts her flask in my hand.

What if I refuse? Will I be buying myself a ticket to loser town with them?

This feels like high school all over again.

"Hey, can you guys save us seats on that couch by the fire?" Rachel asks. She hooks her thumbs under her panties and pulls them until they drop to the ground. Both she and Katie stand front and center in the room, buck naked, seemingly without a care in the world.

On our campus, girls changed before heading to the shared bathrooms, and they covered themselves with towels.

Another thing I'm going to need to get used to.

I bring the flask to my mouth and take a big, wince-inducing gulp.

"So, you're an es... esthe..." I can't get the name out, and I'm not sure if it's because of the word or the alcohol that Tillie's been pumping into me.

"Esthetician. Yes." Katie giggles, flipping her silky mane of blonde hair over her shoulder. "I worked for the Hilton for a couple years, but I got laid off last December. Wolf hired me on contract for this job. We'll see how things go. Maybe I can get transferred to a permanent location when the season's over. They have hotels all over the world."

"What exactly does an esthetician do, again?" The closest place I've been to a beauty salon is Sheila's Clip 'N' Color shop on Main Street, back home. Sheila, my mama's childhood friend, has been trimming my hair for as long as I can remember.

"Anything related to beauty and grooming. That's me. That's what I love." All it takes is a once-over of her to see that. Perfectly shaped and painted nails, glowing skin, shaped brows. "Facials, chemical peels, mani-pedis, waxing, makeup application."

"I've never had *any* of those things done," I admit.

"Really?" Her blue eyes slide over my face. I don't think

she's all that surprised. "You should let me do your eyebrows. It takes, like, ten minutes. Tops."

"Does it hurt?" I glance around, suddenly embarrassed that someone can hear this conversation. I don't see that happening, though. The staff lodge has come alive with laughter and music as compared to an hour ago when I was cramming in dinner. A guy with a beanie sits by the fireplace, strumming an acoustic guitar. If there was a piano here, I'd try to match his notes. That's one thing that I will miss about not being back home for the summer: access to the piano in our family room. I've been playing since I was six; mostly church hymns though. Sometimes, when Old Mollie Simmons isn't feeling well, Reverend Enderbey asks me to play at Sunday service.

"Not really. Well, not your brows, anyway." She laughs. "It's so worth it. Especially for the summer, when you don't want to be worrying about stubble under your arms or bikini line. I can do it all for you, if you want. I do Rachel's all the time, and she loves it."

"But she's *bald* down... there," I blurt out, then blush because I've basically admitted to checking her out earlier.

"It's a good look, trust me. Just say the word and I'll clean you right up." Katie winks. "And guys love it, too."

Jed said he didn't understand why a woman would want to make herself look like a little girl. He thought he'd prefer some hair. I wonder if he still prefers that.

Then again, I'm not doing anything for Jed anymore. Still... "I'd have to be drunk."

She clanks her glass with my bottle of water. "Well then, cheers to that."

"Hey, Abbi. I'm turnin' in for the night. We have to be up in a few hours."

*Few hours?* "What time is it?" I squint at my watch; the hands are blurry.

"It's two. Training starts at nine, and if you don't want to wait in line for a shower, you need to get in there before seven."

Shit. How am I even still up? Especially with the time-zone change. "Okay. I'm coming."

Katie squeezes my thigh affectionately, the simple touch making me feel all the more comfortable in this group of strangers. "We're not too far behind you. Night."

I stand. And take several stumbling steps into a tall guy.

He wraps his arms around my waist to steady me, but he doesn't let go. "Whoa there, little lady. You okay?" He sounds like he's from down south. He has that charming southern drawl, but it's different from Tillie's.

I tip my head back and peer into smiling emerald-green eyes. "Yup. But thank you for saving me anyway."

He grins at me. "You sure are a cute little thing."

"I don't want to be cute," I grumble. "Cute gets left on the sides while "hot" gets bent over the couch by my boyfriend because he can't control himself."

That wasn't meant to be spoken out loud.

"Whoa." The guy holds his hands in the air, palms out. I peel myself away from him and stumble to Tillie, my face burning, whispering, "I blame you and your devil juice for this."

"I've got your water. You're gonna need it." She hooks an arm through mine and leads me out the doors and into the night.

"It's warmer out here than it was before. How did it get warmer?"

Her chuckles float into the darkness as we make our way

down the path, lit with lampposts every twenty feet or so. "The magic of Jim Beam, that's how."

"I love your accent. You know that? Like, I could kiss your accent if it were an actual thing. It's that hot. Isn't it beautiful out here? I mean," I let my head tip back, "look at this sky. You don't get this kind of sky just anywhere."

"I keep readin' about those northern lights. I'm hopin' to see them before I leave."

"Aurora Borealis," I murmur, closing my eyes and smiling, letting her lead me. That would be a sight.

Voices and laughter ahead catch my ear.

"Damn...," Tillie murmurs appreciatively, and I follow her eyes to see what has caught her attention. Three guys stroll out of the men's shower room, the white towels wrapped around their waists glowing in the dark. Each one of them is broad and hard and rippled with muscles.

I've only ever had eyes for Jed. Since February, I've had eyes for no one at all, uninterested in giving anyone a second's thought. Maybe it's the distance or the foreign world up here, or maybe it's the alcohol, but I am appreciating this view. The alcohol is definitely giving me the confidence to ogle them shamelessly.

"And that would be your Outdoor crew." A few steps closer, Tillie calls out with, "Good evenin', gentlemen. It's a little bit cold to be prancin' 'round half-naked, don't you think?"

The one closest to her, a blond with a casual swagger in his step, slows. "You offering to warm me up, Tillie?"

I guess they've already met.

"That's what the robes in your cabin are for." She flashes a deceptively sweet grin back at him. It must be a southern thing, because all the women from the south have that smile down pat.

He steps into her personal space—and, by default, mine, since our arms are still linked—but she stands her ground. "But you're so much warmer." His pretty blue eyes turn to settle on me. "And who's this lovely young lady?"

"This is Abbi from Pennsylvania."

"She another roommate?"

"That's right."

Turning his gaze back to Tillie, his eyes settling on her perky chest, he murmurs, "What I'd do to get into that cabin of yours."

I can't tell if he's talking about literally coming to our cabin, or if he's being figurative, but I do know that either way, it involves sex.

"Like a fox in a hen house, right? Y'all have a good night, now." Tillie leads me around him and farther down the path.

I glance over my shoulder and see them still watching us. The blond winks at me and I can't keep the stupid grin from taking over my face. "How do you know them?"

"I met Connor last night. He's as smooth as freshly churned butter, that one. Watch out for him, if they sort out your job situation. He'll charm the pants right off of you by lunch hour."

"Maybe that'd be a good thing. Jed is taking his pants off for the jezebel every day now and he wants me to cross my legs until he's ready to come back. Why should he get to have all the fun?"

"Jed? The ex-boyfriend?"

"Ex-fiancé." I'm still numb to the earned title of "ex." "He cheated on me and broke my heart, but I'm supposed to wait for him to get her out of his system. That's why I'm in Alaska." The knot that normally springs up in my throat at the mention of Jed stays down and out of sight for once. That's a relief. Maybe this is the trick to getting over him. Alcohol and scantily clad hunks.

"Ouch." She gives my arms a squeeze. "Well, don't you worry, hun. There is plenty to choose from here to make you forget about Jed and the jezebel."

"Jed and the jezebel. That could be the title of a play or something."

"I'd rather watch the 'Abbi Gets Even with A Hot Dude' play."

I laugh. Tillie's so sweet, and caring. I really like her. And I feel the urge to wrap my arms around her and give her a giant hug, so I do.

Her melodic laugh carries through the night. "Oh, dear Lord. Maybe not so much Jim Beam next time. You may regret it in the mornin'."

"But it'll have been worth it, because I had so much fun tonight." Mama clearly hasn't ever drunk before, because if she knew how much fun it is being drunk, she wouldn't want to deprive me of it. I've become so comfortable around the other Wolf staffers so quickly.

"Yeah, we'll see. Make sure you finish that water before bed. And maybe take some Advil."

Cabin seven arrives too soon, and I'm feeling alive for the first time in forever. "I'm going to hang out here for a few more minutes, enjoy the fresh air. It's helping me clear my head."

"All right. But be quiet when you stumble in, you hear? Lorraine went to bed already." Tillie swipes her key card and disappears inside.

I want to go for a walk. The staff village is behind the lodge and separated from the guest section by a thick cedar hedge and decorative fencing. It's a bit like a secret garden. I'd like to investigate it during the daylight. Right now, though, I wander along the path, pocket flashlight in hand in case I need it, my sneakers crunching beneath the gravel. Even in the middle of the night, it's beautiful. The paths are well lit, and there are security cameras everywhere. I feel safe. I'm not normally so comfortable with walking around alone at night. I'm sure once the hotel opens in a few days, I won't have the luxury of this absolute quiet.

A squirrel leaps from its branch and runs across the path in front of me, giving me a moment's pause. Do I have to worry about coming face-to-face with a wild animal? No. Belinda mentioned the electric fences around the perimeter.

I make my way past the hedge and over to the main guest area, eyeing the honeycomb of balconies above me. Each will be alive with guests soon. Apparently they all have hot tubs. I've never been in a hot tub before. These ones are for guests only, though. As are both the indoor and outdoor pools, and the hot springs. Basically it sounds like the only thing the staff is allowed to swim in is the bay, at the small staff beach I haven't yet seen.

I wonder how cold the water is. Is it warmer than the air?

I could dip my fingers in and check...

Before I can think it through, I turn down the path toward the docks that I arrived on earlier, stumbling over a rock before I manage to regain my footing. I'm drunk. I need to be more careful if I'm going near the water.

The dock at night is picturesque, marked at the edges with lanterns, as well as several coach lights. Beyond that is nothing but darkness and stars.

My feet hit the cedar planks with a thump. "Shh!" I warn, and then laugh, because no one's out here and I'm talking to myself. Down the long path I go, past the ferry, past a sizeable white boat, the waves lapping quietly at its side to make a soft thumping sound, to the end, marked by a tall rod with a light on the tip.

Dropping down to my knees, I lean forward, stretching my fingertips outward.

My glasses slip off my nose and plummet into the deep waters.

"No!" I cry, stretching my arm far in my useless attempt to grab them.

A sudden pounding of feet behind me is the only warning I get before hands seize my waist and yank me back and to my feet.

"What the hell are you doing?" an angry male voice exclaims.

"My glasses fell in!" I cry.

"Forget them. They're gone."

"I can't forget them!" They're my only pair and I can barely see ten feet in front of me without them. Sure, I brought contacts because I wear those while working outdoors, but I *need* my glasses.

"They're gone," he reiterates. "What on earth are you doing out here, anyway?"

"I wanted to see how cold the water was." His hands are still gripping my waist as if afraid I'm still going to fall in. I try brushing them away but they're like vise grips.

"I promise you, it's freezing. Though you almost took a nosedive in and found out for yourself."

I scowl. "You're exaggerating."

"I was watching you the entire time. I'm surprised you even made it on two feet this far."

I squint into the light to see exactly who is scolding me, but his back is to the lamppost and his face is cast in shadow. All I can see is a dark mop of hair and a beard.

"Why are you lurking out here in the middle of the night, anyway?"

"I wasn't lurking," he mutters. "I was enjoying a peaceful night on my boat and I heard you stumbling up the dock."

I frown, peering over at the boat in question, now even blurrier than before. "I didn't notice anyone there."

"Not surprised. Come on. You need to go to bed." His hand slides around my lower back and prods me toward shore.

A rare defiant streak surges. I didn't fly thousands of miles away from my overbearing mama only to be scolded and ordered around by a stranger. I jab his chest with my finger. "You can't tell me what to do. You're not the boss of me. The boss is the boss of me. And he can boss me." I'm not sure that made much sense.

"And who is he?" Amusement laces his tone.

"I don't know. Some arrogant big bad wolf billionaire who sleeps with Victoria's Secret models and changes women like underwear. He sounds like a complete jerk. But you're not him. You're..." I'm leaning against his chest now. A broad, solid chest, his muscles hard against me. I reach up with the hand I used to poke him to touch the few weeks' worth of growth covering his face, my fingertips scratching across the coarse hair. "A lumberjack."

"A lumberjack."

"Yes. With this beard and this," I rub my hand over his flannel checkered jacket, sitting open, and then to the shirt beneath, reveling in the ridges of his stomach. "Definitely a lumberjack. Did they hire lumberjacks to cut wood for that giant fireplace in there? They've hired people for everything else. I mean, seriously, who comes up to Alaska to get their pubic area waxed and their hair colored? And yet there's a full-service salon!"

His hands have found my waist again. He takes several steps backward, pulling me along with him.

But I dig my heels in. "I'm not going anywhere until I check the water for my glasses! I have a flashlight!" I yell, earning his shush.

He heaves a sigh. "Will you let me take you back to your cabin *immediately* after?"

"Once I do that, I will happily go to bed with you. Not with you. I'll go to bed. I'm not going to bed with a lumberjack." My tongue feels thick and slow as it trips over my rambling words.

"Fine. But I'm holding on to you the entire time. The owner doesn't need any of his employees drowning."

"Deal."

He leads me back to the edge and drops to his knees with me. "Sit your ass right down or you'll end up pulling us both in."

"That's no way to speak to a lady."

He snorts. "It is when she's as stubborn as a mule and as drunk as an Irishman."

Damp cold from the dock seeps through my jeans as I follow his order. He has large, strong hands and they grip my slender middle tightly as I lean down, shining the small beam of light from my pocket flashlight against the murky waters below. His hand that's closer to the water slides up to rest underneath my breast. I briefly consider telling this burly lumberjack that he's touching me inappropriately, but a part of me doesn't care right now.

"I can't see them." The water level is much lower than I expected. I can't even skim the top with my fingertips. I would have fallen in, had he not been there to grab me.

"No shit." He hauls me up with seemingly no effort, the

quick movement making the world spin a bit. "Where are you staying?"

"Cabin..." My words trail away as I finally see his face for the first time, bathed in a stream of light. Steely blue eyes stare down at me. Even with heavy scruff covering his face, I can tell that his jaw is strong and angular. And that mouth... I am utterly riveted to those plump lips. I can't help myself. I reach up and graze them with my fingertips, wisps of hair around the outside edges tickling my skin. They're as full and soft as they look and they part for me slightly, enough that my fingertips get wet, and warm breath skates across my skin.

My stomach bursts into butterflies as my own lips part.

I've heard people say that alcohol can change your perception, can make you believe that someone is better looking than they are in the sober light of day. I think they call it beer goggles. But I haven't been drinking beer and, besides, for my eyes to deceive me like this would be a cruel trick by Satan himself.

I've never seen such a handsome man in real life.

"You're beautiful," I whisper, and then my face flushes when I realize that I said that out loud. But it's okay that I did, I tell myself. It's true, and he needs to know.

I gather my nerve and shift my attention from his mouth up to his eyes to find his intense gaze weighing down on me, skating over my features before resting on my mouth. He leans down, his lips reaching for mine. My heart begins racing, anticipating the feel of them on me, wondering if they'll be firm or soft, demanding or yielding. How does a man like this kiss?

I want to let go, to let this complete stranger do whatever he wants with me.

He pulls back and gives his head a small shake. "Let's get you home. Which cabin are you in?"

"Seven." I pause, peering up again, my eyes roaming that handsome face. "Seriously, do you know how beautiful you are?"

"All right, let's get you home *fast*." He hooks an arm around the backs of my knees, one around my shoulders and hoists me up into a cradled position, earning my surprised yelp.

"I can walk!" Though, being in this man's arms, with my arm wrapped around this big, strong neck and my body pressed against this chest, is so new and exciting.

"Slow and stumbling and blind, yeah. But I need to be rid of you now."

"Be *rid* of me? Am I that awful?"

His focus is locked on the path ahead of us. "You're drunk and I know exactly where this is heading. It can't, that's all. Don't take it personally."

"And where exactly is this heading?" Was he seriously about to kiss me? No, that's not possible. A guy who looks like this doesn't try to kiss a girl like me, lumberjack or not.

His dark, low chuckle fills the night air. "I can't tell if you're playing coy right now, or if you're actually that clueless." When I don't answer, his gaze flitters to meet mine for a second. "To places a girl like you shouldn't go tonight."

I snort. "Great. You're protecting my virtue, too, now? Did my mama call you?" I stare at him as he walks on, ignoring me. "How old are you?"

"Thirty-one."

Ten years older than me. Thirty-one and a face like that; I'll bet he has slept with lots of women. I'll bet he's experienced. I'll bet he could teach me all kinds of things with those fingers that are currently clutching my body tightly. Things that Jed couldn't, or didn't want to. Thoughts of Jed make my stomach tilt. I quickly push them away. "Do you have a girlfriend?"

He seems to hesitate. "No."

"Neither do I. A boyfriend, I mean. I *had* a boyfriend. Well, a fiancé, actually. His name is Jed. We were going to get married next summer, but he cheated on me with the jezebel." The gravel crunches beneath the lumberjack's feet as I ramble on. "That's what my mama calls those kind of women—jezebels. I saw her. She's beautiful and sexy, so I guess I know why he'd leave me for her. Anyway, I'm supposed to wait for him to sow his wild oats. He asked me to wait, said he'd come back. Our families are so sure he'll come back to me."

"And you'll take him back, won't you." His tone mocks me, as if he's both unsurprised and repulsed by the idea.

"No. I mean, I don't think so." I sigh. Who am I kidding? It's the reason I held on to that ring instead of casting it into the deep waters. "I can't help but hope that he'll realize what a mistake he's making and come crawling back, begging for forgiveness."

"And you'll give it to him." Again, not a question.

"No!" A moment later, I admit with a grumble, "Maybe." Not because I forgive him; not because he didn't hurt me so badly. "He's all I've ever known. He's been a part of my life for so long. We had everything planned out. Now, I'm lost."

Lumberjack doesn't want to be listening to this; I can tell by the steely look across his face. But I haven't talked about it with an impartial person before. My friends tell me that I should despise Jed, and everyone back home tells me to bide my time.

Somehow dumping all this on a complete stranger feels therapeutic.

"I don't *want* to be pathetic. I don't *want* to be there for him if he does come back. I want to be over him, moved on." Sadness fills my chest. "But it's hard to get over someone you've loved since you were five years old."

Lumberjack doesn't say a word. It's annoying.

"How do I do that?"

He turns to meet my gaze, his mouth mere inches away in this position, so close that his sigh skates across my skin. That's the only answer I get before he turns his focus back to the path.

Now that I've opened up to him, I can't seem to stop. "That's why I came to Alaska. I wanted to get away from my life for a while, at least until I have to go back to college. I don't know what I'm going to do after. Jed and I were going to move back home, get married, and take over the farm. And have lots of sex. Sex, sex, and more sex. It's all about sex with you guys, isn't it?"

He takes a deep breath and adjusts my body tighter into his arms.

"So now he's busy parading the jezebel around *my* home town, probably having all kinds of sex in our private spots, while I'm in Alaska. He asked me not to be with anyone. Can you believe that? He's screwing around with this other girl and yet he asked me to wait for him, to save myself for our wedding night. Can you believe that? Would you ever expect your ex to wait around for you like that? I should just go and do it with someone, so that if he does come back, I can scream, 'too late! No virgin wife for you.' I don't want to be a virgin anymore. I need to find someone who will have sex with me here."

Lumberjack's footsteps falter and I squeeze his neck tightly, afraid we're going to fall in a heap. "You're a—How old are you?"

"Twenty-one. I hate that part of me still loves him. We have so much history. But then part of me..." I tip my head back to look at the vast expanse of stars above. I know they're somewhere up there, but I can't see them anymore.

He nudges my head with his shoulder. "No passing out on me."

I pull my head up and lean it against his body, burrowing in until my cold nose is pressed against his neck. I inhale deeply. "You smell good. Expensive. Is that cologne, or aftershave, or soap, or—"

"Christ," he hisses. "Do you normally talk this much?"

"No? I don't think so. It must be the alcohol. I've never been drunk before. It's fun."

Now he does chuckle, a low rumble that I feel deep inside my chest, and farther down, into the pit of my belly. "You might not think that tomorrow morning."

*Where was I? Oh, right... Jed.* "A part of me hates his guts. We were supposed to be each other's firsts and then he went off and did it with someone else, after all this time because he's a guy and he's too weak to wait. If he'd asked me, if he told me he couldn't wait, I would have done it. Why wouldn't he just ask me?"

When Lumberjack doesn't answer, I press. "Do you not know how to carry on a conversation?"

His stern face cracks with a smirk. "Is that what we're doing?" He looks down and when he doesn't see me smiling back, his face smooths over.

"I don't understand." A sudden unexpected wave of emotion hits me, and before I know what's going on, hot tears are streaming down my cheeks. "Is it because I'm not pretty enough for him? He always said he liked me like this, not like those other girls who plaster their faces with makeup. But then he turns around and starts dating one of them! Maybe I need to wear makeup?" I gaze at the lumberjack's face, his eyes locked straight ahead. "Do you think I need to wear makeup?"

His jaw tenses. "No."

I wipe away my tears with my free hand. "Do you think I'm pretty? I know I'm plain. I've just never been into all that girly stuff."

Finally, his blue eyes shift from the path to meet mine, where they rest for a long moment before sliding down to my lips and farther, to where my breasts press against his chest. "He would have cheated on you whether you fucked him or not. Be glad you didn't."

I don't know if that brings me any comfort. I do know he didn't answer my question. "So, should I..." I stall over the word he used, unable to bring myself to say it. "Should I *be* with someone else? Or should I wait?"

His bottom lip disappears between his teeth, as if he's holding back his words.

"How do I get over him?" My voice is almost pleading.

"By spending the next four months fucking someone in every position imaginable."

I'd be lying if I said I hadn't thought of it, more than once. But it was always from a place of pain and rejection, a place I knew would drive me to have regrets down the road. "I don't want just 'somebody.'" Right now, the way my body's responding to him, I want the lumberjack.

I trace the back of his neck with my fingertips. His arms are so strong, his body is so tight, his face so striking. Every fiber of my body is in tune with his, my skin prickling with the thought of these hands touching my bare skin. What would it be like to be naked with someone so big and masculine?

I twirl the little curly wisps of hair within my shaky but unusually bold fingers. "Have you ever been with a virgin?"

He inhales with a light hiss. "Not for a long time."

"Why not?"

"I prefer women over little girls."

I swallow against the burn of that rebuff. He's calling me a little girl. "So inexperience bothers you?"

"It's never appealed to me." A wicked smirk touches his lips. "Though you wouldn't be inexperienced for long."

A flush races through my entire body almost instantly, the heat building between my legs at the way he talks, as if sex is a real possibility between us. Pressing my lips together to try and hide my nervous grin, I reach up to run my fingers through his beard again. What would that feel like against my skin if he kissed me? I've never kissed a man with a beard. I've never kissed anyone but Jed. "I'll bet if you shaved your face, you'd be even more beautiful." His jaw tenses as I caress the edge of his jaw slowly, imagining what he looks like beneath.

"Maybe I don't want to be more beautiful."

"You know what I mean, Lumberjack." I rest my head against his broad frame again, burrowing my face further into his thick neck because it feels so nice and warm in there. I notice one of the buttons on his shirt has popped open. I reach for it, intent on fixing it for him, and accidently tug another one open in the process. "Oops. Sorry." My fingertip skates across hot exposed skin as I try to fix it one-handed. *Oh my God. This guy's chest.* I understand what "rock hard" means now. His skin is smooth, with a faint line of hair trailing down the middle. "Are you staying here, in the village?"

"Sure."

"Which cabin?"

"Why?"

"Because maybe I want to find you tomorrow?"

"You won't."

"How do you know?"

A cocky grin flashes. "Because if you remember any part of tonight, you'll be avoiding me for the rest of the summer."

I scowl into his neck. "You think you have me all figured out. What if I just want to say hi?"

"I'm sure I'll see you around."

"Fine." My lips have been skating across his skin while I talk. Now I run my tongue along them, because it's the closest I can get without actually licking him. "You taste salty."

A shaky breath escapes him and he speeds up.

Did I just turn on the lumberjack? Jed used to breathe like that when I sucked on his earlobe. My ego sure could use the boost right now. "What if I wanted to find you for other things?" *Man, alcohol makes me brave.*

There's a long pause. "What other things?"

I let my cool nose brush back and forth against his neck. His neck muscles strain with a hard swallow. "You know..."

"You can't even say it, can you?"

"Not when I'm sober," I admit. "But you've got drunk Abbi tonight, which means you're in luck."

"Then say it," he murmurs, his tone suddenly low and taunting.

We've entered the village now. I'll be at my cabin soon, and my time with the lumberjack and this uncharacteristic bravery will be over. Taking a deep breath, I lift my head enough for my mouth to reach his ear. "Would you fuck me if I asked you to?"

His chest rises against me and then he exhales. "Maybe."

His already deep voice has grown husky and I feel that one word right between my legs. "And what else?"

My giggles are laced with embarrassment. "There's more? I don't know. I've never passed first base. I've never even had a guy touch me down there."

"Here we are. Cabin seven."

Before I realize what's happening, my feet are hitting the ground, and I've lost the pleasing warmth of his body against me. I reach out and grab fistfuls of his jacket, the ground unsteady.

"Where's your key?" he whispers, seemingly in a rush.

"Back pocket." I frown at the gravel. It's moving.

His arms wrap around me, one settling on my lower back. Warm fingers slide against my butt as he searches my right pocket.

"Wrong one." I giggle, the wide grin on my face no doubt idiotic.

His hand quickly retreats and searches the other one, pulling out the card.

"You touched my bum. You should at least tell me your name."

He pauses, his eyes on the key and the door. With a sigh, he offers, "It's Henry."

"Hmm... Henry." I lean—okay, fall—against his chest and rope my arms around his waist in a hug. Tipping my head back to see his striking face illuminated under the cabin door light, I whisper, "So, about that thing we were talking about."

His jaw tenses but in his eyes, I'm sure I see amusement dance. A gentle tug against my braid has my head dipping farther back. My lips part as he leans down, preparing myself for a kiss. "Stop baiting me and go to sleep."

I give him my best pout, but truthfully I'm beginning to

feel dizzy. I need to lie down now. "Fine. Thank you for getting me home and not letting me fall into that icy water. By the way, my name's Abbi. Some people call me Abigail, but I hate it. So, if I ever see you again, don't call me that."

His perfect mouth is right there, so close to me that I can smell mint on his breath. And I want to taste it. I don't think I've ever wanted anything so bad in my life as I want to feel and taste his lips right now.

Before I lose my chance, I stretch up on my tiptoes and skate my lips over his, the edge of his scruff tickling me. He exhales against my skin and I close my eyes, shivering with the sensation. He hasn't pulled away yet though, and so I forge on, running my tongue over his lips once before pressing my mouth against his, capturing his top lip between mine in a hesitant, sweet kiss that I hope he'll reciprocate.

He pulls back a touch, enough that his mouth is out of range, and slides my card into the reader. The unlocking mechanism sounds and the light flashes green. Pushing the door open for me, he prods me in to the darkness. I'm brimming with disappointment and on the verge of tears over the rebuff.

Just as I step across the threshold though, a strong hand palms the front of my waist. He leans in, his cool nose skating across my ear, stealing a tiny gasp from me. "Apparently *some* people call me the big bad wolf," he whispers. "But I kind of like it."

I'm inside the cabin, the door's shut, and my lumberjack is gone before the words truly register.

"Oh my God!" I yelp, slapping myself in the forehead.

A round of growls and shushes sound out in the room.

# five

I groan inwardly, my forehead resting against my palms, waiting for a full day of training to begin. All I want to do is crawl back into bed.

"You should eat something," Tillie suggests, pulling apart her bagel. "Here."

I sneer at it. "Last night was so not worth it." I don't know what was worse: waking up to the taste of putrid breath and disgrace in my mouth and the head-splitting ache between my temples, or knowing that I humiliated myself in front of the owner—my boss.

Things are still a little bit foggy, but from what I remember, he had to save me from almost-certain drowning, carry me home because I couldn't stand on my own two feet, listen to me babble about Jed, and endure me hitting on him shamelessly.

Until I forced myself on him with a pathetic attempt at a kiss.

"Would you just tell me what happened?"

"Nothing." I refuse to give her—or anyone—the details. I'm too embarrassed.

"Huh." Suspicion drips from that single sound. "Sounds like you got the post-drunk-flashback blues. They're somethin' terrible. We've all had them, so spill it."

Is that true? Does everyone feel this shroud of shame and mortification after a night of drinking?

"It'll make you feel better. Promise."

I'll do anything to feel better right now. "I cried on a guy last night," I finally admit.

She smiles triumphantly, as if proud of herself for making me break.

"It was awful."

"Yeah, well... girls get emotional when they're drunk. Who was he?"

I avert my gaze to hide the lie when I say, "I have no idea."

"You didn't even get his name?"

I shake my head.

"Well, I assume nothin' too wild happened, seeing as nothin' causes limp dick faster than a crying girl."

"What else would—"Another memory hits me and I gasp, staring wide-eyed at her. "Oh my God!" I basically asked him to have sex with me.

And told him that I'm a virgin!

And that I've never been so much as fingered.

Saliva begins to pool in my mouth. "I'm going to be sick." This is why I'm not supposed to drink. Mama's right. Satan does live at the bottom of a bottle of booze.

"Don't worry. If you see him again, apologize. I doubt he gives a shit."

"I hope you're right," I mumble. I'm still having a hard time believing that the big burly man in the plaid jacket is the billionaire, Henry Wolf. But that's my kind of luck.

I called him a lumberjack.

And stroked his beard.

I groan again, as the petite Texan brunette at the front of the room claps her hands several times to gather everyone's attention. There are close to fifty people in this room by Tillie's count; the vast majority of them women.

"Welcome to Wolf Cove Hotel, a Wolf Hotels establishment! My name's Paige," she chirps. "Y'all have been chosen to join this team because of your exceptional experience in high-end accommodation establishments, your exemplary ethics, and your dedication to put this hotel into a league of its own."

Tillie leans in next to me, her strong perfume wafting into my nostrils as she murmurs, "Or maybe because we're all gorgeous people."

I stifle my snort, though I can't help but agree with her. It was all the more evident at breakfast in the lounge this morning. Even though some were clearly nursing a hangover, myself included, every last person employed at Wolf Cove, right down to the cooks and plumber working on the public restrooms this morning, has something going for them in the looks department.

I'm pretty sure there's a profiling lawsuit brewing somewhere here.

But honestly, how did *I* end up here? I mean, I filled out an application, answered a few questions, and was hired a week later to do a job that I have no experience in.

And I seem to be the only one without respectable credentials. Everyone in my cabin has worked for a large chain hotel before, if not for the Wolf itself. Autumn was a concierge at the Seattle location and Lorraine normally works out of the Wolf Chicago spa.

And that's the whole experience angle. The looks angle... Let's just say I'm the only one here with braided hair and thick, ungroomed eyebrows, now emphasized because I'm forced to wear contacts in order to see ten feet in front of me.

If I let myself think about it for too long, I start to believe they screwed up when they hired me. There was an accidental shuffle from the "reject" pile to the "hire" pile.

"Okay! Let's get down to business. Everyone in this room has been hired for the Cove's housekeeping services. You've all done this kind of work before, some of you within the Wolf family, some outside. For those outside, we want to make sure that each and every one of you knows exactly what's expected of you at Wolf Cove, and I'll promise you that our standards are high."

"I don't need a lesson on cleaning toilets," Tillie mutters.

She may not need one, but I don't want one. I sigh and glance over my shoulder at the clock. It's 9:00 a.m. I swung by the reception desk before the session, but Belinda wasn't there yet. This has to get fixed. As nice as it would be to work with Tillie, this is not what I signed up for. My own bedding is sitting in a heap, back in the cabin. I'm pretty sure that wouldn't meet Wolf standards.

Paige goes on, and I lose myself in the spectacular backdrop out the wall of glass behind her—trees and water and, far in the distance, white-capped mountains. I can see why they would build a ballroom here. What an incredible wedding reception location this would be.

Jed and I were supposed to have our reception in the old barn out back, the one we use to store all the tractors and farm equipment. It was going to be rustic and romantic, with flowers strung along the beams, and candlelit lanterns on the tables.

I push that thought aside in time to hear Paige say, "Mr. Wolf has every intention of earning a Five Diamond and

Five-Star rating for Wolf Cove. Y'all play such an important role in making that happen. We need you to work hard and make each guest's stay memorable. That's why he's here to speak to you this morning."

My heart rate spikes.

She gestures to her left and everyone's heads shift as one.

The air grows thick as a man enters the room from a door off to the side and saunters toward the podium, the pant legs of his tailored suit falling gracefully with each step.

My mouth drops open.

It wasn't the alcohol. He *is* that dazzling.

*And* he shaved his beard off, leaving only smooth skin and a stunning profile behind. The man's face has been carved by the gods themselves, with chiseled edges and a small cleft in his chin.

"Dang. Autumn wasn't kidding," Tillie murmurs. "Hello, soaked panties in two seconds, flat."

*Mine, too.* I stare at him unabashed, remembering how good he smelled last night; how the salt from his skin tasted. How his arms felt wrapped tightly around me. I was being carried by an Adonis and I was too drunk to appreciate it. Instead, I babbled his ear off about my ex and virginity and all kinds of mortifying things.

He towers over Paige, who's in three-inch heels and staring up at him like a child in awe. Everyone seems to stare at him in awe, their attention riveted on his frame as it fills the space behind the podium, his upper body broad and solid in the gray suit and yellow tie.

He looks every bit the billionaire.

And that hair... It's a rich chestnut brown, combed back and curling at the ends. My fingers twitch, remembering playing with them at his nape. What would it feel like to run my hands through that thick mane?

He clears his throat and reaches for a tall glass of water. Takes his time drinking it, the muscles in his neck pulsing with each swallow. His eyes wander over the group, seemingly unruffled as we all watch.

I shrink down a little in my chair, hoping to avoid his notice.

It doesn't work.

That steely gaze of his settles on me. I freeze, my heart rate spiking, my cheeks burning bright.

"Oh my...," Tillie murmurs under her breath beside me.

Finally, he releases me and focuses on the podium in front of him, but not before I catch the tiniest smirk touch his lips. He sets his glass down and, leaning into the microphone, offers coolly, "Good morning, everyone."

His voice is as deep and as sexy as I remember it being.

And, I swear, every last female shudders a sigh at the sound of it. A wave of "good morning" responses roll through the group as people sit up straighter in their seats.

The left side of his mouth kicks up in a sexy smile, like he knows what his voice can do.

"Lord have mercy," Tillie whispers. "I would maul that man in a heartbeat."

*Would you fuck me if I asked you to?*

Panic explodes inside me as I replay the words in my head, my hands pressed against my mouth to hide my gape.

But he said, "maybe." At least, I think he said maybe. Am I remembering that correctly? If so, was he simply toying with me?

"I'm sure Paige here has given Wolf Cove the introduction it deserves, and I trust that she'll provide you with more than adequate training. I wanted to stop in and reiterate how important it is to me, personally, that each and every guest here has an exceptional experience. My family has owned this property for hundreds of years. I've always considered Alaska to be a home to me, even when I'm not here. As such, I want to see this Wolf location prosper." He speaks eloquently, his grammar impeccable, his words flowing. How did I not notice that last night? "It is my dream to make us one of the only 0.3 percent in the world to achieve Five Diamond status. Many people have told me it's impossible; that it can't be done." His perfectly groomed eyebrow arches. "And I tell them that I live for a challenge. This is why I've flown in the most prestigious Wolf chefs, and sous chefs, and I've hired you bright and eager people to help me succeed." His eyes wander through the group again. Where there was plenty of adjusting in seats and bowed-head doodling before, there is only rapt attention on the man now. "I'll leave you in Paige's capable hands. She has helped train hospitality staff at three Wolf hotels so I trust she'll whip you all into shape and you, in turn, will make sure every guest will wish they never have to leave Wolf Cove. I expect the best, and only the best, from each and every one of you." His eyes sail around the room again, and I'm relieved that they skate past me without stalling. "I trust you'll find all of the employee benefits more than fair. Should there be a point when you feel they aren't and you don't enjoy being here, I ask that you let our hotel manager, Belinda Cartwright, know right away. We'll have you on the first ferry out."

Was he this cool last night? He's not exactly Mr. Charming, that's for sure. Intolerant, if I had to choose a word. A man like this must think I'm a complete idiot, the way I rambled on. No wonder he wanted to be rid of me. And here I thought there was perhaps a connection. That, at one point, with my mouth against his neck, I managed to arouse him.

I'm never drinking again.

"Thank you." He turns, but then stops and leans in to the microphone again. "Oh, and before I forget: Please make sure you are well versed in the staff conduct section of our orientation package. The main hotel grounds are meant for guests only. We expect staff to utilize the facilities in the staff village and remain there while off-duty. There has already been one incident of drunk and disorderly conduct. Future incidents will result in termination of employment."

My face burns with his words. That's got to be a warning for me. That, should I ever try to make out with him again, I'll be fired. I guess that's fair.

His humorless eyes graze mine one last time and then, with a small nod toward Paige on his way past, he strides out the door he came in through. I'm torn between wanting to crawl beneath the table and hoping he'll find a reason to stick his head in, so I get a chance to see his beautiful face again.

By the look of it, everyone else in here is wishing the exact same thing.

"Abbi?" I turn to meet Tillie's raised brow. "Did that warning have anything to do with you?"

I sigh. "I don't want to talk about it. Please."

Paige claps her hands again, drawing everyone's attention back to her and, thankfully, ending any chance for Tillie to press. "Okay! So where were we? That's right. Learning about Wolf Hotels' housekeeping excellence."

## *six*

"Why would you want to work outside? It's so dirty," Tillie mumbles as we walk through the main lodge toward the reception desk, the vaulted timber ceiling towering several stories above us. Her pretty face scrunches up, and I notice for the first time the flecks of brown in her otherwise crystal-blue eyes.

"And wiping urine off toilet seats isn't? How about 'disposing of used condoms with discretion'?" I air-quote Paige's exact words with my fingers. The past two hours have been focused on how important it is for guests to know that the staff is discreet. That we will see all kinds of things in these rooms—high-end clientele or not—that may make us take a second glance. We're not to do that. We're to keep our mouths shut, tidy up their rooms, hide the dildos we find in the soiled bedding in the nightstand, and offer the guests nothing more than a polite, nonjudgmental nod should we pass them in the hallway.

Tillie waggles her brows. "I don't know. There's something sinful about being in a stranger's private space."

"Well, I'll let you be sinful while I tend to the hostas and lavender in the front garden." I already took inventory of them on my way in. Professional landscaping mats and mulch will ensure that the weeds are kept to a minimum, but I'm sure there's something that can be done.

"I guess you'll find plenty of entertainment with your coworkers. It's a male-dominated group. Connor sure seemed to take to you."

I snort. "Maybe I can get drunk and hit on him, too."

"So is that what you did? You hit on someone?"

I shake my head. I've already said too much.

"You're gonna have to spill it some time. Either way, it'll get out. You can't keep anything quiet in a place like this, trust me."

"I hope you're wrong," I mutter, more to myself.

Tillie's infectious giggle carries through the lobby, catching several glances. Including Belinda's, who's now behind the desk. I practically run toward her. She has swapped her tight black dress for a red one with a plunging neckline. I try not to look at her breasts when I talk, but they're large and distracting and, I'm pretty sure, not real. "Hey, Belinda."

She stares blankly at me.

"It's me. Abbi Mitchell. You said you were going to look into the mix-up with my position."

"Right." She offers me her trademark forced smile. "I'm sorry. I don't know what happened exactly, but I need you in Housekeeping. We're short staffed. If something changes, I'll make sure to move you over right away."

As rude as it is, I sigh with frustration. "But I was hired for an outdoor position. Is there *nothing* you can do?"

She shakes her head. "I'm sorry. With us opening in two days, we can't be short on housekeeping staff."

Should I remind her that I have zero experience with

housekeeping? Or will that guarantee me a ride back to Homer, never to return again?

"Is there a problem?"

My stomach drops at the sound of his voice from behind me. Fingers take hold of my elbow and squeeze gently. Forcing myself to turn, I take a deep, shaky breath and look into those crystal-blue eyes as my pulse begins to throb in my throat. Eyes so light, they're mesmerizing. And framed by the longest, thickest lashes I've ever seen on a man. I never felt their full impact last night. Now, they make my legs turn to Jell-O. He's not giving anything away though. What he thinks of me, of my drunken stupor, of me trying to kiss him.

His steely mask hides it all.

And yet he makes my knees wobble, all the same.

I give him a small, embarrassed smile. "It's just that I applied for outdoor work and I've been assigned to Housekeeping."

"And you're unwilling to work in Housekeeping?" There's a sharp edge in his voice.

"No. I mean..." Remembering his words from earlier, I'm quick to correct. "I was hired for outdoor work and would be much better suited for it, is all. I'm afraid I won't meet your standards."

His flawless eyebrows arch with surprise. "Outdoor work here is pretty tough."

"I know. But I can handle it."

He turns to Belinda. "How did a mistake like that happen?"

"I can't for the life of me figure it out." Does this reflect badly on her? If it does, she shouldn't be glaring at him like that.

He opens his mouth to say something but stops himself,

his tongue running along the bottom of his lip as if in thought. And I'm hit with the memory of my fingers sliding across them last night. Of my *tongue* sliding across them.

Oh, God, I am truly never drinking again!

"They're preparing the rooms for arrival tomorrow?" he asks.

"Yes," Belinda says. "All the last-minute dusting, care packages, making sure everything's perfect."

"I'm not sure how the hiring team made this mistake, but it's hardly fair that you flew all the way here and we screwed up your position." He pauses, his gaze flickering down the length of me ever so briefly, so fast that I may have imagined it. Still, between that and my spotty memories of last night, of what I said to him with my mouth pressed up against his ear, I'm now struggling to breathe.

He heaves a sigh. "Come to the main gates at 7:00 a.m. sharp tomorrow and someone will see to it that you get some outdoor hours in. You might find that you'll change your mind about housekeeping. Belinda, please ensure Paige knows that Abbi won't be joining in until the afternoon."

Great. He remembers my name.

"Certainly." Belinda's eyes haven't left his face the entire time. How did she get appointed hotel manager? She clearly isn't the right person to enforce a business-attire dress code.

His heavy gaze settles on me. "Does that work for you?"

My head bobs up and down. "Yes. Thank you, so much. I appreciate it. *Mr. Wolf*."

A glimmer of mischief briefly dances across his face and then vanishes. "We'll see."

I hold my breath as he strolls away, heading for the elevators.

With a quick nod toward Belinda, who is now glaring

daggers at me, I spin on my heels and head back toward the training session, Tillie hot on my heels.

"What was that all about?" she hisses.

"I'm not sure. But I think he's trying to help me get a job in Outdoor."

"Oh. My. Lord. That man is somethin' else."

I release the lung's worth of air. "Yes, he is. He seems nice enough, at least." I asked him if he thought I was pretty. *Ugh*! He avoided answering that, which is answer enough.

"What I'd do to be assigned to his room," she purrs. "I'd crawl through his sheets and—"

"He's our boss!"

"Hell, like you wouldn't."

"I wouldn't! You're not allowed to, anyway! Didn't you read the policy handbook?"

She snorts. "There ain't nothin' about getting off in the boss's sheets."

I flush at the thought.

"Well, it's not like either of us is gonna get the chance. Guys like him stay for the opening and then hop in their helicopter and jet off to bigger and better things. He'll be gone in a few days."

I glance over my shoulder in time to see him pressing the Up elevator button, his suit hugging his muscular frame in all the right places. He seems oblivious or indifferent to Rachel and another girl ogling him from behind the bar, where they're setting up bottles of alcohol.

"Really? I figured he'd stay. It sounded like this place was special to him." The thought of him leaving so soon disappoints me. Not that it matters in my little world. As much as I'd love to believe otherwise, a guy like that has no interest in a twenty-one-year-old farm girl from Pennsylvania. Especially one who threw herself at him in a drunken mess.

Still, he sure is something to look at.

"All these guys love gettin' up in front of the staff and telling them how vital they are. I swear, it's like it's in an owner manual. It don't mean nothin'." She pauses. "Then again, you know what I heard? That he personally reviewed each and every video interview made and gave the final approval for hiring. So maybe I'm wrong and he will stay."

"That can't be true." A guy like that couldn't be bothered when he has a hiring team to do that.

She shrugs. "If it is true, then he must love control. Maybe that extends into the bedroom." She waggles her eyebrows suggestively.

I don't understand what that means, but I smile at her anyway.

"Come on." Tillie loops her arm through mine. "Let's go learn about folding towels and checking for bedbugs."

I groan.

# seven

I'm pretty predictable when it comes to sleep. Every night around 3:00 a.m. I'll wake up, lying on my stomach, hugging my pillow. I've done this for as long as I can remember, even when I'm alone in my room, even in dead silence.

Last night was the exception. Tonight, it seems I'm back on schedule. I lie in bed, listening for the shallow breathing of five other women, hoping that'll lull me back to sleep.

At first, I'm not entirely sure what I'm hearing. I know it's coming from Katie and Rachel's bunk, which runs perpendicular to ours. It's set slightly behind ours, and so close that if both Katie and I stretched arms out, we could touch fingertips.

The curtains on the windows dim the cabin well, but they don't completely block the lights shining in from outside. The privacy curtain helps with that. Only, Autumn and my curtain isn't long enough, and there's a gap near my head.

Tonight, Katie and Rachel haven't pulled their curtain

all the way around, and the light glows over the end of the bottom bunk.

It takes a few blinks for my eyes to adjust to being awake, and to process what I see.

A naked woman is bent over Katie's pillow.

I fight the gasp as my mouth drops and my eyes pop wide.

Another voice whispers through a pant, "Oh my God, I've missed this. Don't stop..." and I immediately recognize Rachel, earning my second wave of shock. I knew the two of them were from the same hometown and came here as friends, but I hadn't expected *this*! Wasn't Rachel ogling Mr. Wolf only hours ago?

"Like this?" Katie purrs.

"Yes," Rachel moans.

Katie shushes her with a giggle, followed by a soft moan of her own. "I'm going to come fast if you keep doing that."

I know I should close my eyes and give them their privacy and yet I don't move, because part of me is curious. So I lie dead still and watch them pleasure each other, wondering what it would feel like to have someone's tongue on me like that.

Is anyone else awake? They wouldn't be able to see this, not like I can. Well, maybe Autumn, but I hear her soft snore above us.

"Not yet, you greedy—" Katie's words drift as she begins panting and wriggling. The curtain shifts, something poking the inside of it. Her knee, I'm guessing. She's spreading her legs wide.

I should feel guilty or dirty about spying on them, but I don't. In fact, I can't help the heaviness in my pelvis, the moisture pooling inside my panties, the urge to spread my own legs.

I'm aroused.

Oh my God. Does this mean I'm a lesbian?

A phone suddenly appears. Katie pushes a few buttons and the screen lights up, and anything hidden from my view is now lit for me, right down to the goose bumps on Rachel's slick flesh.

She's selfie-videotaping this.

*Oh my God.*

Katie pauses to pant a few times. "Deeper," she whispers, and my thighs squeeze in response to whatever Rachel may be doing on the other end.

And then Katie wraps her free hand around Rachel's thigh and presses her face into Rachel's mound to muffle her cries of ecstasy. At the same time, I hear Rachel's stifled cry and then her body begins to quiver.

A few moments of silence pass before Katie's head settles back on her pillow and Rachel's lithe body begins to climb backward, over the end of the bed, off Katie.

I close my eyes, afraid of getting caught and painted the peeping Tom.

"I needed that," Rachel whispers, followed by a soft, "Good night." I sense movement right beside my head and then the ladder creaks.

Soon, all is quiet again.

Except now I'm wide awake and mildly traumatized by the private sexual act I watched. Of all people to witness it... Would they be angry with me if they knew I had watched? Embarrassed? I'm guessing not, if they'd risk doing it in the first place. That eases my guilt a bit.

I'm afraid to move yet, so I stay still, replaying what I saw in my head. I guess it's the same thing that a guy would do to a woman. I can't imagine having a man's face down there like that.

A man like Henry Wolf, with that strong, square jaw grazing against the soft skin of my inner thigh. Try as I might, I haven't been able to get him out of my head all day. Would he even do something like that? Or would he find it unappealing? Would I ever be confident enough to allow it? Jed said the idea of putting his mouth on any holes involved in defecating didn't appeal to him. I'm betting that has changed.

It's now 4:00 a.m. Soft, shallow breaths surround me, and I have a terrible throb between my legs that isn't going away. As quietly as I can, I roll onto my back and slide my fingertips beneath the drawstring of my pants, hesitant to do this in a room with five other women, even if they're all asleep. Sure, the curtain and my blankets hide it, but still...

I gingerly draw my index finger through my slit. It comes out slick. I bite my lip. And do it again. And again. And then I begin to flick my clit like I watched Katie do with her tongue, and it makes me wetter.

I haven't done this in months, since before I caught Jed cheating on me. I haven't had the urge, too heartbroken.

The more aroused I get, the braver I become, until I'm no longer so worried about getting caught. In fact, the idea of Katie or Rachel watching me do this spurs me on because I think they'd like it. I push my pajama pants down and spread my legs farther. I'm still under my blanket as I do this, and I'm being quiet. No one will know.

Should I even care? Autumn brought a dildo with her, and I just watched my two roommates eat each other out and stick a plug up their ass only three feet away!

I close my eyes and slowly, gently, back and forth, rub the sensitive nub of flesh, reveling in how soft it is. How good this feels. Like my body has been begging me to do it for years.

I struggle to keep quiet as my heart rate begins to race. I close my eyes and imagine it's not my hand doing this. It's Henry Wolf's hand. His big, strong, manicured hands would probably know how to do it well.

Or his tongue.

The slow build that's been growing in my pelvis now rushes, pushing my legs farther apart, until my covers have fallen away and the cool air touches my bare skin, and I don't even care that I'm exposed within my little cubbyhole.

I close my eyes and imagine myself like Rachel was, bent over Mr. Wolf's face while his tongue and his fingers plunge into me. A rush hits me and I have to press my lips together to keep from crying out as my muscles pulse beneath my fingertips.

Not until it's over do I fully comprehend what just happened.

I brought myself to orgasm thinking of my boss.

# eight

I check my watch for the third time. He said 7:00 a.m.

So where is everyone?

I rushed past that guy, Connor, and the rest of the Outdoor crew in the staff lounge, a croissant hanging out of my mouth and a steaming cup of coffee in a Styrofoam cup. They didn't seem to be in any hurry to get here on time, their forest-green all-weather jackets hanging off chairs. I don't have a suitable jacket besides my winter coat, so I wore several layers plus my vest and hiking boots. I wonder if that'll be good enough. If not, someone's going to have to equip me.

*If* someone shows up. Is this the right gate? It looks like the main gate, with iron rungs and a security booth made of stone and timber on the right. Kind of silly, given I heard there's nowhere to go. The only way into Wolf Cove is by plane or boat. We're surrounded by a mountain range and water, and ahead of us is the Kenai Fjords National Park.

I'm about to ask the guard when a low rumble cuts in to the remote peace. It's coming from a black pickup truck slowly making its way along the service road, a pathway hidden from the lodge's view by a thick cedar hedge.

I step aside to allow the truck past. It stops next to me instead.

"Get in."

His deep, commanding voice—so early in the morning, so unexpected—makes me jump.

I can't seem to form words. I simply stand and stare at Henry Wolf himself. He's traded the tailored suit and styled hair for the red-and-black checked wool jacket and a less-tame head of waves that I remember from the other night, when I called him a lumberjack. The sleeves are rolled up to show off impressive forearms, thick and sinewy with muscle. His eyes hide behind a pair of aviator sunglasses, though it's not nearly sunny enough to need them yet.

"You said you wanted some outdoor work, right?"

I finally find my tongue. "Right."

"Well then, get in the truck."

"With you?" I look around me, waiting for someone to jump out from behind a tree and yell, "Psych!"

"Not if you don't hurry up." There's no mistaking the hint of a warning tone in his voice now.

I scurry over to the passenger side and climb in, slamming the heavy door behind me. A mixture of soap and bug spray hits me and I inhale deeply. I never thought bug spray could be so appealing.

He throws the truck into gear, and it lurches as it begins to move, jostling me around. "Sorry. It takes me a few days to get used to this engine again. My cars back home drive a lot more smoothly."

Cars, plural. Of course. "That's okay. I'm used to old farm trucks and bumpy roads." I try not to stare at his profile, but I fail miserably. He's honestly in a class all his own. His square, chiseled jaw is covered in a shadow of dark stubble, as if he forgot to shave. I've always thought a thin layer of stubble was sexy. Jed couldn't grow it; it'd come in patchy. "Where's home?" Do I address him as Henry or Mr. Wolf?

The security gate eases open and the guard throws a wave our way.

His large hands curl around the steering wheel as he pulls through. "Manhattan, mainly. Though I have a few places I like to spend time in."

I shouldn't be surprised. Of course a guy like this has homes, plural, to go along with his cars, plural.

Henry turns right at the end of the driveway, and onto a single-lane dirt road.

"So," I decide on the more formal to be safe, "Mr. Wolf, where—"

"Call me Henry." He turns to regard me with a smirk, his cheek marked by a deep dimple. "I think we've passed the formal greeting stage, haven't we?"

I release a shaky sigh. "Okay, Henry..." I like the feel of his name on my tongue. "Where are we going?"

"Does it matter?"

"No, I guess not." I eye the twelve-gauge shotgun mounted over the rear windows.

He chuckles and the sound vibrates deep inside my chest. "Don't worry. The safety's on."

"I'm not worried. I just wasn't expecting to see one here." I come from a family of hunters, so I'm comfortable enough around guns. "Why do we need it?"

"Have you ever seen a grizzly bear up close?"

When I shake my head, he shrugs. "I have. And that's why we need a gun."

"I thought they won't usually attack." That's what the orientation video said.

"You're right. They won't, if we're not stupid." Henry's eyes scan the brush by the side of the road as we drive, one hand resting on his thick, powerful thigh. The hand I was picturing on me last night, as I was coming. Just the thought makes me squeeze my thighs tightly together now. "But nothing is 100 percent. I like to be prepared for all possibilities."

"So you're a boy scout."

That earns me another tiny, sexy smirk that makes my heart skip a beat. "Something like that."

We ride in silence over the steep hills in the road. I do my best not to stare at him, but I can't help glance intermittently, to catch a glimpse of his blue eyes, the color of the morning sky above us. He keeps seeing me do it, too, forcing me to veer my gaze to the road.

Only to wander back moments later.

Finally, he clears his throat, and I'm sure I've made him uncomfortable.

"So you decided to shave your beard?" I ask in a rush.

"I have some important people coming tomorrow. I figured it was time. And one of my employees mistook me for a lumberjack."

I grin sheepishly. "I'm sorry about that. To be fair though, I was *really* drunk."

"Yes, you were."

"And you didn't introduce yourself to me as my boss."

"No, I didn't."

I wait for an explanation. When it doesn't come, I go on. "I wish you had. Maybe I wouldn't have made such a complete ass of myself."

"Maybe you wouldn't have been yourself then."

"That was *not* me. That was me drunk for the first time

in my life." I wince, recalling how utterly wretched I felt yesterday. "And the last."

"Probably a good thing, considering you nearly went swimming. Aside from that, you were entertaining."

"Entertaining?" I turn to face the window so he doesn't see my red cheeks, recalling some of the things I said and did. "It didn't sound like you were amused, given the whole employee-code-of-conduct speech yesterday morning." I read through it last night. Section five states no romantic relationships between management and their subordinates. It doesn't specify anything about a drunken subordinate hitting on the hotel owner, but I'll bet they're adding that in as we speak.

"I didn't have a choice. I can't have my employees stumbling around drunk."

*Or trying to kiss you.* "You could have told me who you were, at least."

He sighs. "Sometimes I need a break from all the Mr. Wolf and the nervousness and people walking on eggshells around me."

"I crushed every eggshell there was."

His chuckle fills the truck and my heart swells. I like making him laugh.

It would be easy for me to get lost in the nature around us, unlike anything I've ever seen before, the forest thick and lush even in early spring, the snowy ridge in the distance. If not for the man accompanying me, I would. But I still can't seem to keep my eyes off him for long.

"You're managing without your glasses?" he finally asks.

"Yes. Contacts." As if reminded that they're there, I blink repeatedly. I'm not used to wearing them all the time.

"Good. I was afraid you'd be blind." He glances over at me. "You look different with them off. Your eyes are..."

"Too big for my face?" Kids used to tease me about them growing up, especially the boys. They called me "Bug Eyes" and "Owl."

He doesn't answer. Instead he asks, "How is everything so far? The food, the accommodations? Do they suit your needs?"

"Everything's great."

"Everything can't be great. Everything's never great." His lips purse. "Tell me the truth."

"Is this Mr. Wolf asking? Or Henry?"

He turns to spear me with a glare.

"The food is great. The cabins are good, if not a little bit crammed."

"And your roommates?"

"Um. They're...fine." Thankfully Katie and Rachel were still asleep this morning when I ducked out.

He frowns. "That doesn't sound convincing. We've never utilized a staff village like this before. I was worried about such close quarters, but my team promised me it would work out, with the way scheduling will be managed. Why? Are you having a problem with someone already?"

"No. Not at all. It's just..." I hesitate. I shouldn't be telling him this, should I?

"It's just..." he pushes. I glance at him, and see the genuine worry etched in his face.

"I think two of them have sort of a thing going on."

"Oh." Henry's brow pops over his sunglasses as realization dawns on him. "And it's making you uncomfortable?"

"No. Well, not really. Last night, I kind of saw them in bed together." I can't believe I'm telling him this. I had no intention of telling anyone. But apparently I don't have to be drunk to say inappropriate things around this man, after all. "I didn't mean to, but their bunk is right next to me, and they didn't pull the curtain around." I blush with the memory. "One of them crawled into the other one's bunk."

He pauses for a moment, his eyes trained on the road. "So you saw two of your roommates fucking?"

Just the way he says that, so casually, sends heat through my core. I can't believe I'm reacting this way to his words alone. I clear my throat. "Yes."

"And you have a problem with that? Two women?"

"No! Not at all."

Henry's mouth opens then closes several times. When he finally speaks, his voice has turned low. "So you watched them?"

Is that an appropriate question for the owner of the hotel to ask me? I look out the window, my cheeks heating. "I didn't mean to." *Please don't ask me if I enjoyed it.* Now that the moment's over, I'm embarrassed about what I witnessed last night, and what I did afterward. But I also can't ignore how alive it made me feel, how in tune with their pleasure my body was. How much I wanted to feel that.

How I came thinking of the man sitting right beside me.

"That must have been a shock for someone like you."

I frown. "Someone like me?" It takes me a moment to understand what he's saying.

A virgin. Someone who's never even had a guy's hand in my pants. That's right. I told him that, too.

Henry pulls the truck to a stop near a logging road on my right. "Hold on. It's going to get a little bit bumpy." Throwing it into four-wheel drive, he then eases the truck through the deep divots in the muddy ground.

"Whose land is this?" I ask, grabbing on to the door with one hand and wrapping my other arm across my chest, the rough bouncing hurting my breasts.

By Henry's sideways glance, he notices and slows down a touch. "Mine."

"Your family's?"

"No, mine. My grandfather left it all to me."

So I guess that particular rumor was accurate. As we ease deeper into the woods, I can see the devastation where chainsaws cut into hundreds of years of growth, mowing down mass clearings. "This is so sad."

"The hemlock and cedar used for the lodge was sourced from in here. Why buy from someone else what I have right in my backyard."

"Yeah, I guess. You're going to replant it all, though. Right?"

"Eventually. When I have the staff to do it."

The wheels in my brain are turning. "I could do it."

He stops the truck next to a fallen tree and turns the ignition. The deep rumbling stops, leaving us in eerie silence. Peeling his sunglasses off his face, he turns to level me with his beautiful eyes. "You're going to plant all these trees yourself?"

"I could. It would take me all summer."

His head tips back with his laughter, and I marvel at the sight of his Adam's apple, the way it juts out. "You *really* don't want to be in Housekeeping, do you?"

My giggle escapes me unbidden. "Like I said, I'm better suited to the outdoors."

His gaze does a lightning-speed assessment of my body before muttering, "Come on."

The second I crack the door, a cloud of mosquitos swarms me. It's like they were waiting for fresh blood. I swat as I walk around to meet him in front of the truck. The bugs are way worse out here. "You'll need these." He tosses me a pair of work gloves. "And this. The stuff they gave you isn't strong enough." A can of bug spray sails through the air.

I quickly douse myself from head to toe while Henry disappears behind the truck. He emerges with an ax.

"We're cutting wood?"

"Have you ever swung an ax before?" He strolls over to a massive stump nearby and rests the blade against it.

"No."

"Then *I'm* cutting wood. You're going to stack it in the back of the truck."

"Really?" The guy's a billionaire and he's out here, chopping wood?

"Do you think you can handle that?"

I snort. "I bail hay at harvest. I can handle this."

Again, another quick scan of my body, only this time his gaze slows over my thighs. I was in such a rush to get out of the cabin this morning, I grabbed a pair of jeans that are a tad too tight for outdoor work.

He gives his head a little shake. "There's a cooler of water in the cab, if you need one." He slides a bottle from his pocket and, unscrewing it, brings it to his mouth, his plump lips wrapping around the end.

My thoughts from my drunken night come sailing back into the forefront of my mind.

What would it have felt like to have him kiss me back?

Or to have his tongue working me like I saw Katie do to Rachel. Or more?

Is this well-groomed billionaire in front of me into the kind of kinky stuff that my roommates are clearly into? Is that what everyone's into, and I'm just that clueless?

I don't realize I'm staring until he turns to face me. "Is something wrong?"

I feel my cheeks burn bright. "No. I was just..." Imagining

the owner—my boss—sticking his tongue in me. There is no good answer here, so I let the words hang and head for the truck to grab a bottle of water. The air is still chilly, but I'm sure once I start moving, I'll break a sweat.

There's a small pile of split wood off to the side, so I move for that, cradling a piece. "What's this for, anyway?"

"What is firewood usually for, Abigail?"

I don't miss the hint of mocking in his tone. "It's Abbi. And I figured you'd have firewood delivered."

"Because I'm wealthy?"

"No, because it's a big hotel." *And because you're wealthy.*

I watch him bend and heave a large piece of tree trunk onto the stump, wishing he didn't have that bulky jacket on so I could watch his muscles strain. If the feel of his body wasn't a drunken illusion on my part, then he's got plenty of them, and they're nicely honed.

He grips the ax handle. "We do have logs delivered for wood-burning fireplaces. Today is for me. It's great exercise, and I like to come out here to clear my head. The quiet is like nothing, anywhere else. Especially when I'm stressed." With a mighty swing, the blade of his ax cracks the hunk of wood, splitting it in two pieces. The sound ricochets through the valley, sending several birds squawking away.

"You're stressed right now?"

"I have a hotel that cost me twenty million of my own money opening tomorrow, with plenty of investors' money tied up and my family's name behind it. What do you think?"

I try to move past the astronomical dollar figure. "You hide your stress well, then."

He doesn't answer. He simply adjusts the pieces of wood. With another powerful swing, he brings the blade down on the wood, splitting it evenly with one swing. He makes it looks so effortless, like it's nothing to hit the wood the right way. I know for a fact, from watching my father, listening to a string of cuss words from his mouth every time he messed up a split that it's not.

A thought hits me. "You really are a lumberjack."

He doesn't say anything, but I catch the deep dimple settle into his cheek with his smile. I take that as my sign that he wants to work, so I purse my lips together and focus on loading up the truck while Henry chops wood.

Wondering why he brought me here for his "me" day, as he called it.

I've helped my dad stack a lot of wood; our old century farmhouse is heated in the winter by a woodstove in the kitchen and a stone fireplace in the living room. It's a lot of work, and after an hour of mostly silent labor, under a sun that finally offers some real warmth, my body's coated in a light sweat. I sling my vest and zip-up sweater over the side of the truck, leaving me in a North Gate College long-sleeved shirt.

"You go to a Christian college," Henry says, setting his ax down. It's a statement, not a question, like he's familiar with North Gate.

"Yeah."

He tosses his gloves onto the stump and then wipes his forehead with his forearm. The hair at his nape is damp and beginning to curl. "What's that like?"

"I don't have anything to gauge it against. I guess college, but with the integration of faith. It's meant to ensure you don't lose yourself or your core beliefs."

"And how's that going for you, now that your ex left you to fuck someone else. Have your beliefs changed?"

Again with that word. A word I've always found offensive

but now don't seem to mind coming from his lips. "I've definitely begun to question some things."

"I noticed." He says it so casually, like this is a normal conversation to have between the two of us.

None of this is normal.

I reach into the cooler and hold out a bottle for him. "Water?"

He eyes it, then me for a long moment, and I can't even begin to read what's going on in his mind. Finally he walks toward me to accept it, his steps graceful and confident, his entire aura one of ease and power. His fingertips stall over mine for a few brief seconds. "Thank you."

I force myself not to stare at his mouth this time by zeroing on the sharp protrusion in his thick throat, and how it bobs with each gulp, and how all the muscles in his throat tense, until he's emptied the contents.

Good grief. Had I known whose neck I was burrowing my face into, and tasting, I doubt I would have had the guts to do it, drunk or not.

Henry steps into my personal space and I automatically take a step back, until my back is hitting the truck.

A brief smile touches his lips before he tosses the empty bottle into the truck bed, his gaze on the tidy stack I've already built. "Looks good." His gaze drifts down. "How are your arms? Your back?"

"Fine. I could do this all day with you." The second the sentence replays in my mind, I grimace, my cheeks bursting with heat. "I mean..."

He starts to laugh. "You *are* different when you're sober, aren't you?"

I dip my face to avoid his heavy gaze. "Isn't everyone?"

His hand nudges my chin, forcing my eyes back up to

his. "You don't need to be so hesitant around me." His eyes flicker to my mouth before drifting back up.

"Yes, I do. You're the boss, even if you don't want to be." Having him stand so close to me, the smell of his clean sweat filling my nostrils, is making my heart rate accelerate and the tingling between my legs intensify. It's making me not care that he's the boss.

"I *am* the boss and you're my employee, and I know you won't try anything like you did the other night again. So relax. Please."

Finally he backs away. Unfastening his jacket buttons, he peels off his plaid coat and tosses it into the truck. Beneath it he's wearing a black long-sleeved shirt. One made of that clingy material that's supposed to absorb your sweat. And it's clinging. Oh my God, is it ever clinging.

Henry is all muscle. He has a lean, athletic build, full of contours and bulges, right down to the ridges of his abdomen. When he heaves a giant log onto the stump I can see his arm muscles straining beautifully.

Watching him is exhilarating.

"Come here."

My legs begin to move of their own accord, until I'm standing next to him. I let out a tiny yelp as he grabs me by the hips without warning and pulls me in front of him, my back to his chest. "What are you doing?"

"I'm going to teach you how to swing an ax."

"You assume I want to learn?"

"What do you think the Outdoor team does all day? It's not all about pulling weeds and, as I'm sure you've noticed, there's little grass to cut. That's where your landscaping expertise lies, doesn't it?"

My mouth drops open. I don't dare turn around. "You checked my references?"

"We checked everyone's references."

I finally glance over my shoulder at him, to find his cool eyes watching me. "Then why would your team hire me?"

"They didn't. They passed you over."

I frown, confused. "Well then, why am I here? Was it a mistake?" I knew it! I was hired in error.

He jerks his chin toward the wood, drawing my attention back to it. Bringing his arms around to either side of my body, he lifts the ax in front of us, setting the blade against the stump. "Because *I* hired you."

An odd nervousness courses through my limbs. "I don't understand."

"Take the handle," he instructs, not elaborating.

I do, and he adjusts my gloved hands to have one on the end and one a few inches below. "Don't ever cut wood with nails or curvy pieces. You're just asking to get hurt. And skip the ones with knots in them until they dry out, unless there's a good line away from the knot where you can split the wood."

I'm still focused on the part about him hiring me. "Did you watch the interview videos?"

"I skimmed them."

"Did you see mine?"

The heat radiating off his body so close behind me is warming my back, and yet his breath, skating across my neck, is sending shivers through me.

"Yes." He pauses. "It was compelling."

I frown, trying to recall what could possibly be so compelling. I did almost cry in it.

"You want to aim for the lines in the wood. Like this one here." He steps away to lean forward and run his hand over the vein in the hunk of wood. "That's where it'll split easily. And you want to aim closer to you, rather than on the far side, so you're not hitting the wood with the handle should you miss. You'll hurt your arms that way."

"Okay." I'm doing my best to listen, as I should considering I'm about to swing an ax for the first time.

He repositions himself behind me. A slight gasp escapes me as he fits his big, muddy boot in between mine and nudges my feet apart. In a lower voice, he directs, "You need to adjust your stance. A bit wider. Yeah, like that."

The farther apart my feet shift, the deeper the throb between my legs becomes.

"Now you lift the ax straight up above your head, and keep your arms straight." His arms come around me again, his huge body dwarfing mine, to cover my hands and grip the ax. With his chest pressed against my back and my body seemingly enveloped in his, he helps me to lift the ax straight above my head, the strain from the weight working its way through my muscles. "Let the weight of the ax be your muscle." We bring the weapon down on the piece of wood, hitting it square on the line he pointed out earlier. It makes a nice divot. "It'll take you a few good hits to get all the way through."

As frazzled as I am by his proximity to me, I push that aside. "Let me do it on my own."

He steps away and to the side several feet, his arms folding across his chest in a way that makes his biceps bulge even more. I ignore how self-conscious I feel under the weight of that gaze and mimic the steps, bringing the ax down on the exact spot, the impact jolting my arms.

"Good job. Try it again."

I do. A dozen more times, until sweat trickles down my back, and finally I hear the splitting sound.

"A couple more hits should cut through the last bit, there."

He's right. Finally, I rest the ax head on the ground and smile triumphantly as two chunks lie on the stump. "Where's the next one?"

He chuckles, closing the distance to take the ax out of my hand. "Let's work your stamina up. Your body's going to hurt tomorrow, and we need you on your game. For your job in housekeeping."

I step back as he takes his position in front of the stump, setting up one of the pieces on its end. He swings the ax over his head and brings it down, splitting the wood in one stroke.

I can already feel the heaviness in my arms, and I split one piece of wood. He's been swinging that ax for an hour straight. "You must have high stamina." The second the words leave my mouth, I realize what else it could imply. I shut my eyes and fight the burn in my cheeks. All I seem to ever do around him is blush with embarrassment.

When I crack a lid, I find him setting a fresh piece of wood on the stump.

"My stamina is exceptional," is all he says before getting ready to swing the ax again.

I'm sweating now, and I'm not sure that it has anything to do with outdoor work anymore. Peeling off my college sweatshirt, I leave it on the side of the truck beside my vest and smooth down my black, long-sleeved shirt, wishing for the thousandth time that my breasts weren't so cartoonishly large for my slender body. I've had them since I was fifteen. I remember coming back to sophomore year after summer break and being accused of having a boob job by the nastier girls in school. A ridiculous suggestion, but I guess I can understand why. I *did* go up two cup sizes in two months.

I duck my head and turn my focus to the small woodpile. It takes another half hour to load everything into the back of the truck, and I do it quietly, afraid of what else may come out of my mouth.

I'm finishing up the last few pieces when a rash of noisy bird caws sound nearby.

"Abbi."

"Yeah?"

"Get in the truck. Now." Henry's tone is low and even, but I hear the warning in it and I don't stop to ask questions. I climb into the passenger side. He's already walking slowly toward me, ax gripped in hand, his gaze focused in the distance. I scramble over as he climbs in behind me, slamming the door shut. He seizes me by the hips and, with seemingly little effort, shifts me onto his lap and then over, swapping seats to put himself on the driver side.

Unease slides down my back. "What's wrong?" As the words come out of my mouth, I spot the brown body emerging from the tree line, some hundred feet away.

# nine

"That's a grizzly bear." The telltale hump bobs up and down as the beast saunters toward us. I spent plenty of hours reading up on those as part of my research.

Henry remains perfectly still, his gaze locked on it. "A teenager. They're more brazen than the older ones. More likely to come out to investigate." He's speaking softly, calmly. "I saw tracks around here last week."

"You *knew* there was a grizzly bear wandering around here and you brought me?" I can't help the accusation in my tone.

"Relax. He's just curious. I won't let him do anything to you."

A small part of me relishes the protective words, but it's overshadowed by the bigger issue at hand. "I read they can break into cars."

"He's not the Incredible Hulk, Abbi. He's not going to smash through the glass and grab you in one swoop." Henry chuckles softly. "As soon as I crank the engine, he's going to bolt. Trust me. And even if he doesn't, we'll drive away. Sit back and keep calm. You get to see nature up close today. Something none of the other staff is likely to see."

I try to mimic Henry's ease, settling back into the seat, even though my heart is hammering inside my chest and my breaths come out ragged and my voice sounds shaky. "So that's a teenager? As in, it's not full-grown?" I can already see that its back easily lines up with the truck's hood, even from this distance.

"He's going to be a big one. I'm guessing close to a thousand pounds."

I watch it move, the power in its steps. "How do you know he's a he?"

"See the way he sways as he walks, with his hind legs farther apart? Males do that in the spring, during mating season."

"You know a lot about bears."

The grizzly is maybe twenty feet away. Henry lowers his voice to a whisper. "I spent my summers in Alaska when I was growing up."

The bear is coming around to my side.

"Oh my God," I hiss.

"Slide closer to me if you're afraid," Henry whispers, but I'm paralyzed, the grizzly no more than ten feet from my door, his gaze on me. You're not supposed to look it in the eyes and yet I can't help it. They're narrow and assessing me.

"Why's he doing that?" I ask as the bear steps from side to side, like he doesn't know which direction to go. Suddenly he charges straight for my door. I yelp and scamper backward across the seat toward Henry.

Onto Henry's lap, into his arms.

The bear veers to the side, taking several steps back.

"He knows we're here and he's wary. Stay still," Henry whispers into my ear, the words skating across my skin.

"No problem." The fact that I'm in my boss's lap hasn't escaped me, but I'm temporarily distracted. Thankfully, he hasn't pushed me off.

Yet.

"See?" Henry's hand sits on my trembling thigh, rubbing it soothingly, but I only have eyes for the side mirror, where I can see the bear now approaching the truck, where my vest and sweatshirt hang off the side. "He's curious."

"Oh, shit," I mumble, realizing what he's after. "I have turkey jerky in my vest pocket."

"Turkey jerky?"

"Yes. I always get hungry midmorning and I didn't know what I'd be doing today."

"But, *turkey*?" Henry mutters something about beef but I'm not listening, too focused on the bear.

Sure enough, the bear tips his head to sniff the air around it. Then he's up on his hind legs, his massive front paws landing on the side of the truck, rocking us and earning my nervous yelp. His nails drag along the side in a scraping sound that can't be good for the paint. He starts rubbing his nose along my vest, leaving a trail of wet against the soft pink.

"Do you think he'll take it?"

The bear drops to all fours, and my vest vanishes with him. Seconds later, I hear the sound of material tearing, and then he's swaggering away, putting about twenty feet of distance between us and him, with his prize and pieces of pink fabric dangling from his mouth.

My initial terror has abated somewhat as we watch him hunker down on his rump and work away at the wrapping. "That must be hard for him, with those giant paws."

"He'll manage just fine," Henry whispers, chuckling softly.

Heat on my thigh reminds me that his strong hands are resting there. Quite provocatively, too; halfway up, his fingers splayed. I glance down at them, deciding if this is okay.

"We should get back," he murmurs. "We won't be getting any more wood split today."

"Right." I'm disappointed and I don't do a good job of hiding it from my voice. The morning with Henry was fun and therapeutic, and exactly what I needed to ease my conscience about how I acted with him that first night. Maybe that's why he invited me to tag along.

I need to climb off his lap before I do something to add to my track record of inappropriateness around this man.

I make to move but his hands tighten their grip, pulling me back a touch, until I can feel something hard press against my ass.

My heart begins racing, pumping adrenaline into my veins.

I may be inexperienced, but I'm not stupid.

Is this happening?

Henry has an erection. Is it simply because I'm sitting on him? Or is it *for* me? Maybe his cool exhales against my neck aren't intentional, either. I feel the urge to grind myself against him. Would he be okay with that? No, I don't think so. He made a point of saying that he trusted me not to try anything when I'm sober.

But now he's pinning me down in his lap and his erection is digging in to me, and his shallow pants fill the truck to compete with my own.

"Did you tell anyone about the other night?" Henry's deep voice has turned soft and seductive.

I'm shaking my head before I can manage any words.

"No. I mean, Tillie figured out that *something* happened with someone, but I didn't tell her that it was you."

"Why not?"

My eyes dart to the rearview mirror and I find myself pinned down by his gaze, the look dark and daring. "I don't know. I was embarrassed, I guess?"

"What exactly were you embarrassed about?" His voice is so melodic, as if coaxing me to respond.

A strangled sound escapes me. "I don't know. That I was drunk. That I said all kinds of stupid, crazy things about my ex-fiancé and... other things."

"Other things, like when you asked me to fuck you?"

I struggle to form a coherent answer. He must know this makes me uncomfortable, that I'm mortified. So why is he tormenting me? Does he like making me squirm? Or is he punishing me for my behavior? Or did he bring me out here because I asked him to have sex with me and now he wants to deliver?

What would a man like Henry Wolf do to a girl like me?

He did promise me that I wouldn't be inexperienced for long with him.

He also said that I should spend the next four months fucking someone in every position imaginable. Is he offering to be that guy?

Would it be four months? Or one night? If it's true that this guy goes through women like underwear, why would I want to give away my virginity to him, to be used and tossed aside?

I wouldn't. Of all things, that I'm sure of.

And this is the owner, I remind myself. He could have me on the next flight back to Chicago if I do or say the wrong thing here. Or worse, Pennsylvania.

I finally free myself from his gaze to stare ahead.

"You look perplexed. Why?"

"Because this feels like a test."

A ghost of a smile passes his lips. "Maybe it is."

For five pounding heartbeats, with his grip on my thighs tightening, and his body leaning in until his mouth is a hairsbreadth away from my neck, I make myself believe that I'm not delusional, that his hard dick is for me, that Henry Wolf has invited me here for more than to simply help him stack wood, and that I could actually deliver on that.

My breaths turn ragged, waiting.

"Watch this," he whispers, reaching for the ignition. The bear has finished my snack and is now on all fours, eyeing us. With one flick of Henry's wrist, the sudden, loud rumble of the engine sends the bear bolting for the tree line at speeds I can't fathom for a body that big.

"And that's why you should never try to outrun a bear."

He leans back and releases a heavy sigh. His hands slip from my legs, one reaching for the heat dial, leaving my thighs cold and me instantly missing his touch. Warmth blasts out from the dashboard.

I slide off him and shift to my spot in the truck. The air is still tense and I can't stand tension, so I clear my throat and say the first thing that comes to mind. "I've changed my mind. I don't want to plant trees. Leave the land barren."

The truck fills with his deep laughter and I instantly relax. His laugh is beautiful and it reminds me that, above all else that he may be, Henry Wolf is still human.

"Should I leave my vest here?" I stare out at the tattered remains lying in the mud.

I feel his gaze on my chest before I even turn back. It sits there for five racing heartbeats, intense and probing, until my nipples begin to tighten. I'm sure he can see them poking out of my thin cotton sports bra. "For now. I'll get you a new one," Henry promises, as the truck lurches into motion.

The drive back goes much faster than on the way out, and I find myself wishing we were still stacking wood. "How long will you be staying in Alaska?" Is this it? Will I see him again before he leaves? Wolf Cove suddenly feels lonelier with the idea of him not being here.

His fingers strum the steering wheel. "I'm staying for the season."

"Seriously?"

"Yeah. Why?" He glances over at me, curiosity in his eyes.

"Don't you have other hotels to open, or something?"

"I have a lot on the go, but I've decided to focus on Wolf Cove for now and work remotely on everything else. It's important to me that it succeeds."

Inexplicable happiness fills my chest. Does that mean almost four months with Henry? Will we be doing any more of these private little trips? Or is that just wishful thinking?

"Why are you smiling?"

"No reason." My cheeks flush.

He pauses. "Does me staying for the summer make you happy?"

I bite my bottom lip, deciding whether to be honest. I finally settle on, "Maybe."

He says nothing, turning into the driveway.

"You're back to being Mr. Wolf when we pass those gates, aren't you?"

"Yes." No hesitation.

"Well, then it was nice to spend this time with you." My eyes drop to my lap.

"I trust you know where you're going this afternoon."

"To set the rooms on the fourth floor, and then collect

my uniform." The instructions appeared in my inbox last night during dinner.

A secretive smirk touches his lips. "Don't worry, I doubt you'll find it as awful as you expect."

"We'll see what your guests have to say. I don't think I've ever actually made a bed properly."

"Huh." He mutters something that sounds like, "I'll keep that in mind," under his breath. The wheels squeak as the truck rolls to a stop where Henry picked me up this morning. The hotel is alive with workers now, carrying supplies from the docks, raking the beach, and I'm sure a thousand other things I'm not even aware of. Grizzly bear or not, the morning was much more peaceful than what I anticipate the next few days will be. "Do you need me to help you unload the wood?"

"No. I have the Outdoor crew for that."

I shoot him a glare, earning his smirk.

It quickly falls off his beautiful face, though. "I'm glad I can trust you to keep things to yourself. I'd like to ask that you continue to do so. If anyone does ask, tell them you helped me load wood. *If* anyone asks."

I frown. "That's all I did. Do you mean about the bear? Or..." My eyes inadvertently drift to his lap before I snap them back and swallow hard.

A wicked smirk touches his lips. "You can respect that, right?"

"Yes."

"I thought so."

"Maybe I'll see you around."

"Maybe."

I reach for the handle, but then stop, the one unanswered question still ringing in my ears. "You said that *you* hired me? Why?"

He stares out the windshield for the longest time. When he finally turns, it's to settle a dark, heated gaze on me. "Because it looked like you really needed this."

"I did. I do." I clear my voice to get the shake out of it. Lord, he can be intimidating at the snap of a finger.

"Well then, I wanted to give it to you."

The mood in the truck has turned dark and palpable, and I feel the sudden urge to escape. I slip out and head toward the main lodge, replaying his words. It would be easy to believe he meant that I really needed this job, or I really needed to get away to the peaceful wilderness of Alaska.

Something tells me he's talking about something else, though.

I glance over my shoulder to find him watching me quietly from his truck. That stare, it's almost... wolfish.

# ten

"Fifth floor needs ten more corkscrews and shoe polish kits!" Shelley, one of the room service supervisors, hollers. "Can you ladies bring those up? Last request, then you can go get your uniforms and call it a day. Promise."

"Sure thing," Tillie answers for us, strolling past me to grab the corkscrews from the supply bin against the wall to our left. All the major staples—bottle openers, extra pens, batteries, adapters for foreigners, the special custom-made Wolf Hotel branded chocolates—are sorted there for easy access. "Maybe you should carry these, with those broken arms and all." She winks and dumps the corkscrews into my appreciative hands.

I guess being in Chicago all year has softened my muscles, because only hours later—albeit long, arduous hours of shuttling extra pillows, towels, and hair dryers all over the hotel and, yes, wrestling with bed sheets—my arms are aching something fierce.

I'm exhausted. All I want to do is curl up in my little bed, and as soon as I'm able, that's exactly what I'll be doing.

"That's what you get for disappearing into the woods with Mr. Wolf," Tillie hisses as we head toward the staff elevator.

I spear her with a warning glare. Tillie's the only one who knows who I left with, and that's because she badgered me until I let it slip. In trying to respect Henry's wishes, I asked her to keep it to herself.

"Oh, relax. I'm not gonna say nothin'." She hits the Up button with her elbow and then stands back. "I can't believe you spent all morning watching that man cut wood and did not take one picture. Did he sweat? Oh, I bet he was sweating."

"I didn't notice," I lie. "I know that *I* was sweating. It was hard work."

"Why'd he ask you, anyway? I mean..." Her eyes roam my tiny frame.

"I think it was a reality check for outdoor work in Alaska. So I'd shut up and be happy in Housekeeping."

"Lugging wood would do it, I guess." A woman passes us in the corridor, her maid uniform slung over her shoulder. "Not bad, hey?" Tillie says, nodding toward it.

As far as frumpy housekeeping uniforms go, I'd say we lucked out. The French-inspired dresses are classy yet functional, all black with cap sleeves and cowl necklines, trimmed with white lace. Someone was modeling it earlier. It's flattering. Nothing too revealing, and comfortable enough—though I haven't scrubbed any toilets, yet.

The elevator doors open just as someone calls out, "Abbi, wait!" We turn to see Belinda speeding toward us, her heels clicking furiously.

"Go ahead. I'll be up in a sec," I tell Tillie, watching her disappear behind the doors.

"Did you get my message?" Belinda pants, like she's out of breath.

I frown. "No. But I don't have my phone on me." I've enjoyed not carrying it, being disconnected from the world. Mainly from Greenbank.

She waves it away. "Not a problem. We have a solution to the role mix-up."

Dare I hope? "You're moving me to Outdoor?"

"No." Her lips purse together. "But I'm sure you'll enjoy it." Is there a hint of bitterness in her voice? "Beginning tomorrow morning, you'll be covering Penthouse One."

"Penthouse One." I frown. "I don't understand. What does that even mean?" And how is that better?

"Here." She thrusts an iPad at me. "All the information you need is in there. Guest programs, amenities, procedures. It'll take you a few days to digest it all, but you'll have time to do that."

"But—"

"You'll need a liaison's uniform. They should have something that fits you."

I stare at the iPad. "Okay?" I'm starting tomorrow and yet the hotel manager has admitted that it'll take me a few days to know what to do. "Are you sure I'm the best person for this job?"

Again, that lip pucker. "It doesn't matter what I think. Mr. Wolf insisted on it."

My eyebrows must jump halfway up my forehead. "He did *what*?" Clearly he's not as smart of a businessman as I thought he was if he's going to put me with his most valuable guests.

Belinda hands me a key card. "Each penthouse has its own uniquely coded liaison card. You know where the penthouses are, right?"

I nod absently.

"To the right of the guest door is another door. That is the one you use. You'll be expected to arrive on site tomorrow morning at 7:00 a.m., sharp."

There are so many questions flying through my head that I don't know where to begin.

She taps the iPad in my hand with her nail. "Watch the video, read through the training sections, and if you have any more questions, Paige will help you."

I watch her stalk away as if in a rush, checking her watch as she rounds the corner.

A rash of nerves floods my stomach. What on earth was Henry thinking, putting me in this job? I thought he cared about his hotel?

I wish I knew how to find him so I could talk him out of this. But I don't have time to hunt him down. I need to drop off these kits, get my new uniform, and get back to the cabin to familiarize myself.

I have a feeling I won't be sleeping tonight.

"*The* Cabins?" Autumn looks as shocked as Tillie did when I told her. "You need *years* of experience kissing rich people's asses to be put there. Only superstar seasoned Wolf employees get that kind of gig."

"Yeah. I don't get it either." I sigh, studying my new "uniform"—a breezy white blouse and plum-colored pencil skirt with a provocative slit up the back—that hangs in its dry-cleaning packaging on my hook.

I'm neither seasoned nor a superstar and yet the owner of Wolf Cove Hotel wants me catering to the needs of the most elite guests. Why? "So, what am I going to be doing there?" If anyone would know, Autumn would.

"Oh, man." She unfastens a pearl earring and tosses it into a jewelry box. "Well, you're basically there to cater to every need that your guests may have. You're available to them at all times. All Wolf hotels have servants' quarters on the same floor as the penthouses. Here, I heard that they've built little quarters inside each cabin, where you stay until you're needed. Bring a book," she warns, with a knowing stare. "And, depending on how demanding the guest is, you may be expected to stay overnight and cater to them at 3:00 a.m. if they buzz. When they want room service, you order it for them. When they want to eat at the restaurant, you make their dinner reservations. You make their excursion arrangements and spa sessions; you recommend activities, you ensure their liquor cabinet is full at all times, their coffee and tea is poured, their dishes are always cleared, their rooms are cleaned."

"You wipe their asses if they ask you nicely enough," Tillie murmurs.

I feel my face blanching. I hope she's kidding.

"And the best part?" Autumn goes on. "You don't even have to do the actual cleaning. You dial up Housekeeping when it's convenient for the guest and someone else comes and does the work. Consider yourself a butler, only female."

Well, that's one blessing. But... "I'm supposed to book excursions?" My head is beginning to spin with all the things I need to know that I won't, not before the morning. Why do I need to be there so early, anyway? No one's going to be there at 7:00 a.m.

"Yes." Autumn grins, climbing to the top bed. "Through your friendly concierge. And if you're lucky, they'll take you on one. You know, because they need a servant while they watch Kodiak bears and view glaciers."

Mention of bears distracts me from my current agitation, bringing me back to this morning. And Henry. He has invaded my thoughts all afternoon and into the evening as it is.

"Penthouse guests get what they want, when they want it. Honestly, it's the country club of the service world. At least, it is for a Wolf employee."

"He's insane." I groan as I ease my sore body into the bottom bunk, having already showered and readied for bed.

"Who's insane?"

"Mr. Wolf. Apparently, he's the one who put me in this job." I've been wracking my brain for the last half hour, trying to figure out why he would. There is nothing that happened today that should give him the false belief that I can do this job. A dark thought crosses my mind. Maybe he wants me to mess up so he has an excuse to fire me. I quickly dismiss that, though. It makes no more sense than anything else.

"She knocked Wolf on the head with a piece of wood when they were out earlier today, is what I think," Tillie says, grabbing her robe and her shower caddy.

Autumn's face suddenly appears beside me, her hair dangling in wet, freshly washed tendrils. "Wait, you were with *Mr. Wolf*?"

I sigh. So much for Tillie keeping her mouth shut. Thank God I didn't tell her anything more than I was supposed to. "I helped him load firewood."

She frowns. "Why? He has the Outdoor crew."

"Don't know, but who am I to say no to the boss." I doubt I'd be capable of saying no to him, regardless of request.

"And because I can't say no, I'll be down here, studying up on my role as liaison to a bunch of rich people all night."

"You best suck it on up then because any of us, including me, would murder to be in your place. You're gonna double your salary this summer, girl. I, for one, am green with envy," Tillie mutters, heading toward the door.

Autumn, at least, offers me a sympathetic smile and yanks on the privacy curtain to close us in.

I slide on my headset and get ready for a long night.

# eleven

My black Tieks pad softly along the stone path, sheltered from the drizzle by the elaborately constructed wooden canopy above. The covering stretches all the way from the main lodge to the cabins, easily three hundred feet away. In one hand I hold a paper cup filled with staff lounge coffee, in the other the iPad, to hopefully catch up on everything I didn't read when I passed out last night.

Unlike yesterday at this time of the morning, Wolf Cove is buzzing with life, staff preparing to meet the first wave of guests at noon with glasses of champagne and swift check-ins. Again, I wonder what I'm supposed to do until my guest arrives.

Ahead of me, the covered path splits off into three smaller paths, each leading toward an elegant and detailed timber cabin, small replicas of the main lodge. An ornate bronzed sign points me to the right.

Penthouse Cabin One and its grand mahogany door stand before me. As Belinda promised, the servants' entrance is next to it. Inhaling deeply, I stick my key card into the slot and wait for the telltale beep and green light to allow me in.

The liaison's room is a small nook. On my left is a basic office: a desk, phone, computer, stationery supplies, and the like. Across from me is another door. The one, I presume, that leads into the suite. To my right, shelving with extra supplies—towels, bedding, every toiletry you could imagine, wine glasses—line the wall, along with a shiny stacked washer and dryer. There's a doorway at the far end. I wander through it and find a small powder room and a twin bed tucked into the corner. I guess that's where I'll sleep, if I have a guest who insists on it?

I'm not crazy about this idea.

With a nervous sigh, I set my things on the desk and survey the space again, scanning over the bulletin board. It's neatly plastered with all kinds of information: the restaurant and room service menus, full alcoholic beverage choices, and phone numbers to all facilities, as well as a checklist of all expected duties, along with timelines.

*Place newspaper in mail slot by 6:30 a.m.* Does that mean I need to be here by six thirty every morning? And how does Wolf Cove even get newspapers that early?

*Deliver new vase of fresh-cut flowers each day with breakfast.* That, I can remember.

*Turndown service at 8:00 p.m. or when the guest requests it, if they are staying in.*

When does my shift here end? Obviously I'll be handing off at some point... right?

Suddenly the door to the suite opens and I spin on my heels.

"Good, you're here," Henry says, filling the doorframe with his body.

It takes me a moment to respond, my mouth hanging

open in shock. "What are you doing here?" I scan him from head to toe, and excited butterflies fill my stomach, making me forget my current stress levels. He's as intoxicating as ever to look at, his black pants custom-fit to a body that sees the leg press at the gym regularly, no doubt. His dress shirt is still hanging open, revealing a white V-neck t-shirt beneath, the material thin and fitted enough to highlight his pectoral muscles and a six-pack beneath.

"I live here."

"You *live* here?" My gaze drifts past him to catch glimpses of a white couch and fur rug, and a rustic-hewn side table.

"While I'm in Alaska, yes." Mesmerizing blue eyes float over my uniform, unnerving me. I was already feeling self-conscious in it. My skirt hugs my body from my hips right down to my knees. It's a good thing that bending won't be easy in it because the slit up the back is deep. The blouse is more fitted across the chest than I had expected, and I don't know if that's the design or my disproportionately ample boobs. It's missing at least two buttons off the top for what I'm comfortable with. I won't be able to lean over without exposing myself. All in all, it's a modest, professional outfit that's not so modest or professional after all. But I guess all the female liaisons wear it, so I need to suck it up.

Henry takes several steps back—his feet are bare—and gestures for me to come in.

I follow him, the smell of soap and aftershave filling my nostrils. His hair is still damp from a shower.

I finally force my eyes off him—because I'm staring—and train them on the full wall of floor-to-ceiling windows on the opposite end. The vast expanse of water stretches beyond. "Nice place." Inside, the cabin walls and ceiling are made entirely of wood. I can't be sure of what kind, but it has a grayish coloring, which complements the soft decorative palette of whites, grays, and creams. It's obvious that a topnotch designer had a hand in every detail.

My head tips back to take in the double-story vaulted ceiling, and the thick beams running the length on either side. "Steep."

"I like high ceilings," Henry explains easily, wandering over to the dining table, where room service dishes rest. He pours himself a coffee. "Would you like one?"

I hold up my paper cup in answer.

A sexy smirk curls his lip. "I promise, this will be better."

While he's pouring into a second cup, my gaze drifts toward a sliding door to the right, half-open. Behind it I spy the bedroom, a mess of bed sheets strewn over the bed. My body begins to hum with the mental vision of Henry's body tangled within those sheets. Does he wear something? Or does he sleep naked?

"Abbi?"

"Yes?" My head whips back to Henry, to find him holding the creamer over my cup.

"Cream and sugar?"

"Yes, please."

He prepares it wordlessly and then sets the cup in front of me.

"Thank you." I take a long sip, releasing a soft moan. He's right—the stuff from the staff lodge tastes like mud by comparison.

He quietly watches me savor my coffee, one hand resting over the damask-upholstered dining chair, until I begin to squirm under the weighty gaze.

"Why did you tell Belinda to move me here? I don't know the first thing about serving your wealthy guests. I'm going to disappoint people." *You, most of all.*

He sets his mug down. "You're not here to serve my rich guests. I want you to work for me."

I frown, confused. "I thought I already was working for you."

"Not as Wolf Cove staff. As my personal assistant."

"Your personal assistant," I repeat, surprise numbing my senses.

"I lost my assistant recently, and I need someone to keep me organized. Someone I can trust. And, frankly, I need someone to take care of me. Look at this place; it's a disaster."

I scan the room again at his prompt. Aside from a few loose newspapers and empty dishes, I don't see anything amiss. "What would you need me to do?"

"Basic admin work, like managing my calendar and e-mail, booking my meetings, booking excursions with investors and other important clientele that come in. Attend management meetings with me. Liaise with Belinda to make sure the grand-opening event goes smoothly. That is especially important. There will be a lot of media here."

"I have no experience."

"That's not what you said in your interview. You worked in the church office, managing your reverend's calendar and helping organize events, right?"

I laugh. "That's nothing like what you're asking me to do now!" A weekly coffee with Edith, the ninety-two-year-old organist. The first of the month food drive in the church basement. Not exactly on par with the CEO of a luxury hotel chain's daily schedule, I'm sure.

He pops a grape into his mouth and chews slowly. "I called the Reverend. He spoke highly of you."

"Reverend Enderbey? You *called* him?" I squeak. "When?"

"A few days after the job fair."

"You wanted me back then?" His eyebrows spike and I replay my words in my head. "I mean, for this job," I quickly correct, flushing.

He flashes the tiniest, most devilish of smirks, and my stomach flutters. I'm beginning to crave those smirks. "I began considering you for the position then, yes." With slow, measured steps, he closes the distance to me, circling me. "I called your aunt, too. We spoke at length about your work ethic, your reliability, and your values." There's a hint of mockery with that last piece, and I wonder if that has to do with his own lack of faith, or my poor demonstration of those values to date. "She told me all about your painful breakup with the Reverend's son."

"Wait a minute." It dawns on me. "So, that night on the dock, you already knew who I was and that you'd hired me to be your assistant?"

Henry stops directly behind me, forcing me to turn around. I find him on the edge of my personal space, like a sly animal closing in on me. Confusion and wariness compete for my attention. What kind of game is he playing here?

"I hadn't made my final decision yet and, honestly," his steely blue gaze flickers to my mouth, "after that night, I wasn't sure that you would be a good fit for me."

Because I practically licked his neck and asked him to sleep with me. Will I ever live that night down?

"That's why I took you out yesterday morning. I needed to spend time with you, sober, to make sure that this would work."

"And you think it will?"

"Obviously."

*Obviously*. "So, then... Hiring me for the outdoor team—"

"Was never going to happen. When I found out, I made Belinda change you in the system before you got here. There is no way I am putting you in there with those guys. It'd be like dropping a lamb into a pack of wolves."

So Belinda was in on this from the beginning. That explains her lack of concern or compassion. "I can take care of myself," I argue, feeling more than a little annoyed at being deceived all this time.

He reaches up to touch my braid, his fingers skimming down the length of it until he lets it fall. "Really? And what do you think would have happened to you that night, had one of them found you on the dock instead of me?" Amusement slides off his face, replaced with a hard look. "Drunk and broadcasting that you're a virgin, your hands all over the guy's chest, whispering in his ear... asking him to fuck you." I gasp at his words, more inappropriate now than when I said them to him that night. "Your night would have ended with you bent over the table in the utility shed, I can promise you that. Most men don't have the kind of control that I do, not when you dangle that kind of bait in front of them."

What is he saying? That he needed to exercise control that night? Was I maybe not imagining things? Was this beautiful, sexy, all-consuming man in front of me considering acting on my request?

I push that thought aside because it no longer matters, if I'm going to be working as his assistant. And because it's plain ludicrous. Still, I struggle to regain my composure. My voice wobbles when I speak. "What if I don't want to take this job?"

Surprise flickers across his face. "You don't want to work with me every day? I thought you were happy that I was staying."

"No, that's not... I'm not saying..." I stumble over my words. "I mean, what if I'm not convinced I can do this job?"

He smiles now. "*I'm* convinced you can do it. You're smart. I think you know when to jump at an opportunity. Fake it 'til you make it, right? Or something like that."

I *did* lie to get this job. Though, they saw through it immediately.

I nod. "So, administrative stuff?"

Another three heartbeats pass and then he moves past me and back toward the dining table and his coffee cup. I sense his demeanor shifting back to a more professional one. "And personal assistant help, too. I dragged a guy out of bed last night at midnight to dry-clean my suit because I didn't get a chance to bring it down earlier. I need someone who's going to be on top of those kinds of things for me."

On top of dressing Henry? What about undressing Henry... I grit my teeth to keep the smile at bay. "That, I think I can do."

His hand waves through the area. "And keeping this place in order, clean. I don't let staff in here. I have too many confidential and private things lying around."

"You don't trust your staff?"

"No." Not a moment's hesitation answering that.

"But, why hire people you don't trust?"

"I have my reasons," he says, and I can tell he's not going to elaborate. "But I do trust you."

"Why?"

"Because my gut tells me that I can, and I make decisions based on my gut." He pauses, his eyes dipping down over my outfit again, that thick fringe of lash a thing of beauty. "I'm your boss, and you're my employee, and I know you won't cross any lines. While you're sober, anyway."

So, again, it all comes down to sex. And women wanting

him, perhaps. Spoken by any other man, I'd write him off as an egotistical douchebag. But it's *this* man standing in front of me, and I've already seen and heard firsthand how his employees talk about him, like he's a piece of meat they'll do anything to sink their teeth into.

"This job means spending a lot of time with me. Being in my living space with me while I'm rushing in and out, getting ready for meetings and events. Putting up with me while things are stressful. Do you think you can handle that?"

I can't ignore how my heart hasn't stopped racing since he opened the door, or how the flutters of excitement have only increased with every word out of his mouth. Or how I keep inhaling deeply, to absorb the fresh, clean smell of him. Or how I keep replaying the feel of his arms around my body and his erection against my ass.

Is this a good idea? Am I setting myself up for constant frustration? I'll probably become a champion masturbator by the end of the summer.

What's worse, the way he asks it, it's like he knows exactly what's going through my head right now. I don't want my boss to know that I'm attracted to him in a major way. A way I didn't believe I could be. A way that has all but shoved Jed from my thoughts.

I have to clear my throat, afraid my words will come out shaky. "Exactly how much time?"

He levels me with a look. "I want you available to me day and night, unless I say otherwise. Some days will require more than others. Some early mornings, some late nights. You'll be paid a flat salary that more than covers an hourly wage plus overtime."

I frown. "But..." *Day and night?* "How will that work?" It dawns on me. There is no staff shift trade-off.

Henry frowns. "You look worried."

"I'm just taking it all in. Will I have to stay in there?" I glance back toward the staff quarters, to the little hobbit room. I'm not sure how I feel about that. On the one hand, it's my own room. On the other, I won't get any sleep knowing Henry is so close.

He smiles. "I'm not a tyrant. I will give you time off, Abbi." He strolls over to the desk that sits in one corner, overlooking the water, and collects paper and pen. "Before we go any further, I need you to sign this confidentiality agreement." He sets it on the table in front of me. "It's pretty standard."

"I've never signed one of these," I admit, picking it up.

"No?" His fingers move absently over his shirt, fastening his buttons. "I've signed a thousand in my lifetime already. Take your time and read through it. I need to finish getting dressed now." He disappears into his bedroom, leaving me to the paperwork.

It's pretty easy to understand. Basically, I'm not to talk about Henry—anything he says or does—or he can sue my ass.

"I do require that you not drink while you're working for me," he calls out from his room. "Given what I saw the other night, it's too risky."

"I think we've already covered that I won't ever be drinking again." I scroll my name along the bottom, set the pen down gingerly and take a deep breath. This feels somehow monumental.

"Done?"

"Yes."

"Good. I need you in here."

My heart skips a beat. He needs me in his bedroom. "Coming," I say, my voice shaky. All kinds of visions float through my head that I didn't even know I could conjure up, but that make blood rush through my body. Henry stripped down. Henry, lying on his bed, waiting for me.

I find him standing in front of the dresser mirror, holding two ties in his hands. "Which one should I wear?"

I sigh with relief. "I like the charcoal-and-silver one with that suit."

"This one?" He holds the navy one up and I frown, earning his laugh and swap. "I'm color-blind," he admits, looping the one I chose around his neck, tossing the other onto the bed. "So don't be surprised if I ask you to help me match my socks and ties on occasion." He pauses. "Are you good with tying ties?"

"I think so." I tied Jed's ties all through high school and into college. I make my way over, slowing to take in the wall of glass and the water beyond, hyperaware that I'm about to help Henry get dressed. "What a view to wake up to every day," I mumble, trying to diffuse my nerves.

"It's something, all right." I feel him staring at my face as my fingers begin flying, making quick work of the silk, all while my heart feels like it's going to leap out of my chest at any moment.

My hands are trembling.

"You have freckles," he murmurs. "I never noticed them before."

I scrunch my nose with the reminder. The light smattering across the bridge has always bothered me. "My glasses usually cover them."

"I'd offer to get my wetsuit on and dive for them, but I don't think I want to. You should keep wearing contacts. They suit you better."

I don't know what to say to that, so I say nothing, focusing instead on pulling the end of the tie through, only to find that I've made it way too short. "Hold on, I have to redo."

He waits quietly, as I loosen and adjust, and then go through the steps again, my fingers grazing against his body occasionally. Each swipe makes my skin tingle and my breathing more uneven.

"There. I think that's perfect," I whisper, taking a step back to admire him. God, he is stunning. I honestly can't tell which look I like more: the businessman or the lumberjack. Both are equally hot.

But I'll bet neither can compete with Henry Wolf, naked.

I've never even seen a man naked and I'm thinking about that right now? Ten minutes in to being his assistant? How on earth am I going to work alongside him for the next four months and maintain my composure?

"Good?"

I duck my head, smiling shyly. "Yes. You're definitely ready for... whatever you're doing today."

He laughs. "Exactly how I expect the person managing my calendar to answer. Come." His fingertips brush the small of my back, the heat from them searing my skin, as he ushers me past his rumpled sheets. "You can make my bed for me later." There's amusement in his voice.

Now the comment he made in the truck yesterday after I admitted to not being able to properly make a bed makes sense.

Henry leads me to the desk. He digs out an iPhone from the drawer. "So I can reach you at all times. It works everywhere on the property. And here are my passwords to my e-mail accounts and my voice mail. Save them in your phone and then shred this note. You can access my e-mail with my computer. Feel free to open any e-mail that comes in unless it's marked confidential in the subject line. Those are not to be opened. Belinda will be by with a laptop and I believe she has already given you an iPad."

"Yes, last night." So I could study hours of useless information to be a liaison, it would seem. Why wouldn't she tell me that I was going to be Henry's assistant?

"Good. You're all set then. I have about forty conference call requests in my inbox. Please get them booked in for this week, between 5:00 and 8:00 a.m. Pacific time. Whatever length of time the requester has set, cut it in half." He scans his watch. "A few key people are arriving this morning. I need to meet them at the helicopter pad shortly." He collects the suit jacket that lies across his couch and slides his taut, muscular arms into it. "The suit hanging behind my door needs to go to the cleaners. Belinda has already made arrangements for the day, but make dinner reservations for three at Lux for 7:00 p.m. Ensure Cedric is available to us for wine selection, and that Phil is ready with the plane for our excursion tomorrow morning at 8:30 a.m."

My mind is spinning as he's firing off instructions. Grabbing a pen and pad, I quickly jot down the important names and times, because those will be the first I forget.

He stops at the door. "Oh, one other thing. In here, when it's just the two of us, it's okay to call me Henry. But outside of these walls, it's Mr. Wolf at all times. Is that understood?"

"Yes. Understood." It's a good reminder that this man is my boss. I need to douse whatever fire my body wants to stoke for him.

"So?"

"So..."

"I assume you're accepting this job."

This is my chance to get out of this predicament.

Oh, who am I kidding? "Yes. Of course I am." I tuck a

strand of hair behind my ear, nervously. "I hope I'm what you're looking for."

"To be honest, you are not what I was expecting." He pauses, and a flash of something dark flickers in his eyes. "But I think you're *exactly* what I'm looking for while I'm here."

What *exactly* is he looking for then? Because if it's me, then it's not a competent, experienced assistant. But I will try.

A knock on the door sounds. "That will be your employment contract." He opens the door and Belinda steps through.

She smiles and then, seeing me standing there, sets the paperwork and a laptop down on the side table. "Abbi, please read over and sign this as soon as possible. The laptop is to stay here at all times."

"Okay. Thanks."

She looks to Henry. "Can I have a word with you? *In private*?"

That's my cue. "I'll take that suit to the cleaners," I offer, rushing to his bedroom to grab it and head for the servants' door. That was one of Paige's strict directives: always use staff entrances and exits wherever possible.

I've stepped outside, suit slung over my shoulder, and the door is about to close when I realize that I left my key inside. My hand blocks the door just before it shuts and locks on me, relieved that I don't have to start off on the wrong foot by ringing the doorbell to gain entry.

"I still don't understand why you wanted *her*. She has no hotel or corporate experience," I hear Belinda say through the servants' entrance, still ajar to Henry's cabin.

I freeze, knowing they're talking about me, but unable to keep myself from listening.

"She has *some* experience. And she's a college student with exceptional grades," Henry offers.

I'm a straight-A student. *But how does he know that?*

"She didn't interview well. She shook through the entire interview, wringing her hands like a worried mother hen."

"She was nervous."

"She's awkward. And frumpy."

I don't think there's anything worse than eavesdropping while someone talks negatively about you. I should go, but now I'm afraid they'll hear the door creak open again, and figure out that I was still here all this time.

"Not everyone looks like you, Belinda," Henry says, and I can hear irritation in his voice beginning to mount. I don't know if I should find comfort at his words.

"She doesn't fit the Wolf employee mold. Did you see that cheap small-town special she wore to the interview?"

I didn't think it was *that* bad.

"You're making some bad choices lately, Henry."

"What the hell is your problem?" he snaps.

*Yes, exactly.* What does Belinda have against me working for Henry? I've never done anything to her!

"Is this about Kiera?" she asks.

*Who's Kiera? Henry's ex?*

Silence hangs in the room and I take a step closer to the door, afraid I'll miss his answer.

"I heard things got ugly. And expensive." Belinda's voice has turned soft, more cautious, as if she knows she's treading on thin ice. "I got a call from your father a few days ago."

"For fuck's sakes," he grumbles, and then heaves a sigh of exasperation. "A *few days* ago? Why didn't you tell me right away? What did he want?" This is a new Henry, and not a happy one at that.

"He asked me if there was anything going on up here that he should be worried about."

"And you told him what?"

She clears her throat. "That everything was going smoothly."

"Good. Let that be the answer every time he calls."

"And will it be the truth?"

"I don't like this version of you, Belinda. You work for *me*."

"I work for Wolf, and right now that's still William Wolf, until he officially hands the company over to you. And I've worked too hard for this company to have it all go down the drain because you're fucking some farm girl. She's twenty-one!"

My mouth drops open in shock with the suggestion. She thinks he... we're... *why would she think that?*

Henry starts to laugh. It's not a happy sound, though. "Is that what this is all about? Are you jealous of Abbi? What's wrong, Belinda? You're starting to panic about the big forty coming up?"

"Fuck you." The contrite woman is gone again.

"Don't forget who gave you this job," he warns through a growl. "I chose the farm girl to avoid any more headaches."

"Well, she's not exactly *ugly*."

"No, she's not," he agrees. "But she is a *girl*, pining for some spineless dickhead who dumped her and is never coming back. Insecure, stupid little girls don't attract me, Belinda. You know that."

My cheeks burn with hurt and confusion. He just finished telling me that I was a smart woman, and I lapped it up. Now I'm an insecure, stupid little girl?

"Maybe I need to be reminded."

I frown at the suggestive tone in Belinda's words.

There's a long, lingering pause, unsettling my nerves. "Wolf Hotels will be mine next month, and you won't have a job here if you don't inform me the second my father calls next time." Henry delivers that threat in a curt, no-nonsense tone that I never want him to use with me. "And if you ever feel like giving him truths, how about you tell him how much you loved having my dick in your mouth while we were opening that hotel in Istanbul. Find out if he thinks that was professional."

*Oh my God.*

He's her boss. Isn't that against the rules?

Above my shock, though, envy erupts in my chest. Now I know why she hates me so much. Though it's ridiculous.

Belinda's heels click along the tile and then the main entrance door opens and shuts. I steal a peek through the tiny window in time to see Henry marching two steps ahead of her down the covered path.

I'm alone.

I drop the suit over the desk chair, the high of being hired by Henry as his assistant dampened. While I never truly believed that Henry could be attracted to me, I must have been holding out some hope, some fantasy, that he might be. Now I know for certain that the looks, the moments, the erection pressing against my ass, were all wishful thinking on my part. I feel all the more ridiculous that my subconscious ever entertained such thoughts.

At least hearing it straight from his mouth will help me keep myself grounded and my head out of the clouds.

I shouldn't let it get to me. I *am* a farm girl. I *am* insecure, especially after what happened with Jed. I wish I wasn't so. And I would be stupid to believe that anything that's happened equates to his attraction to me.

But the idea that he sees me as an insecure, stupid little

girl pining for a spineless coward has slipped under my skin like a bothersome sliver.

Because, deep down inside, I know he's right.

Enough already. It's been three months, and Jed is dating someone else. I need to move on. I'm twenty-one years old, I'm in Alaska, and I need to let go.

And become someone that Henry not only trusts, but respects. After all, I'm going to be spending the next four months working for him.

He's given me a job—a gift, really. I'm going to be the best assistant he could ask for.

Marching back to the desk, I collect the scrap of paper. "Cedric... Phil..." I read off my notes, all chicken scratch. Nearly illegible, even to me. "Oh, you're going to regret this, Henry." I dial the concierge desk.

"How may I be of assistance, Mr. Wolf?" A deep male voice croons.

"It's not Mr. Wolf. It's his personal assistant." I try that on for size. It sounds weird. "Is Autumn there yet?"

# twelve

The main doorbell rings.

I pause mid e-mail. Is Henry expecting someone? I know he doesn't want anyone in here.

A bellhop stands outside with a large rectangular box in his hand. "Delivery for Abbi Mitchell."

"Me?" I frown, taking it from him. He trots off down the path, leaving me staring at the box with the Patagonia logo on top. It's so light, it feels empty. I open it at the dining table to find something wrapped in tissue and a handwritten note sitting on top. My heart flutters as I recognize Henry's writing from earlier today.

*Deepest apologies for allowing a grizzly bear to eat your clothing.*

*And your turkey jerky.*

*P.S. They didn't have pink, but I thought this would look nice on you.*

I can't keep the stupid grin from my face as I unwrap and pull the lightweight silver down vest out and hold it up in the sunlight. It's soft and luxurious and the feel of it beneath my fingers tells me it's probably three times more expensive than my Target special. Beneath it is a North Gate College black zip-up sweatshirt to replace the one dragged through the mud by the bear.

Warmth spreads through my chest. The ever-busy billionaire, who has a hotel opening today, took the time to order this and have it brought here. I can't even say his assistant did it for him, because he didn't have one until today. How did he find the time to take care of this? And so fast!

Something weighs the right-hand pocket down. When I reach and pull out a package of turkey jerky, I start to laugh, and it helps break the dark cloud that's been hovering over me all morning.

A FLUTTER of nerves erupts when Henry strolls through the door at five, and my pulse instantly kicks into high gear.

The moment his eyes touch me, I begin apologizing. "I'm sorry. I've spent all day with your e-mail and calendar. I haven't done much around here."

His fingers fumble with his tie as he heads for his bedroom. "What does this week's schedule look like for me?" The friendly tone from this morning is gone. He's all business now.

I grab my iPad and quickly punch in the code to open up his calendar, something that took me hours to sort out. "I'm waiting for confirmations from a few people, but you will be booked solid from 5:00 to 8:00 a.m. every day." He has, on average, seven meetings each morning, some of them for only fifteen minutes. I wouldn't want to start my days like that, but I guess that's why he's so successful.

"Let me see the schedule?"

I step past the door as he's reaching over the back of his head to pull off his t-shirt.

My breath catches at the sight of his smooth upper body, so perfectly honed with muscle. If this were a magazine picture, I'd assume it had been embellished, but he's right here, in the flesh, his biceps and triceps bulging, his abdominal muscles a washboard of ripples, the grooves around his neck and collarbone begging for my fingers to touch them.

Henry makes Jed look like a scrawny boy by comparison.

And then there's that trail of dark hair that runs downward, disappearing beneath his belt...

"Abbi?"

My eyes snap up to his face with the sound of my name. "Yes?" My voice is a croaky whisper.

He tosses his t-shirt into the hamper—which reminds me that I need to do his laundry—and then extends a large, manicured hand my way. "The schedule? Can I see it?"

Giving my head a shake, I rush forward, stumbling over the white fur rug but regaining my footing. "I color-coordinated the meetings based on area: green is the EU, blue is North America, yellow is Asia, pink is England."

"Pink? Why pink for England?"

I shrug, blushing. "I like pink, and I've always wanted to go to England."

A small frown zags over his brow. "Why England?"

"To see the royal family," I admit, sheepishly. Ever since I was little, I've been fascinated by the idea of a real-life king and queen in a palace.

"Of course," Henry mutters, and I instantly feel stupid.

Of course the silly little girl would want to go to England to see the queen, who's not even *our* queen.

He studies the screen quietly, each moment passing

twisting my stomach into tighter knots. I worked hard today. "This is..."

I hold my breath.

"Good. Very good. I had a feeling you'd hit the ground running."

My chest warms with pride. I didn't screw that up, at least. "I went through all of your e-mails, too, marking the time-sensitive ones and the progress reports. There were a few that I don't know what to do with. I've dumped those into a folder marked 'Needs Henry's attention'."

He hands the iPad back to me, our fingers grazing in the process. "You've picked up even faster than I expected."

Honestly, I had no idea what I was doing, but I just poured myself a coffee, sat down, and began clicking. I'm glad it worked out. "I've ordered coffee delivery for 4:50 a.m. sharp and your poached eggs and fruit for six thirty." Because, after tracking down the room service supervisor, I was able to confirm that that's what he's ordered the last few mornings, and I made an executive decision that that is what he'd have tomorrow. "If you want something else, please let me know. Cedric is on standby for 8:00 p.m. tonight and Phil will have the plane ready by 8:30 a.m. sharp." *Thank you, Autumn, for confirming that Cedric is the head sommelier and Phil is the pilot for the bear touring flights.*

"Great. I need you to bump the dinner reservations up to six. The guys want an earlier dinner, given the time difference."

*Shit.* "Lux might be full." It *is* full, according to Rich, the reservation guy I spoke to. With the online dinner reservation service, today's first guests have been booking for the past two weeks and the early spots filled up first.

"You'll figure it out," he says simply.

I sigh. I don't know how.

A playful smirk touches his lips as his gaze takes in the freshly made bed. That, at least, I managed to get done. "Was it as bad as you expected?"

I smile shyly. "No." Thanks to yesterday's room prep marathon, I'm now an expert at making beds whether I want to be or not. Paige did spot checks in each of our rooms, to ensure we weren't being lazy. She said my corners were on point.

And, oddly enough, I found I didn't mind hiking up my curve-hugging skirt and crawling over Henry's mattress to fight with the fitted sheet that wouldn't stay in place, because I knew he'd be the one sliding into it tonight.

Maybe naked.

Hopefully alone.

How often does Henry have sex? He said he doesn't have a girlfriend. There obviously isn't one here. A summer without sex never seemed impossible to me because I have no idea what I'm missing. He said he's staying up here for the summer. Will he not have sex all summer? Or will he find someone? Belinda, I guess.

Or maybe he'll have friends fly in and "visit."

I'm thinking far too much about my boss having sex while I'm in his bedroom and he's shirtless. And uninterested in me.

I promised myself that I wouldn't allow this anymore.

I clear my throat once again, afraid of what my voice may sound like. "Thank you for the vest and sweater. They were a nice surprise."

He slides his watch off and tosses it on the dresser. "It's the least I could do, and you need them up here." His hand begins unfastening his belt.

My eyes widen. I guess that's my cue to leave. "I'll go

make that reservations call now." I spin on my heels and march for the door.

"Abbi."

I stop, but don't turn around. "Yes?" Why must my voice sound so needy?

"I need to jump into the shower so I'll give you my suit. I spilled some Coke on it earlier. Please take it to the cleaners and then you can call it a day."

I listen to the jangle of his belt and slide of material, and know that he has taken his pants off. I am 99 percent sure this is considered inappropriate behavior for a boss with his personal assistant, but I'm 100 percent sure that I don't mind.

I keep my eyes away though, letting my gaze wander over to the en suite bathroom. It's a fishbowl, with a hall down the center dividing the area in two: the toilet on the right, behind a glass-and-tile wall, and a massive walk-in glass stall to the left that houses the jacuzzi tub and a shower area that could easily fit five people. A pocket door separates the bathroom from the rest of the room.

I hazard a sideways glance to see him strolling toward me in a pair of black boxer briefs, suit in hand, powerful legs tensing with each step. I hold my shaky arm out and he drapes the suit over it gently. "Thank you."

"I'll see you tomorrow," I say, my voice suddenly husky, and then I duck out. I hang the suit over a chair and head for the desk phone to change dinner plans, acutely aware that Henry has left the door ajar as I punch the reservations desk button.

"Good afternoon, Mr. Wolf. How may I help you?" Rich says in his deep, melodic voice. He could be a phone sex operator. I can't wait to meet him in person.

"It's Abbi again. We need to move Hen—" I catch myself, "Mr. Wolf's dinner reservations."

He groans. "This is the longest day of my life already, and dinner hour hasn't started."

I cringe. "I know. I'm sorry."

"Please. You've been hiding out in your little palace over there, reading Cosmo."

I snort in response. "I heard the commotion." Wolf Cove has two ferries to transport guests; the small one that John brought me in on, and then a much larger, fancier one that reminds me of a small cruise ship, with an indoor section, set with cafe tables and chairs, and a waiter to serve drinks. It made several trips back and forth, arriving loaded with guests each time. A few planes also landed in the bay and propelled to the docks to deliver wealthy, elite guests. Helicopters made use of the pad as well.

Apparently, the hotel is nearly at capacity for its opening week, with off-season special rates enticing faithful Wolf chain patrons. The big grand opening ceremony with media is next week. Enough time, hopefully, to iron out any kinks.

"I don't know how to make this work. Do you have any suggestions?"

"Of course I do. That's why I'm doing this job." I hear him clicking away at keys. "Not a lot of time to work with, though. Okay, here we go. Rooms 43 and 44, table of four at 6:00 p.m."

"What are you gonna do?"

"I'm going to swap their reservations for 8:00 p.m. and go up to their rooms to kiss their asses with a bottle of reserve wine and a charcuterie board to tide them over another two hours. Oh, how I love kissing ass." The sarcasm drips from his tone.

"Thanks, Rich."

"Anything for Mr. Wolf."

I hang up with a sigh of relief. There. That problem is fixed. Now I can take his suit to the cleaners and go home. To sleep, after a mentally and physically long but exciting day.

I move for the suit still draped over the chair. As I get closer, I catch the sound of the shower in Henry's room running.

"He's your boss, he's your boss, he's your boss..." I chant as I fold his clothing over my arm, inhaling the smell of his cologne that clings to the material. He smells divine. What I'd do to burrow my nose in his neck again.

Turning to leave, my eyes can't help but veer to the narrow space where the bedroom door doesn't quite meet the wall. It's a perfect sightline to the bathroom. I expect the pocket door to be pulled closed.

It's not.

And the shower room is so large that the steam doesn't do a good enough job of fogging up the glass.

Henry's back is to me, his hands working shampoo through his hair, the soap running down in rivulets over hard round ass cheeks and down sinewy thighs. I don't know when he works out but he must—religiously—to have a sculpted body like that.

My mouth drops open.

I can't be watching this. He shouldn't have left both doors open, but maybe he did that because he trusts me *not* to spy through the five-inch opening. I reach for the door handle to give him his privacy, but before I can will myself to pull it shut, I let my greedy eyes find Henry again.

An "Oh my God," escapes my lips as I watch him turn to

face me, the water streaming over his bowed head. He adjusts his stance, spreading his legs farther apart. I can see *all* of him now, including the cock that juts out in front of him, the swollen end of it stretching toward his navel, almost reaching it.

I'm frozen, half in panic, half in awe as I watch him reach down and fist the base of it and then begin sliding up and down it, slowly, from root all the way to the purplish, round tip.

I gasp. I'm watching my boss jerk off.

And I can't stop.

First Katie and Rachel, now Henry? I've turned into a complete pervert.

And yet I can't pull my eyes away. This is different from watching Katie and Rachel. Their bodies didn't turn me on, as attractive as each of them are. It was what they were doing, and the pleasure they were deriving from it, that had my blood flowing.

But here, now... I know I'm reacting to all that is Henry. To his solid, golden form, drenched in water and soap; to the sharp V of his abdomen, leading to a patch of dark hair and the first fully grown man's penis I've ever seen in person; to the highly vulnerable position I've caught him in.

Muscles in his forearm cord as his hand picks up speed, sliding down to the base and all the way up, over and over again. He's huge, so much bigger than what I know of Jed, with my limited experience through his pants. How that would even fit inside a woman, I can't imagine.

But the dampness in my panties and the deep throb between my legs tells me that I'd like to find out.

Did he mean to leave both these doors open? He knew I was still here, phoning to change reservations. I wasn't on the phone that long, was I?

My lips part as his hips begin to sway with each stroke, until he's more thrusting his body than his hand actually doing any work, his balls beneath swinging with the jerky motion. They look heavy and full. That's what Jed said happens when he's about to come. He admitted to me that he rubbed himself off in his room sometimes, especially after we'd been kissing or touching.

Above the sound of the showerhead running I can hear Henry's deep groans, and I find myself licking my suddenly dry lips and panting along with him, wishing those hands were on me, wishing it was my fist wrapped around him, pumping him like that. I don't even know if my hands are big enough.

I'm now practically leaning against the door, squeezed within the narrow space so I can see him, praying that the glass remains clear enough to watch. He looks almost savage, the way he tugs violently at himself with one hand, while his free hand presses flat against the glass. My legs shake with anticipation as I watch, feeling my breasts grow heavy and my nipples tighten with the anticipation. What will Henry orgasming look like?

Thirty seconds later, I find out as Henry's lips part and he lets out a series of guttural moans followed by a cry. His powerful naked body stills as white cream shoots out the tip of his cock in streams, hitting the glass wall. His hand slows as he milks himself, his chest heaving in and out with his deep breaths.

This is definitely when I should leave. Heck, I should have never peeked through that narrow space in his room in the first place. I should have grabbed the suit from the chair and kept going.

So when Henry abruptly looks up, as if sensing someone

watching him, and our gazes lock, my stomach drops to the floor like a rock.

For three long, heart-stopping seconds, I stare into Henry's piercing blue eyes. And then I bolt out of Penthouse Cabin One, clutching his suit to my chest.

# thirteen

How long before Henry fires me? Will it be tonight? Or tomorrow morning? Will he do it himself, or have Belinda give me a shove off? Something in my gut tells me she might not mind that.

He trusted me and I let him down.

The water in the stall next to me shuts off.

"What is that delicious smell?" Katie calls out.

I smile despite my anxiety, lathering my sore, stressed body. I always take pride in someone fawning over a product of mine. "Mint soap. Homemade." After a nerve-wracking day, there's nothing more soothing than creamy coconut-oil-based herbal soaps and a hot shower.

"Homemade as in *you* made it?"

"Yup."

"You know how to make that kind of stuff?"

"Yeah. It's pretty easy." If I were in Greenbank, I'm sure I'd be occupying my time and broken heart by making truckloads right now. I kind of miss the process, but I couldn't bring my supplies here. No way Alaska Airlines would have let me fly with a vat of lye. Plus, I figured I wouldn't have the facilities or time to make anything.

My shower curtain suddenly glides open and I gasp, one arm flying to do a poor job of covering my breasts, my free hand fanning between my legs.

Katie adjusts the white towel that's wrapped around her body. "Relax. I see naked women all day long, Abbi." She rolls her eyes and laughs. "Can I see the soap for a minute?"

I uncover my breasts reluctantly and hold out the hand with the bar. I can't say the last time anyone besides my doctor has seen me naked. *People are meant to change behind closed doors, alone.* More sage advice from Bernadette Mitchell.

Katie takes it from me and holds it up to her nose. She inhales deeply, then runs her thumb over it. "Heavenly. And it doesn't look gross, like other homemade soaps."

"I guess not." I pause, the hot water streaming down my back as the front of me gets chilled with the draft. "You know you could have waited until I was done."

She slaps the bar back into my hands. "I wanted to see how it lathers. If you have any extra, I'd love a bar. I forgot my organic soaps at home and I couldn't find anything in Homer." Her crystal-blue eyes drop to my naked body, dancing over my arms and neck, lingering on my breasts for a moment, before lifting to my face again. "You should be more confident in your own skin. You have no reason to hide that body."

"Um... Thanks?" That's the second person who's made reference to my confidence today. Do I really wear my insecurity so openly?

"And seriously, let me help you with that jungle." Her eyes dip to where my hand hides my pubic hair. "I have all my waxing stuff in the cabin. It'll take me fifteen minutes and you'll have an extra neat and tidy little Brazilian when I'm done with you."

"Great." I reach for the curtain, hoping that gives her the signal.

Katie just laughs and strolls away, leaving me feeling equal parts flattered by the compliments of a woman who obviously appreciates the female body, and outright violated.

Then I remind myself that I stood there and watched my boss jerk off in his own shower not more than two hours ago. I have no right to complain. Sure, he could have closed the door. But he said that he trusted me to do my job well and with full discretion.

What I did was the opposite of discreet.

And now I find myself staring down at my pubic hair that Katie called a jungle. That's a bit harsh. Maybe more "burning bush," the color matching my hair color, unfortunately. Sure, I haven't shaved my bikini line. I only do that in the summer, to avoid embarrassing hairs from sticking out of my bathing suit. Am I supposed to do it during other times of the year?

Even in the privacy of my shower, my cheeks heat. How am I so utterly clueless about these things?

"How was your first day in Penthouse One?" Autumn asks. The frame above me jostles as she settles in. Only Lorraine and Rachel are still out, working later shifts.

"Fine."

"Just fine? What are the guests like? Did you have much to do?"

I sigh, dreading where I know this conversation is going to go. "Actually, Mr. Wolf is staying in Penthouse One."

Autumn's body comes rolling off the top of the bunkbed at the same time that Tillie turns to stare at me. "What?" they both exclaim in unison.

"You're *Mr. Wolf's* private housekeeper?" Tillie's pretty face twists with shock and, I'm guessing, envy.

Am I even supposed to talk about this? "He hired me to be his personal assistant."

"*Personal* assistant?" They both echo, their shock only multiplying.

"You guys sound like parrots," Katie chuckles. She's sitting on the edge of her bed in her robe, brushing freshly blow-dried hair, seemingly unfazed.

"Yeah. Stunned me, too."

"What are you doing for him?" Tillie asks.

"I manage his calendar and his e-mail, I clean his cabin, book excursions for him and whoever he's entertaining that day. Honestly, I'm not sure yet." I can't help but glance at the phone he gave me, dread filling me as I wait for my punishment. Will it be a text dismissal or, better yet, a request to see him right away so he can look me in the eye as he fires me?

I shouldn't have spied on him like that for so many reasons, including the visual now firmly emblazoned in my mind of his powerful, savage thrusts and his perfect body. How will I ever face him again?

"You are a fucking bitch," Tillie mutters. When my mouth drops open, she waves a dismissive hand. "Don't mind me. I'm cranky and PMSing and completely jealous."

"Anything juicy to share about our handsome boss?" Katie asks, sliding her robe off her body to reveal a lacy white bra and panties. She reaches for her jeans. I guess she's heading out to the staff lounge.

Meeting people and making small talk is the absolute last thing I want to do right now. I roll onto my back and shut my eyes. "Nothing." Besides Henry's huge cock coming all over the shower glass. I'm going to have to clean that glass tomorrow, and the idea isn't even grossing me out.

What have I turned into up here? This is exactly what Mama was afraid of.

"He made you sign a gag order, didn't he?" Autumn crawls back into her bed, the shock of my new job finally settling.

"Yeah. Why?"

"Figures. I heard he's a bit paranoid. He hasn't let anyone step foot in his room since he got here. Not the maids, not room service. He'll leave dishes outside the door."

"Can't say I blame him after what happened in L.A.," Tillie mutters, giving her eyes a rub. If anyone's had a hard day today, it's the housekeeping staff.

"What happened in L.A.?" I ask warily.

"He came home from a meeting to find a maid naked and handcuffed to his bed. When he called security to escort her out, she claimed he restrained her and forced himself on her." Tillie reaches beneath her uniform and begins peeling her nylons off her body. I guess there is no room for shame when six women share a cabin together. "The accusation was shut down *real* fast, what with her on camera and using her room key to get in, and him being in a meeting all day. Wasn't too bright, that one. I guess she thought she'd be playing out a fantasy for him and when she realized he wasn't interested, she panicked to try and save her job. Gorgeous girl, too, from what I've heard. A Miss Venezuela runner-up, or something like that."

"That's not true. How do you know all this?" Autumn demands.

Tillie's smug smile tells me she enjoys being the hub of dark and dirty secrets. Once again, I'm relieved that I never divulged details to her about that first night. "Also, he had an assistant in the New York office until a few months ago. He fired her for hitting on him."

Is that the headache he was talking about with Belinda? The headache he wants to avoid? He did say that he hired me because he knows I won't try anything. When I'm sober.

"Okay, seriously. I've been with Wolf for two years and I've never heard any of this!" Autumn exclaims, oblivious of my internal torment, her doubt evident. "Who is your source?"

"My cousin works for the Wolf head office. She has a way of hearing things."

Will she hear about me spying on Henry in the shower today? Will I be the subject of conversation in a few weeks: the personal assistant who was fired on her first day for being a pervert?

And after he just went to such great lengths to find an innocent little farm girl who he thought he could trust?

"Well, I've heard that he's pretty secretive to begin with, which makes me think he's hiding something," Katie offers, waggling her brows. "Maybe some serious kink."

Of course Katie would be the one to suggest that.

Katie and Tillie turn to stare at me expectantly. "I saw nothing... kinky in his room," I offer, my cheeks burning. I'm stepping dangerously close to the "don't talk about me" line that Henry drew. I reach over to turn off the little wall lamp by my bed. "I'm not feeling well. I'm going to get some sleep. Good night, everyone."

After a moment, Tillie pulls herself off her mattress and

reaches for her shower caddy and robe. "Well, he won't ever have to worry about you doing something inappropriate, like handcuffing yourself to his bed. You may be the only one of the females at this place who can say that honestly."

I'm not sure if she's trying to make me feel better, but I'm not feeling better.

Now, I'm feeling much, *much* worse.

# *fourteen*

I take a deep, nervous breath as I step through the servants' entrance into Henry's place, my stomach in knots after barely sleeping all night. There were no texts or e-mails this morning when I dared check my work phone, cringing. Nothing from Belinda.

Will he address it? Or will he pretend it didn't happen?

Do I apologize?

I'm afraid that I'll burst into tears the moment he looks at me.

But Henry's not there.

Evidence of him is there. His half-finished coffee, his breakfast dishes, emptied and stacked. And a note, with elegant scrawl that reads:

*Reschedule today's 7-8am meetings.*

*Book dinner for seven. Eight people.*

*H.W.*

That's it.

But where is he? His trip to Kodiak Island isn't until eight thirty.

I sigh, disappointment and relief taking over where only

pure dread resided moments ago. Maybe he's too angry to face me right now. Or maybe he's embarrassed by what I saw him do. Would a man be embarrassed by that? I know I'd want to die if he—or anyone—caught me touching myself like I did the other night.

Maybe I'm making a bigger deal of this than it is, though. Maybe he doesn't care.

I sigh and pour myself a cup of coffee. For as long as it took me to organize his calendar yesterday, it's going to take me all morning to reorganize it.

The canary-yellow Otter coasts in to the plane docks, the Wolf Cove brand proudly displayed on the wing. I watch from my chilly perch—the porch off the front of Cabin One—as the small door creaks open and one after another, bodies jump out. Seven men later, Henry's large frame emerges, crouching to escape.

My heart begins racing. A nervous giddiness brews deep within the pit of my chest at the mere sight of him, even from this far away. He's dressed casually—in jeans, his plaid jacket, and a charcoal vest peeking out from beneath, his chestnut-brown hair covered in a beanie. So incredibly sexy, but not exactly proper attire for the upscale Lux restaurant.

Which means he'll have to come here to change.

The nervous dread that dulled hits me like a tidal wave now.

They're all talking and laughing, slapping each other on the shoulders. I guess they enjoyed the tour.

Henry trails behind them, chatting with the pilot. Philip, I gather. He hands him something, to which Philip seems appreciative, bobbing his head and shaking his hand before he heads back to the plane.

I hug my body tightly, my breezy white blouse not nearly warm enough with highs of fifty, and watch until Henry disappears from view, all the while holding my breath against the hope that he'll glance up here.

But he doesn't so much as bat an eye.

Ducking back inside, I rush for the desk, scrambling to make sure any last minute e-mails are opened and dealt with before he arrives, squeezing my thighs together as my bladder threatens to spill.

But Henry never appears.

Two hours later, with no sign of Henry and my nerves sufficiently frazzled, my work phone texts with a message.

**Henry:** *Come to the Summit at 2.*

I groan. This is it. This is where Henry and Belinda sit across from me at a table and explain in painstaking detail how what I did was not only wrong but disgusting.

I glance at the clock. I have ten minutes to find this room. Not enough time to grab lunch, but I doubt I could stomach anything anyway. Collecting the iPad and my work phone, I scramble out the door.

I'm going to miss Alaska.

I'M PANTING by the time I find the Summit boardroom, one minute past two. My heart leaps into my throat as I take a quick scan of its inhabitants—a stony-faced Henry, Belinda, Paige, and four unfamiliar faces sitting around a ten-person table.

They all turn to regard me as I knock meekly against the door.

"Take a seat." Henry gestures to the chair next to him. I scramble toward it on wobbly legs, my hands shaking with nerves. Do all these people need to be here in order to fire me?

I feel Belinda's calculating eyes scour over me, the disdain on her face barely concealed.

I'm so unnerved, I barely notice that Henry has changed into the suit I dropped off for dry cleaning yesterday. The ends of his hair are damp, suggesting he had a shower. But where, and when?

"Paige, status update, please," Henry demands, leaning far back in his chair, his one leg crossed over the other at the knee, his fingers lightly tapping a polished black shoe. He must have done that himself. I know I didn't. Am I supposed to polish his shoes, too? "Abbi, take notes."

I simply stare at the tiny Texan woman as she begins talking about housekeeping and hospitality issues over the past twenty-four hours, highlighting minor guest complaints and some process changes she has already put in place.

It's not until Henry reaches over and softly taps my thigh with his knuckle that it registers. I haven't been called to the Summit Room to be fired.

I'm here to scribe.

My body sinks into my chair with relief. I quickly tap out bulleted notes, focusing intently as one by one, each manager gives Henry an update on their area. Sally, a kind-looking blonde in charge of guest amenities, including the spa; Jean, the tiny Asian lady sitting across from me who coordinates all guest tours and programs; Pierre, the kitchen manager; and a thirty-something year old man named Ryan who runs all facilities and maintenance. He would have been my boss, had I ever worked a day with the Outdoor team. He has a big job, ensuring everything from the tulips in the garden to the float planes by the docks are in perfect working order. He also looks like he hasn't slept in days.

Belinda interrupts every so often with a question of her own, or an instruction on how to handle. I'm not at all fond of her and I already know she doesn't like me, but I'll admit she sounds smart and sophisticated. I can see why Henry put her in that role.

And probably why he slept with her, seeing as he's not attracted to silly little girls.

But I'm here to scribe notes, I remind myself with a small smile. That, I can handle.

"Any major complaints about facilities?" Henry asks Ryan.

"A few guests on the top floors have complained that their showers take too long to heat up."

"Where is their hot water coming from?"

"Third floor."

Henry's jaw tenses. "I'm no engineer, but that sounds like a design flaw."

Ryan clears his throat. "Yes, sir. I already have the plumbers working on installing additional hot water heaters specifically for that floor and rerouting the pipes. There is space in the fifth floor maintenance area."

"Minimal disturbance to our guests, I hope?"

Belinda steps in smoothly. "I've already sent Cristal to their rooms. For those who complained, I've comped their first nights' room stay."

That's thousands of dollars, just like that. Does it matter to a guy like Henry? To a hotel like this? I can't comprehend the magnitude. To me, it sounds crippling.

Ryan's expression is tentative as Henry regards him silently for a moment, cool and calm. "Do the same for the fourth floor." He then turns to me. "Abbi, schedule a call with George Duncan for later today. He's west coast."

I mark it in my notes, pretending I know who that is. Hopefully I can find something in Henry's inbox that tells me who George is. By his tone, I'm guessing the conversation isn't going to be pleasant.

Henry moves on, dominating the meeting in a no-nonsense fashion, the tension radiating from him almost tangible. He is under a lot of pressure. Rightfully so, I guess. I can't imagine what it'd be like to open a luxury hotel.

Each person around that table keeps their eyes glued to him, like they don't want to miss a prompt. He intimidates them. That would make sense, seeing as he intimidates the hell out of me. He's an entirely different guy from the patient one who taught me how to swing an ax, and the sheepish one who smiled as he held up the wrong tie and admitted to being color-blind.

And the vulnerable one I watched come apart by his own fist.

His hand sits on his brawny thigh, his fingers strumming a slow, rhythmic beat. The hand that was gripping his cock so tightly yesterday, pumping it from root to tip until he came.

I give my head a shake, scolding my filthy thoughts for veering that way so easily.

His hand suddenly stills. I feel that cool and yet iron-hot gaze on my profile, and my cheeks flush in response. It's like he knows what I'm thinking. "Bookings?"

I force my mind back to the meeting.

"We are nearly booked solid through to August," Belinda announces proudly, as if she single-handedly had something to do with that. "We have guests calling and asking about cancellation wait lists."

Henry's lips twitch. The only indication that he's pleased. "The grand opening. Give me an update."

Belinda punches something into her iPad. "All media outlets have RSVP'd and rooms have been assigned to ensure we have them prepped adequately." She goes on to list names of people I don't know but who must be critical attendees for the event, which sounds like a lavish ball.

Henry scribbles something on his notepad while she talks, and sets it on my lap, his knuckles brushing against my thigh.

*Make sure my tux is in my closet. I don't remember packing it.*

I make a note to check when I get back to the cabin. It's such a simple but personal request, and I find myself reveling in the fact I get to root through his closet for him.

Belinda is still talking. "You and I can go over the dossiers on everyone—"

He cuts her off with, "Send Abbi the rundown of each member attending. She'll brief me directly."

The corners of her mouth twitch. "Fine." It's curt and not at all pleasant.

"Any staff issues?"

"None so far." Her eyes flicker toward me and I promptly avert my gaze. Would he have told her about yesterday? She seems to be in on everything else so far.

"Okay. Thanks, everyone. Abbi will send out a meeting request for tomorrow's update."

Just like when the bell rings in class, everyone scrambles to gather their things, ready to run.

Everyone except Belinda, who remains in her chair with one leg crossed over the other, the side slit in her skirt so high that it reveals the end of her garter. "Can I have a word with you?"

Henry gives her a fleeting gaze. "About?"

"Your father."

He heaves a sigh and, resting his elbows on the table, he hooks his hands behind the back of his neck and bows his head. "Abbi, summarize and send out those notes to the group. Also, there are a few presentations I've printed out and made notes of in the margins sitting on my desk. Please summarize and send those off to the names listed on them for follow-up by tomorrow. And see if you can get me an hour-long in-room massage with Michael for this evening before dinner."

"In-room?" He said he didn't want anyone in his space.

"Yes. Text me with the time." He sighs. "Okay, Belinda. What is it?"

I take that as my cue to leave, unscathed and still employed, and I take it without another word.

# *fifteen*

"Michael?" A towering man dressed all in black, his t-shirt stretched across a fit, lean body, stands outside the cabin, folded table at his side. He must be at least six-foot-four.

"That's me." He holds up his employee badge to prove it, the deep dimples in the picture matching the ones he flashes at me now. He has a disarming smile.

"Come in." I step back, ducking my head to hide my inevitable blush, the one that burns any time an attractive man's eyes are on me.

His arms strain as he lifts the table over the threshold before setting it back and running a hand through his sandy-blond cropped hair. "I'm guessing Mr. Wolf wants this set up over there?" He nods toward the windows overlooking the water, then looks to me, waiting for an answer. I catch his eyes dipping down to my chest but they shift back to my face quickly.

"Honestly, I have no idea," I admit, trailing him to the far side.

"I'll move it if he wants. Damn, this is a nice place." His

eyes graze over the space, landing on the massive stone fireplace. "You want a tip to impress your boss? Get that thing going."

"Now?" It's only five and not nearly cold enough.

"Maybe not right now, but on a cold night, definitely. Trust me. Whenever he's visiting the Aspen location and he brings me in, he always has a fire going. He said it reminds him of being at his grandparents' place up here."

"Thanks for the tip." Maybe I'll surprise him with one tonight. It's the least I can do after what I did yesterday.

"No problem." Michael has the table unfolded and set up in seconds. He's obviously been doing this for a while.

"So you work at the Wolf in Aspen?"

"Yup. Here, help me with this sheet?"

I hide my grimace and grab an end. We stretch the elastics around the ends, covering the mattress board. "Are you from Colorado, originally?"

"Nah. Just outside Pittsburgh. Small town called Stipling."

My face breaks into a wide smile. "No way! Seriously?" There's comfort in finding another person from a small town in Pennsylvania, especially given I'm so far away from everything I know. "I'm from Greenbank. Have you heard of it?" Most times people haven't but by Michael's matching grin, I already know what his answer is going to be.

"Hell yeah! I played baseball up there every year."

"Seriously?" Now I'm giddy. "I may have watched your games. My fiancé played, too. I was at the diamond all summer. Wait, how old are you?"

"Twenty-seven."

I laugh. "Okay, maybe not."

"Still, small world." He shakes his head, smiling down at me. I grin back, snatching the end of the loose sheet to help him lay it over the table, a new sense of ease slipping into my body.

"So, does your fiancé still play?"

"No. And... ex." I waggle my naked hand, ignoring the sudden thickness in my throat at that admission. It's not as bad as in the past, at least.

"Oh, sorry." He shrugs. "I have one of those, myself. Glad we pulled the plug on that one. It would have been a mistake."

I sigh wistfully while I help him stretch a cream-colored wool blanket over the top of the sheet. Will I ever be able to say that about Jed and me so casually? Will I see his betrayal as my way of dodging a bullet?

"So how did you end up here, being personally requested for massages by billionaire hotel owners?"

He chuckles. "I specialized in sport massage therapy in college, but was having a hard time getting a job so I applied for an opening at the Wolf in Aspen. Figured a lot of skiers meant work. Mr. Wolf was there one winter and he injured his leg on the slopes, so they sent me up to his room. I helped him through it and now he always asks for me when he's in town. He personally offered me a job here, which is great seeing as Aspen's dead in the summer." Michael stretches his long arms over his head, bending them at the elbows, as if warming up.

"Lucky you, getting hand-picked by the big boss," I tease, though I suppose I was handpicked, too.

"You wouldn't believe how many of my female coworkers have begged me to play sick so they can take my place." He snorts and shakes his head. "Dude's got it goin' on."

*I think I can*. Given permission to rub your hands all over

Henry Wolf's body? I can't even imagine it, but I'm suddenly jealous of Michael.

And Henry, I accept, as I reach up to knead my own sore bicep absently. Jed used to give me back rubs. I miss them.

Michael picks up on it immediately. "Sore?"

"Nothing a good night's sleep won't fix."

"It's got to be stressful, trying to keep up with his schedule. Come here." He reaches for me, his long arm span closing the distance with two steps. Grabbing me by the waist, he hoists me onto the table as if I weigh nothing at all.

"Is this okay?" I tense as one of his large, strong hands runs along the top of my back, from shoulder to shoulder, his fingers splayed slightly.

"You have a few knots," he says, not answering my question. He begins gently kneading my muscles. I close my eyes and relish the feel of his strong hands over me because this feels oh so good. So much more skilled, so much stronger than Jed. "Is this just stress? Or were you doing something physically straining?"

"I was stacking wood the other day. And I swung an ax, too," I mumble, letting my head fall forward as his skilled fingers apply a touch of pressure along my neck.

He starts laughing. "An ax? Interesting assistant job you have. Are you right-handed?"

"Yes."

His hands move to my right arm, one gripping me at the elbow while the other slides beneath the collar of my shirt and along the ball of my shoulder. "You have some pipes on you for such a tiny thing."

The feel of his strong, warm hands against my bare skin sends shivers down through my chest and my nipples tighten. I hope the padding in my bra is thick enough to hide it because the shirt sure isn't.

"Relax." That one word comes out in a soothing voice, his deep voice crackling.

I can't deny that as flustering as it is to have this handsome stranger touching me, this feels incredible. And he's a professional, so this is okay. He's just doing his job. What would an hour of this feel like? "So, how much trouble would we get into if I took Mr. Wolf's appointment right now, because this feels *amazing*," I joke through a groan and a giggle.

Michael chuckles. "Well, I'm off work at ten tonight. I don't normally offer this, but if you want, I can come over to your cabin and—"

The front door slams shut, the sudden noise making me jump. I look over to find Henry standing in the doorway, his eyes boring into me.

Unamused.

"Hey, Mr. Wolf, good to see you again. You must be overworking your assistant. She's full of knots. You should send her to the spa for a rubdown." Michael is oblivious to the palpable tension in the air.

"I'll be ready in five. Abbi, a word." His tone is clipped, his jaw tight as he strolls toward his bedroom, yanking at his tie. He waves with two fingers for me to follow him.

I know I'm in trouble and I'm not entirely sure why.

"Shut the door behind you."

I slide the barn door to the edge, but remain where I am, watching him quietly as he tosses his tie and suit jacket to the bed and begins pacing. He pushes a hand through his hair, sending it in wild disarray.

"Do you want that dry cleaned?" I finally dare ask, hoping that might dispel whatever has made him so angry.

"No. I do not want that dry cleaned. What I want is to

come home and not find my massage therapist trying to fuck my assistant."

*What?* My mouth drops open. "I... He noticed me rubbing my sore arm and he was just trying to help me. That's all that was." How did *that* possibly look like sex?

He shakes his head, muttering something to himself. When he meets my eyes again, there's only wonderment there. And something else I can't describe. Something dark. "You honestly believe that, don't you?"

"Yes?" I frown, panic flying through me as I replay my conversation with Michael from the beginning. Nothing—*nothing!*—about it was sexual. Henry is acting worse than my mama right now. I hear myself mumble an, "I'm sorry," though I don't entirely know what I'm sorry for.

"Michael, out there? He doesn't want to rid you of your sore muscles. He'll gladly fuck you. Any guy here will."

"No... he was just..." I stumble over my words, shocked by his. "Our hometowns are close to each other. He's being nice."

Henry's chuckle is menacing as his feet close the distance, slow and measured, until he's within my personal space. "Don't be so naïve, Abbi. Trust me. He can smell that virgin pussy from a mile away and he wants it."

I inhale sharply, his words building a throb between my legs, despite my unease. Did he just say that to me? And is he right? Michael is attracted to me? "So what if he does want that?"

"Is *he* what you want?" There's a challenge there, sitting on a razor sharp edge that I'm afraid to near. Several painfully long seconds pass, the tension in the air thick and heady and then a wicked smirk captures his lips. "Did you enjoy yesterday's show?"

It takes me only a split second to know what he's referring to with the whiplash-fast change in topic.

My mouth hangs open, incapable of speech. How do I answer that? With the obvious truth? Yes, I loved seeing Henry naked. Yes, I loved seeing him—the powerful and controlled Mr. Wolf—vulnerable. Yes, the sight of him stirred desires that have haunted me ever since.

But I can't admit to any of that. He hired me because he isn't attracted to me. He hired me because he wanted an assistant who would understand boundaries, like the ones I've already crossed.

"I shouldn't have... I mean, I didn't mean to..." I stumble over my words.

"Are you sure you didn't mean to?" He inches closer. He's too intense, this is too much. I avert my gaze, but his finger finds my chin, prodding until my head tips back to meet his penetrating eyes. Those cold blue eyes aren't cold anymore. They're raging. "Not even two days."

"What?" My voice cracks.

"I knew I shouldn't have hired you," he whispers absently, as if speaking more to himself.

"Does that mean you're firing me?" I fight against the tears that begin to well.

Henry merely shakes his head. The relief with that simple gesture is nearly paralyzing.

His finger slips from my chin. He begins working at the buttons of his dress shirt until he's peeling it away from his body and tossing it on the bed. His t-shirt comes off next.

His gaze, it never leaves me, even when mine can't help but drop.

Dear God, that chest. It's tanned and hard and I want to slide my hands all over it, feel the ridges of his collarbone, the soft skin of his nipples. The burn of his naked skin under my fingertips.

"There should be an e-mail from Belinda in my inbox," he says, switching smoothly back to work.

I avert my eyes to the view beyond the window, still bright and so "off" for the mood in this room. "Why do you make me come in here while you're undressing?" I whisper. It's so inappropriate for him to do this. Not only because he's my boss.

He *knows* I'm attracted to him.

In my periphery, I catch his brow lift in surprise. "I told you that your job would involve being in close proximity to me. I like using my time efficiently." A pause. "Do you want to leave?"

*No.* I like being near him, even when my stomach is doing complete flips.

"Why do *you* think I ask you in here while I'm undressing?"

There's only one reason I can come up with. "Because you like to see me squirm."

"Look at me."

My eyes snap back with his command and I find that sexy dimple waiting with his smirk. He can read my attraction to him plain as day. "You're right, I do. And maybe I like testing you."

"Why?"

His gaze drops to my mouth, and my lips instantly turn dry. "Because every time I'm sure I have a handle on you, you surprise me."

A "handle" on me? Abigail Mitchell from Greenbank, Pennsylvania? I'm pretty uncomplicated. And, by the way he talked about me to Belinda, it sounded like he's already figured that out.

I guess maybe he never expected me to watch him in the shower. To be fair, *I* never expected to have the nerve to do that. Before coming here, I wouldn't. And he's not firing me for it, even though I crossed the line—again—and, this time, sober.

But is he angry with me about it? "How do I surprise you? In a bad way?"

"Some would think so," he answers cryptically. He reaches up to slide the pad of his thumb over my bottom lip.

For someone who finds me unattractive, he's giving off some seriously conflicting signals. Or maybe that's just me, being clueless and stupid and wishful again. Either way... "I'm confused," I whisper.

He meets my eyes again. "I know you are. That's part of your charm, isn't it?"

We simply stare at each other as the seconds pass, my heart pounding, my knees shaking as he hovers, his bare chest begging to be touched.

Finally, his hand drops to his side. "I don't want Michael touching you like that again. Or anyone here, for that matter."

Is he even allowed to demand that? "Why not?"

"Because, you're—" He presses his lips together, cutting himself off. "Because they're not good enough for you."

Michael seems like a genuinely nice guy. If he's not good enough for me, and no one else here is good enough, then how am I supposed to get over Jed? Didn't Henry say that I should spend the next four months fucking someone in every position imaginable?

I can't keep my eyes from his plump, pink lips. Nearly feminine, they're so shapely. I ran my tongue across those wet, soft lips only days ago, when I was drunk and clueless.

What about *the* Mr. Wolf, the man who strolls through

the halls in his designer suits, capturing women's lustful gazes and drawing men's envy?

But he told Belinda he didn't want me.

Fire sparks in Henry's eyes. He reaches back to wrap his fist around my braid. He tugs on it gently, forcing my head back. His whisper is oddly tender in comparison. "You're my assistant, Abbi."

I have to ask it. Instinctively, I know it's the wrong question to ask, but I can't help myself. "And if I wasn't?"

I shiver as his fingertip drags along my collarbone, down along the neckline of my blouse to dip into my cleavage, the simple touch tightening my nipples and making my breasts heavy, begging to be undressed, exposed, touched.

So suddenly, he robs me of his touch and I shudder with the loss.

"I want you to open that e-mail from Belinda and be ready to brief me on its contents." *And he's back to work already.*

It takes me a few seconds and a few tattered breaths to collect myself. Henry has intentionally changed the topic, shuttering his eyes to hide all emotion, even taken a step back.

He has controlled himself.

I struggle to clear my throat. "What time do you want me here in the morning?"

A slight frown touches his beautiful face. "No. Not tomorrow. We need to do it now, while Michael's working on me."

While he's lying naked on the table?

He smirks, unfastening his belt. "What's wrong? *Now* the sweet, virtuous Abbi is too shy to watch? After what you've seen, this should be nothing."

My cheeks burn, but I meet his eyes and see the challenge in them. Did it bother him at all that I watched him in the shower? I'm beginning to think not, which means he's been toying with me all this time, putting me through hell for his own amusement. That's not nice.

With a defiant set of my jaw, I stand my ground on wobbly knees, waiting for him to dismiss me. His hands slow for a moment over his zipper. When I don't move, understanding sparks in his eyes. He cocks his head, amusement taking over.

And then he lets his pants drop to the carpet with a soft swooshing sound.

I keep my eyes locked on his, fighting the compelling urge to look down. I sense rather than see his thumbs running along the elastic of his briefs.

And still I don't move. Where is this nerve coming from?

Stretching the elastic away from his body, he peels his briefs off and lets them drop to the floor, too.

I pretend that having Henry standing naked in front of me has no impact, but I know I'm doing a lousy job of it. My breathing alone—quick, shallow pants through parted lips—is likely enough to tip him off. My heart hammers inside my chest as I stand there, waiting.

I don't dare look down to see the effect this has on him, but I can sense it jutting out in all its swollen glory. It would be so easy for me to reach out and rub my thumb over the tip, to wrap my fist around his length. My palm itches at the idea.

Maybe this is what he's waiting for.

For "sweet, virtuous Abbi" to break.

"Is there anything else you need, while I'm here?" I ask as calmly as I can manage. I don't understand what's happening, but I know what *I* need at this moment. Him.

Henry takes a step closer to me, heat from his body

radiating, his erection now pressing against my stomach, his words stirring my confusion. "Don't tempt me," he growls.

*Oh my God. I'm in so far over my head.* I fight every urge I have to shrink back, to run away. That's what the farm girl would do. But I don't want to be her.

I harden myself. "For someone who's not attracted to insecure, stupid little girls, that sure is a very hard cock you have there."

I can't believe I said that. Nor can I believe that I delivered it in such a calm voice.

I don't think he can either, because first surprise, then alarm flashes in his eyes. Yes, I basically just admitted to listening in on his conversation with Belinda. His mouth opens, then closes several times as he hesitates, choosing his words carefully. "Sometimes I'm forced to say things I don't mean."

Flutters explode in my stomach. Does that mean it was a lie? "So you don't think I'm an insecure, stupid little girl?"

His lips twist. "Oh, you *are* that. Until you prove otherwise, anyway." He exhales heavily, his warm breath caressing my cheek. Some internal conflict twists his features into an almost painful grimace. "Wait for me in the living room," he demands in a hoarse whisper, turning away and heading toward the bathroom with slow, leisurely steps, that glorious backside straining and shifting with each step, his back carved into muscle, the deep line down the center making my knees weak.

I duck out quickly and make my way over to where Michael waits, praying that my face isn't so red that the young masseur figures out what just happened. "He'll be out in a minute," I say, clearing my throat as I grab my iPad and curl up in a nearby wing chair while I search for Belinda's e-mail. Only now do I realize that my hand is shaking. And that my panties are soaked.

"You okay?" Michael asks, his bright green eyes sparkling as they watch me. They look genuine, not lecherous at all. Why does Henry think he's into me? And why would he care if Michael was in to me? I'm not dating anyone, and Henry isn't attracted to me.

Or did he just admit that he is?

I'm still too flustered to wrap my head around what happened and all that was said. "Yes. Thanks," I mutter, offering Michael a smile.

He begins stretching his fingers one by one, warming them up for an hour of labor. "Hey. So what's it like, working this closely with Wolf?"

A strangled laugh escapes my lips before I can keep it in. "Never a dull moment."

Henry appears through the doorway then, a white towel wrapped and tucked around his lower half. It does little to hide what waits beneath and he doesn't seem to care, one way or another.

"So, what'll it be today, Mr. Wolf?"

"Full body, please."

I swallow and keep my eyes on my iPad screen as, from the corner of my eye, Henry removes the towel and tosses it to land on the wing chair opposite me. I could steal a quick, unobstructed view if I adjust my eyes by an inch. Maybe he's still testing me, wondering if I'll take the chance.

I keep my eyes down.

I've seen my boss's cock plenty already.

Henry climbs onto the table, stomach down, and Michael pulls the covers over his lower half. His hands begin their assessment of the expansive slab of muscle and flesh beneath him. "Man, you're tight today. Stressed at all?"

Henry answers him with a low chuckle.

"Abbi."

I swallow against the blip of excitement that stirs with Henry calling my name. "Yes?"

Long seconds of silence force me to glance up, to find him staring at me, the look on his face almost regretful. It appears that both his anger and whatever game he was playing earlier are out of his system. "Yes, Mr. Wolf?" I repeat, as pleasantly as I can.

Another few long moments hang before he quietly asks, "Brief me on the media attending. Please."

"Okay." I exhale shakily, preparing to read from the screen. "Well, first we have Roshana Mafi from *Luxury Travel Magazine*."

"What does she look like?" he asks, without missing a beat.

I scan the picture in the electronic dossier. "Middle Eastern, long black hair. Beautiful," I admit with more than a hint of jealousy. "It says she's thirty-two and lives in New York City."

"Single?"

"Yes." Why Belinda felt the need to include that, I can't say.

"Make sure there are flowers in her room for her arrival. I'll write the card myself."

Almost Henry's age, lives in his city, stunning. Single. I feel like I'm setting the two of them up. That idea makes my stomach clench.

But I scribble down the note on my pad of paper because that's my job.

"Next?"

"Gerard Starsky from *Glamour Hotel*. Short, salt-and-pepper hair. Forty-five years old. Lives in San Francisco.

Married to Rena. One daughter named Bella, aged seven." It's almost disturbing how much personal information is on here. "It says he interviewed you two years ago at the opening in Istanbul." Mention of Istanbul reminds me of Henry sleeping with Belinda. I wonder who initiated that. I'll bet he takes on his sexual conquests as aggressively as he does his business ones.

Anger creeps into my otherwise rattled psyche at the thought of him tormenting me like he did in the bedroom moments ago, seemingly for his own personal entertainment.

"I remember him. Write a note to him that says 'Good to see you again. I hope you enjoy Wolf Cove even more than you did Istanbul'. Try not to make the writing too girly."

So Henry writes personal notes to single women but has me write the rest. It doesn't take a genius to figure out that he's playing up his physical gifts. "And do you want me to send him flowers, too?" I ask as innocently as possible. I can't resist glancing over.

Henry's sharp gaze is on me as Michael works over the deep curves of the middle of his back, the sheet draped dangerously low on his hips. I feel the urge to stick my tongue out at him, but I bite my lip instead. His eyes drop to my mouth and he blinks once... twice... Otherwise, he reveals nothing. "Next."

And so we go through the list, me giving Henry a rundown of every member of the media who will be arriving here to provide either accolades or criticism of a location that Henry himself holds dear, and him instructing me on what to include in the welcome notes to the males. Not the females though. He'll write all of those himself, to include with the flowers I send them in his name. I don't have to ask why.

A personal note from the busy Henry Wolf, himself? Few women would be unaffected by that. Look how I reacted to the one he included with my replacement vest. I internally gushed over it.

What a manipulative ass.

I cover up a yawn as we wrap up the review forty minutes later. Henry looks sleepy too, his eyelids drooping. Michael has moved to Henry's quad muscles, the sheet lifted to uncover his leg. "You can go now. Come back at seven tomorrow." He pauses. "Actually, make it six."

6:00 a.m. I stifle my groan. "Don't forget your dinner tonight."

"Fuck," he moans. "Right."

Michael throws me a wink on my way past. "I'll be at the staff lodge tonight, if you want to meet up."

I glance toward Henry's resting head, replaying his words, his request that I stay away from Michael. That Michael wants my "virgin pussy."

Do I dare fantasize that perhaps Henry wants it for himself?

Because I'd save it for him, if that were the case. "Maybe another night." I collect my things and head for the door.

What a weird day.

# sixteen

The entrance to Henry's suite from the servants' quarters is open a crack for me again. I slip into the room noiselessly.

"This is exactly the kind of bullshit that the future leader can't get caught up in. Your grandfather and I have built this company with the strength of our family values." The gruff man's voice carries through the cabin.

Henry sits at the desk, twirling a pen between his fingers, his jaw taut. I'm guessing that it's his father on the other end of the phone.

"What has legal said?"

"They're still waiting on her to accept the severance package but it's a no-brainer. She's going to sign." Henry sounds drained.

"Good," the man mutters gruffly. "I don't know, Henry. Between this and the Alaska gamble, I'm beginning to wonder about your ability to make sound decisions. Maybe your brother is more suitable."

Henry slams the pen against the desk. "If you want this

company driven into the ground within five years, sure, hand over Wolf Hotels to Scott. He doesn't have an entrepreneurial bone in his body and forget any strategic marketing skills. The fucking idiot didn't even finish his undergrad. I, on the other hand, have a goddamn MBA from Harvard."

"Well, he seems to be doing well with the mines."

"Because they're *mines*. He digs for gold, throws it on a scale, and sells it for market price. A monkey could run that business!" He pauses to temper his tone. "Look, it was an unfortunate situation but it is handled, and it's never going to happen again."

*What unfortunate situation are they talking about?* I know I shouldn't be listening, so I quietly sweep through and collect dirty dishes, keeping my head down while I learn about Henry. He has an MBA from Harvard—impressive. He has a brother named Scott, whom he clearly doesn't think too highly of.

"You better see to it that it doesn't, because one more fuckup like that and you'll be the monkey peddling gold, *if* that. You're already on thin ice with this Wolf Cove project. You're about to embarrass our family with that catastrophic failure. A goddamn seasonal Wolf. I can't believe you talked me into this."

I feel Henry's eyes on me and I can't help but glance over and offer him a polite smile, all the while feeling bad for him for his father's harsh words. I don't see why he wouldn't be proud of his son's accomplishments here, but I'm not a business tycoon. I'm sure it's more complicated than hanging pretty chandeliers and gazing out at snow-covered mountaintops.

"When do you arrive?" Henry pushes out through gritted teeth.

"I don't know. Ask my secretary." The phone line goes dead.

And Henry heaves a sigh, resting his forehead in his palms for a long moment.

"He seems a bit abrupt." I quietly edge in next to him, to where my laptop sits, inhaling the scent of clean soap. He's dressed in cargo pants and a simple black long-sleeved shirt for another bear sightseeing trip with another group of important guests. I wonder if he ever gets bored of it.

"I've been planning this since I was a teenager—long before my father ever handed over the reins to Wolf Hotels. This summer, I will prove to him and every other asshole out there that the Alaska location is a fucking brilliant move." His words are confident—even arrogant—but I sense a hint of fear and unease behind them, too.

"For what it's worth, you've already proven it to me. I'd stay here if I could afford it. I mean, I know my opinion doesn't matter much, but I'd stay."

"You shouldn't do that."

"Do what?" I'm instantly replaying my movements, wondering what I did wrong.

"Discredit yourself like that. Especially if you want your business to succeed one day."

My business? Does he mean my soap business? I frown for a moment, searching through my memory. I never told him about that, did I?

The video. I mentioned it in there. And I guess he remembers.

Reaching for the extra mug I requested with room service—for me—Henry pours coffee into it, then cream and a spoonful of sugar, and slides it over to me wordlessly.

"Thank you." I smile sheepishly. Oh, to have Henry

making my coffee for me every morning. "So, you have a brother?" I ask cautiously, taking a sip.

"Yeah. An older one."

"I always wished I had a sibling." Mama had to have an emergency hysterectomy after I was born, due to complications. She blames that for her excessive weight gain.

"You can have mine. He's a cocksucker. He wants to run Wolf Hotels. Thinks he can do a better job." Henry sighs as he stands, reaching for his red-and-black lumberjack coat.

"Must be a real problem, when you have to fight over an international hotel chain and a gold mine." I let some of my sarcasm slip out, even though I've been taught with years of scolding to keep it in. Sarcasm is "rude."

"You have a bad habit of listening in on things you're not supposed to," Henry murmurs, only his eyes are twinkling with mischief as he peers down at me, his gaze raking over my chest. I'm getting the impression that he's a breast man, for the amount of attention he gives to mine.

His soft reprimand reminds me of the conversation he had with Belinda. It must remind him, too, because the mischief falls off. "There are people, including my own family, who want this hotel to fail. They want me to fail."

He pulls on his jacket, hiding that intoxicating upper body from my view. "The plane needs to leave in ten. I'm heading out."

"Not yet." I rush to his bedroom, eying the rumpled sheets—my daily mental dose of Henry's naked body tangled in them hitting me, making me flush. But I push past that and dig through his dresser drawer. He's waiting for me, mild curiosity making his face softer.

I hold out the pair of black socks, to replace the mismatched blue and brown ones he pulled onto his feet.

"I'm sure the bears don't care about your fashion statement, but I figured you might."

He treats me to a sheepish grin—such a rare sight on his beautiful face—before swapping out his socks and lacing up his hiking boots. There's something decidedly heart-warming about being able to do little personal things like this for him. Things that a girlfriend or wife might do.

"I'll see you later, Abbi." He winks. "Stay out of trouble."

"So no more massages?" It slips out before I can help myself, and I bite my lip nervously, hoping I haven't angered him with the reminder.

"Only from Lorraine," he throws over his shoulder on his way out.

"You know my roommate?"

"Nope." He's gone, out the door, leaving me baffled.

*Date: May 9th*

*Abigail,*

*How are you? Your mom told me that you were in Alaska? That must be something. I never thought you'd be so adventurous! Same ol', same ol' around here. Well, except for the whole Jed thing, of course. The whole town's still reeling over that. I can't believe he had the nerve to bring Cammie to Greenbank. Your mom said that you're devastated but staying strong. We're all glad to hear that. Drop me a line when you get a chance.*

*Lucy*

I stare at the e-mail as I sip on my coffee, stewing in anger over Mama telling people that I'm devastated. Whether it's the truth or not is beside the point. Now Jed and *Cammie* and everyone will think I'm sitting in a corner up here, crying my eyes out. Back when it happened, I didn't care. I wanted people to think that, to feel sorry for me. But now it makes me sound weak and pathetic.

I take in the sunny morning as I consider how I should respond. I haven't talked to Lucy in months. She's a friend of ours from school growing up. She works at the feed store in town, having never left the town borders after high school graduation. Truth be told, she never did well enough in school to even consider applying to college. Punching buttons into a cash register and hoisting grain bags is more her speed.

She's nice enough, but she's a gossip, and I know that whatever I tell her now will spread through town like wildfire.

I smile. Maybe that's not such a bad thing.

*Hey Lucy,*

*Great to hear from you! I'm having an amazing time in Alaska. It's beautiful and peaceful. I could live up here forever. The hotel is pure luxury, and I've made some great friends. I'm actually working as the personal assistant to Mr. Wolf, himself. I'm pretty sure he's the most handsome man I've ever laid eyes on.* ☺ *Have you ever heard of him?*

I do a quick Google search to find a link with an especially flattering media picture of Henry—his designer suit well cut over his powerful upper body, his smile charming—and include it in the body of the email, followed by an airy "talk to you later," sign-off.

I grin. There. Now it's time to work.

# seventeen

Henry: *Come to Lux right now.*

I stare at the text for five long seconds, trying to decipher the tone, before tapping out:

**Abbi:** *On my way.*

I read his text for the umpteenth time as I speed walk through the main lodge, trying not to bump or knock anyone over in my rush. Is he angry with me? Is there something wrong? Did I screw up with the reservation?

With a last glance into a mirror outside the hotel's best restaurant, smoothing my uniform and checking my braid, I step inside.

The tall, handsome man in an all-black suit behind the reservations desk flashes me a polite smile. "Yes?" His voice is as melodic as it was on the phone and I immediately sigh, because I know he's an ally.

"Rich! It's me, Abbi. Mr. Wolf's assistant. He asked that I meet him here."

"Oh, right," he murmurs absently, doing a full once-over of me. "I didn't expect you to be so..."

I wait for it. So plain? So average? So country?

Rich meets my glare and finishes with, "Wide-eyed innocent. Mr. Wolf is at table twenty-two. Allow Mary to lead you there." He gestures to the petite brunette to his right, who's waiting patiently for me in her matching all-black uniform, only she wears a skirt much like mine.

"Thanks, Rich. I'll talk to you later."

He smirks, dropping his voice to add, "Oh, I'm sure you will. I'll be kissing lots of ass for you and the boss this summer."

It takes me a minute to figure out what he means and by that point, I'm halfway through the packed—though oddly calm—dining room, trailing my guide and her perfect round butt, highlighted by the skirt. I wonder what my butt looks like in this thing.

I haven't spent much time investigating all that the hotel has to offer, my time divided mainly between the staff village, Henry's place, and the hotel rooms I prepared before I was moved. But thanks to all the reading I did on the eve of becoming Henry's assistant, I learned that there are three dining areas—Haven, a cozy breakfast café on the first floor that serves gourmet omelets and French-style pastries; Rawley's, a more relaxed though still upscale pub, where you can enjoy microbrewery pints from all over the world as well as hundred-year-old malt scotches while sitting in leather wing chairs and gazing over the mounted works of a taxidermy; and this place. Lux, fine dining at its best, with highly skilled servers and sleek, sophisticated décor. I can hardly focus on the rich silk table linens and million-dollar view, though, as I make my way over toward the table in the far corner. Henry's steely blue eyes are already locked on me, robbing me of my breath.

Lord, that man's gaze... Does he practice that in the mirror?

"He's right over there." Mary waves a graceful hand.

"Right. Thanks," I mumble, leaving her to weave around other dining guests. His attention has shifted back to his investors, his posture casual, his expression calm. He's made no gesture toward me, no indication that I should interrupt him. I don't know what to do, but I can't just stand here, staring at him.

I close the distance to the table, edging up quietly so as not to interrupt the ongoing conversation. The other men—all in their fifties by my guess and dressed in camo, which is so inappropriate for this high-end restaurant, but they're sitting with the owner so I guess it's okay—are talking over each other, their voices loud and boisterous.

"Did you see that one by the river?" A man with a thick Midwest accent asks, spreading his meaty hands wide over a plate of pasta. "One swipe of his paw and your face would be gone! He had to be sixteen hundred pounds easily."

"It's very possible," Henry says, casually validating the man's story while pulling out the spare chair next to him. Finally, he calls me over with a "come here" wave of two fingers. He likes that move. Normally, I would hate it but there's something so commanding and sexy about the way he does it.

I slide in quietly, feeling my cheeks flush under the sudden attention of the other occupants.

"Everyone, my assistant, Abbi. I've asked her here to take some follow-up notes before you all fuck off to the saunas and the bar and forget why you're here: to give me your money."

The table erupts in a loud chorus of laughter, while Henry offers nothing more than a small, satisfied smirk.

And I release a sigh of relief because, again, I've let my

anxiety and my imagination get the better of me. I didn't screw up.

The man directly next to me, a heavyset, graying man with a coarse beard, leans in toward me. "And here we thought he liked us for our personalities," he jokes.

I smile politely as I open my iPad and shift my eyes to the screen.

"I need meetings booked with each of these guys for next week. Contact their assistants," Henry begins. He lists his demands in a cool, even tone, while the others finish their meals, pausing occasionally to interject an important name or date. These men are all CEOs and VPs of big companies that reward their top sales teams with exotic, lavish trips, and Henry wants Wolf Cove to be their destination.

That's the first leg of the notes. The second part is notes on the hotel itself—suggestions on improvements to the rooms and amenities, entertainment packages, and that sort of thing. Things that are ridiculous (a cigar room?) but I say nothing, judiciously tapping away at my screen.

"I think that's it?"

The others all nod their heads in agreement as the server comes around to clear plates.

"Don't know about the rest of you, but I'm ready for a real drink after this morning!" The Midwesterner slaps the table, rattling the centerpiece. The others chirp their agreement.

"Abbi, give us a minute." Henry barely casts a glance my way.

I quietly duck out, smiling at each man before stepping away. But where do I go? Should I stay within easy reach? I settle on the bench by the unoccupied grand piano, set on a stage in the corner.

I'm far enough away that I *shouldn't* be able to hear their conversation. If I didn't have exceptional hearing, anyway.

I watch Henry, leaning back in his chair talking business with these men, his thumb casually rubbing back and forth across the handle of his fork. Yet another sexy, appealing side of him. He's decades younger than them and yet they all obviously respect him.

"How's it going?" Rachel's sudden voice in my ear makes me jump. "I hear you're working for the big boss, now."

I look first at her tray full of drinks, then at her clothes, a version of the black servers' outfit, with a few top buttons missing and a shorter skirt. With her white-blond hair pulled back in a big fluffy bun, her eyes dark and smoky, and her full lips painted red, she looks downright sexy. Too sexy for noon.

I haven't seen her in days, which is crazy seeing as we live together, but that's how these places work, apparently. "Hey! Yeah. Just here to take notes and then I'm guessing I'll be back to the computer."

"You're the talk of the hotel, that's for sure. Everyone's wondering how the virgin landed a job like that."

My mouth drops open. "How does everyone know about that?"

She frowns at me, then recognition fills her face and she laughs. "I was talking about a hotel virgin. But, *seriously*?"

Henry glances over our way and she whispers, "Better go and deliver these. Don't want to make the wolf angry." She stalks over to the table in her black heels, her calf muscles straining beautifully. By her flirtatious giggles and the men's obvious ogling as Rachel sets their drinks down in front of them, I'd say my roommate is a big hit with the executives.

Even Henry's heated eyes linger over her face, along her neckline, down to the swell of her breasts peeking out, only to hold her gaze when she leans over to set his drink in front of him, a seductive smirk curling his lips.

He wants her; it's obvious to anyone watching.

A sharp pang of jealousy throbs within me. He's never looked at me like that. I practically threw myself at him when I was drunk, we had that "moment" in the truck... then there was yesterday, in his room. But he has never looked at me like *that*.

He's not attracted to me.

I don't know exactly how obvious my envy is on my face, but when Henry glances over to catch my eye, a frown flits across his expression. It's followed by a hard look that I can't decipher but makes me nervous. I duck my head and try to refocus my attention on my notes.

Failing. I can't keep my eyes off him.

Rachel leaves, her hips swaying a little too suggestively, attracting all their gazes. Except Henry, who now stares daggers at his glass.

"With that kind of service, who can say no to this place," one of the other guys mumbles, and they all chuckle.

"Surprised you didn't bring your other assistant here," another one says. "Having an assistant like *that* at your beck and call..." His words drift off and his eyebrows waggle suggestively.

"Oh, hell. That leggy brunette. Kiera. Yeah." The burly Carolina man puffs his cheeks out with an exhale. "Don't know how you got any work done with that one around."

"I had to let her go," Henry says simply. "It wasn't working out."

Kiera. That's the name Belinda mentioned the other day. She must be the assistant Tillie was talking about. The one that Henry fired for hitting on him.

While I should be more focused on the bruise to my ego

—in the ten minutes I sat and quietly took notes, they decided they'd rather have the "leggy brunette" Kiera here—my curiosity is getting the better of me. What happened between them, exactly? What did it take to get her fired? Because after some of the stuff I've done, I'm almost positive I'll be next.

And, arguably, Henry hasn't exactly been a saint, either. Did he strip down in front of her, too? Did that send her mixed messages, like perhaps the ones I'm desperate to read?

I pretend not to eavesdrop as they finish up their lunch meeting and unease settles onto my shoulders. With a round of handshakes and "see you for dinner" commitments, the bigwig executives stroll away, their phones in their hands.

"Abbi. Come," Henry commands, with as much warmth as you'd expect from a billionaire calling on his lowly assistant. He turns and strolls toward the exit. I jump up, smoothing my skirt and shirt as I rush to follow him out past guests and the hostess desk.

"See you later, sir," Rich offers. Henry barely acknowledges him, throwing a wave in the air without even a glance. I mouth "bye" toward Rich. He responds with a sarcastic "have fun" look and a salute before pulling the phone receiver to his ear.

"Do you have any questions about your follow-ups to that meeting?" Henry asks coolly, his eyes skating over the lingering guests, some in hiking gear, others on their way to the spa, and yet others simply lingering in the lobby, their hands holding drinks and their speech slurred. It's only two in the afternoon, but I guess when you're on vacation, anything goes, even in Alaska.

"No. I don't think so." I'll have to hunt through Henry's e-mails and calendar to find out who was with him today and their respective assistants, but I can figure that out.

"What was that look back there?"

"Uh...I...what?" I stammer, caught off guard. He likes doing that. "What look?"

"Don't play dumb. It doesn't suit you."

I bite my bottom lip, unsure what to say but feeling summarily chastised and two feet tall.

I say nothing, which seems to frustrate Henry because he stops, turning to glare at me with his arms folded over his chest. He drops his voice. "When your roommate came to deliver drinks. You were upset."

"No, I wasn't," I'm quick to say, averting my gaze.

"Look at me when I'm talking to you."

Swallowing my nerves, I lift my face to meet his gaze again. Cold amusement dances in them as he dissects me, cutting past my poorly veiled attempt to hide my attraction like a well-honed blade against flesh. "You were upset because it seemed that I might want more than just my drink from her."

I shake my head in denial, and that beautiful, hard jaw of his grows taut. He's too perceptive.

"This will all go more smoothly for you if you tell me the truth."

"And what? Get fired?" I whisper.

His brow arches in surprise. "If I were going to fire you, I would have already done that. Don't you agree?"

Why are we having this conversation now, *here,* in the middle of the lodge, where I can feel curious eyes on me like bugs crawling over my skin?

"Remember what I told you? Out here, I am Mr. Wolf at *all* times. You can't be looking at me like some poor, wounded animal. Like I've broken your heart. Do you understand? My staff is *always* watching, waiting for the next juicy detail to gossip about. I can't have them making up stories. It reflects badly on me, and on my company."

"Of course." I hug the iPad to my chest, wishing I were anywhere but here right now. At least my face isn't burning bright. I'm pretty sure all the blood has left my head.

He heaves a sigh. "Please don't allow your crush to get in the way of your job. If you can't control it, then we can't continue our arrangement."

Which arrangement is that, exactly? The one where he strips down to nothing while I stand there and watch?

I nod, not trusting my voice, fighting off the tears that burn behind my eyes as I trail him to the Summit room for our daily meeting.

Feeling all the more like a stupid bright-eyed doe being led by a cunning wolf.

# eighteen

My phone dings with an incoming text. I leap for it.

**Henry:** *You can call it a day. See you tomorrow at seven a.m.*

It's only 4:00 p.m.

**Abbi:** *Do you want me to give you a ten-minute rundown of your revised calendar? I made a lot of changes.*

I wait, biting my thumbnail.

**Henry:** *I'll review on my own.*

He wants me gone before he gets back, that much is obvious. He sent me back to the cabin as soon as the daily update meeting was over, with barely a glance.

Peeling myself off the couch, I grab my jacket and head out, glad to be free of him and whatever game he's playing with my head for a night.

~

"You sure are the talk of the town, Abbi," Tillie mutters beyond the curtain that I pulled around my bunk. I want to hide from the world.

Panic strikes me. I throw the curtain back in time to see her yanking her badge off her neck. "I am?"

She kicks off her loafer shoes. "Sounds like the boss tore a strip off you in the middle of the lodge lobby today."

I guess that *was* what it would have looked like to any innocent bystander watching. And there were plenty of them doing that. The gossip queen hasn't heard the reasons behind it, thank God. I let a small sigh of relief slip. "Oh. Yeah."

"They say he looked pissed."

"Yeah. I screwed up."

"You best be careful."

I want to pull my privacy curtain closed again and curl up into a ball, but that would be considered rude. As it is, I move my attention back to my e-reader. I've been staring at the same page for an hour now, unable to focus on the words. "I'll be fine. I won't make that mistake twice." From now on, my eyes are down and my mouth stays shut. I just want this icky feeling that's taken over my conscience to go away.

"What'd you do to get his panties in a bunch?"

"A scheduling mistake," I lie.

"Don't worry. Guys like him are quick to blow up and even quicker to forget. He won't even remember it tomorrow," Rachel offers from her place on Katie's bed, where Katie paints hot green wax around her brows. "I saw him at the bar about an hour ago, drinking scotch with some suit. He seemed fine."

"Okay. Stop talking!" Katie demands, pressing a white

strip over the spot and then, holding Rachel's skin taut, pulls it off fast, like you would a Band-Aid.

I wince with the action, but it doesn't seem to faze her.

Katie grins with satisfaction. "There. Gorgeous, as usual."

Rachel sits up and peers at her eyebrows in a handheld mirror. They look so thin and neat and tidy. Not like my brows, two caterpillars above my eyes. "They look nice," I offer with a smile.

Katie holds the little wand up toward me, excitement flashing in her gaze as she sizes up mine. "Please, please, please, *please* let me do yours?"

"She won't leave you alone until you do," Rachel says with a chuckle.

"What? I can't help it! I like my women to be well groomed."

*Yes, I've noticed.* It'd be so easy to say yes to her right now. "Aren't my eyes too big to have skinny brows, though?"

"Trust me. Please!" Katie pleads. "You have such an angelic little face. Let me do it?"

"Okay?" I say before I can change my mind. Maybe this will make me feel better. At the very least, it'll distract me.

The broad smile on Katie's beautiful face makes me think I've made her day.

And ten minutes and a few moments of yelping pain later, I'm staring at my face in the mirror, awed, convinced that she has made my summer.

"It makes such a difference, doesn't it?" Katie purrs, admiring her work.

Rachel looks over her shoulder. "Amazing. Seriously."

"My eyes look so different." I'm grinning stupidly at myself. "Why have I never done this before?"

"See? Now all you need is a ginger eyebrow pencil to fill them in."

"I don't have the first clue how to do that." My mama failed me in the "being a girl" department, more interested in teaching me about breeding chickens and milking cows.

"I'll show you," Katie offers.

"Could you?" I've never had friends like Katie and Rachel, so in tune with beauty techniques and style.

She shrugs, as if it's no big deal, her fingers playing with my braid. "You know what? Silvia over in cabin two is the stylist at the spa. I'd bet she'd love a go at this mane."

"Like a trim?" That's all I've ever had. I've had hair down to my butt for twenty-one years.

She peels the elastic out of my hair braid, letting my long, heavy hair fall down across my back. "More like a shape-up. You have beautiful hair. It just needs to be tamed." Her lips twist together. "And Tris over in cabin twelve does color. She could throw some lowlights and highlights into it. That sort of thing."

Color.

"I can't color my hair. I'm a ginger."

Katie's head tips back with her throaty laughter. "Oh, you're so adorable. You *can* color your hair, as long as you have someone who knows what they're doing. Tris knows what she's doing. She was trained at a top school, too. She won't fuck it up, I promise."

"Do you think she'd do it?"

"She will if I ask." Katie winks.

"I don't know..." That's a lot of change all at once. But maybe change would be good.

She sighs, her fingers weaving through my hair. I can't be entirely sure that it's innocent but right now I find comfort in the small act of kindness. "I promise you, it'll make you feel better about whatever happened today with Mr. Wolf."

I guess my misery is visible for everyone to see.

I offer her a tight smile and a weak, "Okay."

~

I CAN'T STOP STARING at the glamorous woman in the mirror, tears welling in my eyes as I meet gazes with the blonde pixie woman's reflection. "Thank you."

"My pleasure!" Tris exclaims, her fingers skating through the silky strands, the dull ginger broken up by vibrant chunks of deep red, copper, and auburn. "Your hair is some of the healthiest and thickest I've ever seen. And this cut Sylvia gave you is perfect. It gives it bounce without sacrificing length."

Sylvia only nods in agreement, busy sweeping the mounds of hair piled on the floor around my chair. My jaw hit the ground when she lopped off six inches from the bottom with a single swipe of her scissors, but by the time she was done snipping and edging with her fancy tools and combs, I didn't care. My head feels about ten pounds lighter.

"Your color took well, but don't wash it too much, if you want it to last, okay?"

"Yes, okay." I want it to last forever. Glancing at the clock, I realize that it's almost nine at night. We've been here for hours. "What do I owe you for this?" Worry gnaws at me. This couldn't have been cheap.

"Nothing. Wolf covered it," Tris says, tidying the work station.

I frown. "What do you mean?"

"I guess he felt pretty damn bad about giving you such a

hard time earlier today," Katie murmurs with a knowing grin.

"What?" I glance around, half expecting him to step out of the shadows. "How does he even know I'm here?"

"We had to get permission. Staff technically aren't allowed to use hotel facilities but I figured, why not ask, seeing as you're his personal assistant. I mean, come on! That's got to get you something, right? So Sally called him and got his okay, seeing as we had no appointments tonight, and he told her to charge it to his account. Tip and all."

I think my eyes are about to fall out of my head. Henry agreed—and paid—for this? "Seriously?"

Katie shrugs. "I guess he can be a decent asshole, too. And seeing as he's a decent asshole..." She grabs my hand by the wrist. "Come on. There's one more thing I *have* to do." I trail her as she pulls me down the hall that separates the beauty salon from the rest of the spa, past the trendy little all-white reception area. "Stacy, do you have a waxing room ready?" she whispers to the receptionist. "I need it for ten minutes. Fifteen, max. I swear."

The girl's eyes flutter toward the three women sitting on a cream-colored leather bench, sipping from their glasses of champagne as they wait their appointments. "They *just* walked in," she murmurs, trying to hide it behind unmoving lips.

"Please!" Katie begs in a whisper.

"Number ten. Be quick!" she hisses.

Katie plants a kiss on her cheek. "You're the best! Abbi, come."

"What are we doing in here?" I ask as she closes the door and locks it, enclosing us in a small room with a padded table in the center.

"We are fixing that issue down there." With a long, pointed finger, she gestures toward my crotch.

My eyes widen as I realize what she wants to do. I open my mouth to say no, but she slaps her hand over my mouth. "Have I led you astray yet, today? Don't you feel a million times better already?"

"Yes, I do," I admit. "But I don't see how doing *that* will help."

"What if you hook up with a guy while you're here? Do you want him to be getting down and dirty and choke on a mouthful of hair?"

I cringe and my face burns bright. "Oh my God."

"Right? Didn't you already hook up with someone the first night you were here?"

"No!" I exclaim. "Where did you hear that?" The second the question is out of my mouth, I know the answer. "Tillie."

"A word to the wise, don't tell that woman a thing that you don't want repeated. She's a gossip piranha. She'll die without her daily dose of it."

I sigh. "I didn't hook up with anyone. I made a huge ass of myself." Big difference.

"Okay, well, whatever. Everyone's fucking like rabbits around here. It's only a matter of time before you are, too. So *please* let me do this for you. I don't have to do a full Brazilian. We can start with something less dramatic."

I can't believe this is happening. "Why do you want to do this?" I try not to sound suspicious, but I can't help it. Why is my lesbian roommate so adamant to get my pants off and rip my body hair out?

She levels me with a flat stare. "Relax. I know you know."

My cheeks burn. "How?"

She slips on a pair of plastic gloves and begins stirring

the pot of green wax. "Because I caught you watching on my camera the other night."

*Oh my God.* I wonder who's more mortified. I don't know what to say. She doesn't seem bothered, though.

"And don't worry. I'm not into you. You're not my type."

Her words prick me unexpectedly. "Why not?"

"You're too innocent and sweet. I like my women bossy and confident."

Hmm. Where have I heard that before?

She laughs when she sees the expression on my face. "Come on. Trust me. The last thing you want to be worrying about is poor grooming when you're about to get it on."

I look at the table in front of me, at the wax and strips of paper waiting.

A small voice in my head—the stupid, clueless, dreamy, crushing side that can't help but fantasize—tells me that I wouldn't want to worry about poor grooming with Henry.

"What do I need to do?"

"Drop your pants."

# nineteen

Henry is sitting at the desk with his back to me when I arrive the next morning, already dressed for the day in a navy suit, leaning back in the chair, a pen within his grasp. Multiple voices carry over the speaker phone.

I move quietly for his breakfast dishes, intent on stacking and clearing them for the service staff to pick up when they come at ten to collect dirty linens and such.

"If we have sound research to show that a Wolf will not succeed in Dubai, then give me even one good reason why we should—" Henry's words drop off. I glance over to find him staring hard at me.

I nod and smile politely, and then quickly move away.

As quickly as my sore crotch will allow me to.

As if being naked from the waist down and splayed across a table under a bright light wasn't bad enough, when Katie ripped that first strip of hair off me, it took everything in me not to scream. And by that point it was too late to turn back, she so kindly pointed out.

She worked fast, mercifully, and within twenty minutes,

I was holding up a mirror between my legs. She'd left a small ginger "landing strip" at the top but otherwise, I'm as bald as Rachel. She even made me spread my cheeks. "You don't want hair there, either," she insisted. By that point, I let her do what she wanted, already past the point of mortification.

The aftercare lotion she gave me helped with the redness. She has promised that I'll have smooth, soft skin within a few days.

I hate to admit it, but she was right. Even if no one ever sees her handiwork, it does make me feel more attractive. And my cotton underwear against my mound feels weird, as if a shield has been removed. If I step a certain way, the material rubs against my clit.

The voices on the other end continue on, a low hum in the background, and I try my best not to disturb Henry's meeting as I shift around the place, tidying up. I duck into his bedroom and find his bed sheets in a rumpled pile. Again, my mind automatically veers to the thought of him in them.

*Don't let your crush get in the way of your job.*

His chastising words yesterday snap me back to reality. Stripping his bed, I gather the sheets, the hamper, and the wet towels, and carry them to the servants' quarters.

Henry's gaze follows me the entire time.

By the time I'm done folding and putting away his briefs and socks—even the man's underwear causes a reaction in me—he's hanging up the phone.

"Abbi. Come here. Please."

I take a deep breath, unsure if I'm ready for whatever he's going to say after yesterday's verbal public flaying. There's an edge of contrition in his tone, at least. "Yes?"

He holds out a purple tie. "Will this work?"

His sheepish grin and his rare vulnerability instantly take the edge off my unease. "Yes."

He waits quietly, tie in hand. He wants me to finish dressing him. I don't understand why he keeps asking me to do this. He *must* know how to tie his own tie. Is this a strange power trip thing?

"How did you manage dressing yourself before I got here?" I accept the silky material and our fingers graze. Electricity courses through my limbs.

"Not as enjoyably." His eyes skate over my hair. "You look different."

"I wanted to try something new. Thank you for giving the okay." I try to avoid his gaze but I can't help steal a quick glimpse. Blue eyes bore into me. "I planned on paying for it."

"Consider it part of your compensation package." He pauses. "For being such a competent assistant."

"Is that what I am?" I loop the tie around his neck, positioning it under his collar just so. Why do my hands always have to shake when I'm this close to him? *Always!*

"You've made some other changes, too."

My mouth drops open. How does he know about *that*?

He nods toward my eyebrows.

"Oh, right." I exhale with relief, earning his curious frown. "My mama always told me that I'd look silly with thin eyebrows."

"She was obviously wrong."

He's acting so different now. But I guess he always does within these walls, and when we're in private. It's when we're out there that the cold Mr. Wolf persona makes itself known.

I like this version—my private version of him—better. I wish we could hide in here all day.

"Have you called home lately?"

"I've had a few calls, but I haven't talked to my mama since the night I arrived." It's a strange question to ask, coming from him. "Why?"

"No reason. I figured you were the type of girl to call home every day."

"Calling home every day means getting a status report on my ex every day. No thanks." Not even the mention of Jed can diminish the impact this man has on me when I'm standing this close to him, dressing him. And who thought *dressing* a man could be such a turn on?

"Still have your mind on him?"

"Not so much." *Not right now.* The throb between my legs has begun again. I work quickly, needing to step away from him, to be alone with his calendar and my coffee and not able to do or say something stupid or unprofessional in front of him.

He smirks, like he knows it. "Are you still afraid that you'll take him back if he comes to his senses?"

"Don't you mean to ask if I'm still the silly farm girl pining over a spineless dickhead?"

He flinches, and it makes me feel good. Maybe he regrets his unsympathetic words. But why is he getting so personal, all of a sudden? "There. Done." I run my hand over his tie to line the two ends together, swallowing hard as my fingers graze the hard curves of his chest. I've seen it bare enough times to know exactly what's beneath his shirt. I'm not sure if that's better or worse. Had I not witnessed him naked, I'd be left only to my imagination, and my imagination couldn't have come up with something as incredible as the real deal.

Henry reaches up to touch a few strands of my hair and I freeze. I usually have it pulled back in a braid, but today I left it down, so in love with how silky it feels, how it cascades over my shoulders and back. "Thank you," he finally offers, a rare softness flickering in his eyes.

His gaze drops to my lips, but it's his exhale I feel skate across them as he sighs. "You understand why I said what I did to you yesterday, right?"

"Because I'm your assistant and people can't get the wrong idea."

His hand curls into a fist around my hair at my nape, tugging it softly until my head tips back. "There's a lot at stake for me here, Abbi. Things are a lot more complicated than you can imagine." He leans in closer, until his mouth is inches away from mine. So painfully close that a tiny gasp escapes my mouth. I can't believe this is happening.

This can't be my imagination or my wishful thinking anymore. Either Henry's a cruel, cruel man...

Or he's attracted to me.

The words are on the tip of my tongue, a plea for him to stop torturing me like this. But I stifle those words, afraid he won't give in, that he'll choose to dismiss me entirely.

"You are so goddamn sweet." His lips skim over mine as he whispers, "I don't even like sweet. I like filthy and unemotional. This wasn't supposed to happen. I'm at a pivotal moment in my career and you are fucking with my head."

"I'm sorry." I close my eyes, silently begging him to press his lips against mine, to let me slide my tongue against his, taste his mouth. It has to be him making that move; I've humiliated myself too many times.

Our hot breath mixes between us, the seconds growing longer as my nipples grow tight and my breasts grow heavy and the throb between my legs becomes unbearable, my panties drenched.

And he hasn't pulled back.

"I need to know that you can keep your feelings for me in check when we're in public. Can you do that?"

*When we're in public?* My heart pounds inside my chest. "What about in private?"

Henry's phone begins to ring and he breaks free of me instantly, almost as if the sound was a warning alarm. I nearly topple over with frustration. Taking a step back to grab his suit jacket, he says, "We have our daily status meeting this morning, right?"

"Right. Because of your afternoon sail." Oh God. Every part of my body is hot now, from my scalp right down to my core.

He lets out a deep exhale, the only sign that the unexpected moment had any effect on him at all. Not the only sign, I realize as he answers his phone and my eyes drift to the prominent bulge at the front of his dress pants.

What the hell just happened?

I trail him out, leaving all my rational thoughts scattered on the floor.

THE MEETING RUNS EXACTLY the same as it did the last two times, only now I'm out of sorts and struggling to pay attention. I've played our moment through my mind a dozen times since our silent walk from the cabin.

Henry nearly kissed me this morning. *Why?* I know my hair looks good, but I haven't changed *that* much.

His knee bobs impatiently, mere inches away from mine. So much closer than he has been in the past. Close enough that I could reach over and touch him. My fingers itch with the urge, but I know that wouldn't go over well.

What is happening between us?

"Staff update, Belinda?"

"We've had a few incidents."

That helps break the spell that Henry has cast on me. I glance up to find Belinda's sharp eyes flickering to me.

But it's Pierre who speaks. "Two nights ago, one of the bar staff members took it upon herself to feed a celebrity guest free scotches all night at the bar."

Now Henry frowns. "Why?"

"Apparently the guest was upset that she mixed up his scotch for a cheap brand, so she figured she'd ease his anger with a few on the house."

"How many dollars' worth?"

"A grand. It was a very rare bottle."

Henry shakes his head to himself.

Now Belinda steps in. "That's not all. Security has her going to his hotel room after her shift was over."

"Bow-chicka-wow-wow," Ryan mutters absently, the only indication that he's paying attention as he scans his phone.

"You've terminated employment?" Henry asks.

"Not yet. I wanted to—"

He cuts Belinda off with "Get rid of her. Get her on a ferry right away. I can't have staff making up their own rules, and we're not running a damn brothel. What's her name?"

"Rachel Avery."

Is that *my* Rachel? I don't know her last name but she works at the bar. Two nights ago... She wasn't in her bed when I got up to head to the showers.

My stomach sinks. It must be her.

And Henry just demanded her firing. I glance at him, wondering if he realizes who she is to me, but he simply stares straight ahead, unaffected. "The other issue?"

Belinda's lips twist, her poor attempt to hide a smile. "This morning, a guest complained that two of our staff were utilizing the spa for their own personal needs last night, while she and her friends were waiting for service." Her eyes settle on me. "I can't say that I blame them for being upset."

My stomach drops. The three women waiting in the lobby when Katie dragged me into the room last night. Without permission. That was them. This is about me.

*Oh my God.*

I'm unable to stop myself from reaching for Henry's knee below the table, squeezing it hard as my heart pounds inside my chest. Henry's gaze flickers to mine. With my eyes, I plead for him not to press, not to ask for details, not to fire me—or Katie—on the spot. Worse, I'll die if Belinda has figured out what "service" Katie provided and *that* becomes a topic of discussion.

He must pick up on my discomfort—anyone would, my face is likely ghostly white—because he dismisses everyone with an, "Okay. That's all."

I could kiss him, right here, right now.

"Sally, Belinda, a word." Everyone gets up. "Wait for me in the hall, Abbi."

I duck out and round the corner, hugging my iPad to my chest, my legs wobbly, my blood rushing through my ears, throwing my balance off even more. I consider running and never looking back.

"Sally? Is this true?" The walls aren't soundproof and, thanks to the empty, quiet hall, I can easily hear Henry's deep voice through the door.

"It's news to me."

"It was your assistant, Henry," Belinda offers, the smug tone glaringly obvious.

"I'm aware that she was in the salon last night. Sally

cleared it with me." Henry's calm voice gives me a false sense of security.

"I did," Sally jumps in. "It was dead in there. Not one person waiting. I can't imagine who would complain about anything."

"And did Henry clear the use of the esthetics room?"

There's a long pause. "I wasn't aware that it extended to that. No," Sally finally offers.

"They were in there for almost twenty minutes."

"Who?"

"Abbi and one of the estheticians."

I squeeze my eyes shut as tears threaten.

"It would have been Katie. She's the one who orchestrated all this. A roommate, I think. She's a bit of a live wire." Sally sighs. "I'm sorry. I wasn't aware. I'll deal with it."

Oh no. I've gotten Katie into trouble. Or worse, fired! Both Katie and Rachel gone?

"Hold off on that, Sally. I'll get back to you. Give us a minute," Henry says.

I take several steps back, so it doesn't look like I was eavesdropping, just as the door swings open and Sally steps out.

One look at me and sympathy fills her face.

"Please don't fire Katie. It was my fault. I made her do it," I whisper. That's not at all true, but I'll say anything.

"Don't worry. I think it'll blow over. And by the way," she gestures toward her own hair, "stunning!"

I offer her a tight-lipped smile, wishing I could revel in the compliment. The moment she turns the corner, I step closer to the door to resume my listening.

"What are you accusing me of?" The venom in Henry's voice is sharp and rank. I've clearly missed something important.

"It doesn't look good, Henry."

"So?"

"Just tell me you're not fucking her," Belinda hisses.

"I'm not fucking her."

"I don't believe you."

"I don't give a shit what you believe."

I know that's a lie.

"This isn't New York. We're secluded here. The future owner of Wolf Hotels fucking his assistant will have everyone's tongues wagging. Do you want that? Because your father will hear about it, even if it's not through me. And I'm guessing he won't be happy."

What *would* happen if *the* Mr. Wolf thought Henry and I were sleeping together? Does he *really* care what his son does? I guess so, if it reflects on his company. By the sound of the phone conversation from the other day, he takes a lot of pride in the Wolf name. Something in the back of my conscience pricks at me about that conversation. I can't put my finger on it, though.

There's a long pause and then I hear Henry ask, "What were they doing in there for that long?"

"What do you *think* they were doing in there?" Belinda snaps, then sighs. "It's a waxing room."

"For twenty minutes?"

I want to crawl into a hole and die. I can just imagine the look on his face.

"I have two guesses. Maybe your little farm girl is loosening up a bit. And if it's not for you, then it must be for someone else."

Footsteps approach the door and I scamper back just as it flies open. Henry steps out and simply stares at me, his face a cold mask. He looks pissed.

Belinda steps out behind him. "I'll meet you on the dock

at one?" Her gaze skates over mine briefly. The woman despises me, and it's purely out of jealousy. It's almost laughable, given who she is and what she looks like.

"Yup," Henry says without turning to regard her. "And please add a conduct warning to Miss Mitchell's file for utilizing hotel property for personal needs."

My face blanches.

I watch her stalk away triumphantly, waiting for her to round the corner before I plead with Henry. "Please don't have Katie fired."

He begins pacing back and forth, his hands on his hips, not saying a word. And then, when he does, it's not what I expect. "Is it for Michael?" he hisses.

My mouth drops open. "No!"

He seems to weigh that single word, his gaze drifting over the length of me. "I'll see you back at my place around five," he says more calmly. "Take care of those follow-ups."

In seconds, he's gone, leaving me standing alone in the hallway.

# twenty

I've always hated nylons.

They're itchy and confining, and, without a doubt, I always end the day with a snag in them somewhere. My mama made me wear them to church growing up, even on the hottest summer days. She said it was improper to go bare legged. Only heathens do that, apparently. I guess my mama and the uniform decision-makers at Wolf agree on something, because one of the requirements is that all females must wear nylons with their uniform dresses.

And I still hate them.

I hate them so much that I sat in Henry's living room and peeled them off with a loud sigh of relief. And the fitted pencil skirt that isn't meant to be worn while wrestling with a fitted sheet? That came off fifteen minutes later, allowing me freedom to crawl around the king-sized mattress because the bloody corners of this ill-fitting elastic won't stay down today.

I don't bother redressing right away. I watched Henry's boat float away with him, Belinda, and a dozen guests on board. He won't be home for hours and, with my white button-down shirt barely covering my panties and my hair pulled up in a messy bun, cleaning Henry's cabin suite has been a hundred times easier and faster, and a hundred times more comfortable.

Now finished, I push the nightstand back to its place and flip the switch to turn off the vacuum. Peaceful silence fills the cabin once again. I heave a sigh, giving my sore neck a rub.

"This is a new take on the uniform."

I squeal and spin around to find Henry standing in the entrance to the bedroom, the nylons that I left on the couch dangling from his fingertips. His normally cool, guarded mask is off, but I can't read the dark and thoughtful look that sits there now.

My face bursts into flames. "Your boat just left. You were on it! What are you doing back so soon?" The whir of the vacuum masked the sound of the door opening. I should probably be diving for my skirt, instead of standing here like a deer caught in headlights beside his bed, but I'm not sure that this moment could get any worse.

"I didn't realize I'd have to check in to make sure my assistant was fully dressed before coming home," he says dryly, loosening his tie with his free hand and tossing it onto his dresser.

"This uniform is not meant for maid work. I should be wearing a maid's uniform, if you're going to expect that I clean this place," I say in weak defense, hiding one bare leg behind the other. There is no excuse for coming home to find your personal assistant half-naked in your suite.

*Shit, shit, shit.* I can't stop screwing up with him. I don't blame him if he finally decides to fire me. I have it coming.

Only, I'm pretty sure he won't.

He reaches behind him and pulls the door, letting it

coast shut. The simple action makes my stomach tighten with nervousness. And excitement. There's something entirely erotic about being caught half-dressed in Henry's room. "One of the guests on the boat had a family emergency that they needed to tend to. Given I had already done plenty of socializing, I decided to hop off when we returned. And I'm not exactly dressed for a boat ride." He takes slow, measured steps toward me, until he's only a few feet away. He slides his suit jacket off to lay it on the bed and I inhale deeply, the smell of his cologne intoxicating.

This is so inappropriate. "I'm sorry. This won't happen again, I promise. Or the shower thing." I swallow. "Or the spa thing." I wonder if that confidentiality agreement extends to cover me from this kind of embarrassing situation.

Are we destined to be one inappropriate situation after the next, for the entire summer?

"That's right. The spa thing." He steps around me, circling me. It's an unnerving, almost predatory move on his part. A shiver runs down my spine. "Tell me what you were doing in that room with Katie Montgomery?"

I swallow. He knows who she is, just like he knew who Lorraine was. Does he know everything about everyone? Or just everything about me? "Some personal grooming."

"Eyebrows and underarms take no more than ten. Legs take much longer. You have no issues with facial hair. So that leaves only one place."

I gasp when his hand slips between my legs to skate across my inner thighs.

My body responds despite my confusion, the throb between my legs that never truly abated since that day in the woods surging again. Is this really happening? Is he touching me there?

"If we are going to continue to work together, we need to be open and honest with each other from now on. So I'll ask you again, because you never answered me the other day." His eyes never leave my face, something dangerous gleaming in them now. "Did you enjoy watching me jerk off in the shower?"

I shut my eyes. He's never going to let me forget that.

"Abbi." It's nearly a growl.

I let myself nod, my eyes still closed.

"Is that something you've seen before?"

I shake my head, unable to find my voice.

"Look at me."

I force myself to open my eyes, to find him smiling. I trail his gaze as it drifts down over my bare legs. I was cursing the blouse's length this morning when attempting to tuck it into the top of my skirt. Now, I couldn't love it more for hiding my ratty white cotton underwear. I need to invest in some new pairs.

His strong hand grips my jaw, gentle but firm, forcing my head back until I meet his eyes. Finally, they're unguarded. Finally, they show something that I recognize and can identify, even if I don't believe it—desire.

*Finally...*

"It was not supposed to be like this. You were not supposed to have this kind of impact on me," he whispers, leaning in to skim his wet lips over mine, never actually kissing me. Torturing me, as he has become so good at doing.

"I thought you didn't like sweet." I don't know how I'm even capable of answering.

He smirks. "I don't. But the idea of turning my sweet little assistant filthy is driving me insane."

I gasp as his hand slides over the curve of my hip, his

fingers curling around and then squeezing my small waist. Am I dreaming all this? Is Henry Wolf—my gorgeous billionaire boss who could have anyone he wants—lusting for me?

He edges around until my back is to his chest, the heat radiating off his body, his hand shifting to my other hip, his fingertips smoothing over my taut stomach. "You were jealous of your roommate yesterday. Tell me why. And be unabashedly honest. Please."

I hesitate. Can I really talk to him so openly? "Because I wanted you to look at me like that. I wanted to be her." But Rachel is fired, so maybe I don't want to be her.

He chuckles against my ear, the vibration coursing all the way down to my nipples, tightening them. "She's a dime a dozen. Do you want to know why I was looking at her like that?"

I nod. Do I? Henry's so unpredictable, I can't be sure that what comes out of his mouth won't be hurtful.

"Because I'm guessing she was one of the roommates who you watched get tongue fucked. That's what you saw, isn't it?"

I open my mouth to deny it, but he pushes, "Don't be shy with me. I don't want shy."

I nod and I feel his smile against my ear.

"I started to picture you getting wet while watching her. And the thought of you getting wet, of this body," both his hands are on my hips, hovering over the elastic of my panties, gripping me tightly, "writhing naked on my bed, with your legs spread and waiting for me to teach you everything you've been missing." The room is beginning to sway with his words. My legs wobble and his grip tightens. He won't let me fall. "That's why I was looking at her like that. I don't want her."

But apparently he wants me.

My skin flushes as one of his warm, large hands dips beneath the elastic of my panties to cup me between the legs. He groans. "Why did you do this?"

"I don't know."

"The truth," he pushes, his hot, moist breath coating my skin. I tip my head to the side, hoping his mouth will find my neck.

"I wanted to be more like Rachel. Someone you might look at." I pause. "Do you not like it?"

My knees buckle as his finger slides through my slit once, so slowly. "So you did it for me?"

"Yes." I don't... It's hard to focus. Henry Wolf has his hand in my panties. *He* wants *me.*

His finger makes another pass, teasing my clit on its way past. "Fuck, you are soaked. Do you want me to stop?"

I should, for so many reasons. "No," I whisper shakily. All of me is shaking, even my legs. But it's not with fear. It's with anticipation. "I thought this couldn't happen."

His hand stills and I'm afraid I said the wrong thing. Oh God, I hope I didn't. These have been the longest days of my life. I can't bear the idea of him stopping now.

I part my legs more, hoping he'll get the message—that I don't want him to stop.

"I don't give a fuck about what we can and can't do." His free hand coils around the back of my long hair. He tugs my head, forcing it back against his chest until I can see him leaning over me, watching his hand work down below. "You said you would give Wolf everything you have."

"I did," I whisper. In my interview, I remember. And he remembers. "So I guess that means I have to give *you* everything I have."

His lip curls into a smirk. "Are you willing to do that? Do

you want to go back to Chicago knowing more than just some spineless idiot who let you go?"

If I give Henry myself—my body—I doubt I'll ever think of Jed again. Though Henry may wreck me for all future men. But right now I don't care about the future. All I care about is the next four months and that Henry's thumbs are working on my panties, sliding them down until they're tumbling to the soft, white rug beneath our feet. I step out of them gingerly. While I still have my shirt covering my vital areas, I feel naked next to his fully dressed frame.

"Abbi, answer me."

I swallow. And nod. Yes, I want this. I want him.

He leads me backward to the edge of the bed by my hips, pulling me onto his lap as he sits, his hard dick pressing against my ass. His hands seize my inner thighs and he pulls my legs apart until they hang on either side of his thighs, and I'm spread wide open.

The full-length mirror that leans against the wall opposite us reflects the shocking image back at me.

"Don't," Henry purrs as my body tenses. His palms hold my thighs apart when I try to pull my legs closed, even pulling them farther apart. "There is nothing about this view that you should be hiding from me. In fact..." He lets go of one thigh to work the buttons of my blouse with quick, expert dexterity. Peeling the two sides away and over my shoulders, I'm soon in nothing but my bra.

With complete efficiency, he reaches back and unsnaps the hook, letting the plain cotton material fall to the carpet.

And now I am laid bare in front of a man for the first time in my life, in an explicit way.

His chest presses against my back with his deep exhale. His heated eyes roam my body's reflection without shame; the sight of them on my breasts makes my nipples tighten with anticipation. "I knew they had to be real but..." His words drift off as he fills his hands with them, the pads of his thumbs running back and forth over my skin, sending shivers right down to my core.

As exposed as I am, I should be ill at ease, and yet his hands and eyes on my body are warming me from the inside out. He lets go of my breasts to skate his hands over my torso and taut belly, his fingers rubbing back and forth over the flat surface. "Are you still sore?"

He doesn't have to elaborate; I know what he's referring to. The light pink skin between my legs.

"A little."

"They say to give it twenty-four hours."

*Twenty-four hours for what?* Katie didn't mention anything about that.

His right hand reaches down between my legs to slide a finger through the slit again, the act so much more intoxicating in my current predicament. But he doesn't stop there this time. A light gasp escapes me as he pushes the tip of his index finger into me.

"Tell me the truth: has *no one* ever touched you like this?" he asks, his mouth pressed against the back of my neck.

"No."

"Not even your ex?"

I shake my head, closing my eyes as my body welcomes the intrusion.

"Then I'm one lucky bastard." He pulls his finger out and then slides it back inside again, just the very tip, over and over, at a painstakingly slow rhythm. "Watch me do it," he commands, and I open my eyes to see the slick moisture coating his skin with each pass.

"You've been wanting this for a while, haven't you?" He

slides a second fingertip in, stretching me gently. I squirm a little against, but he doesn't let up, his thumb reaching for my clit to rub against it. I can't keep the soft whimper from escaping my lips.

"Good. Let me hear that." All semblance of the cold Mr. Wolf has vanished. I have a soft and caring and sensual Henry now, and it makes me open up wider for him and grind my ass into his lap as his fingers probe me, pushing inside, until I feel a strange pressure.

"You're going to give me your virgin pussy, aren't you." It's not so much a question.

"Yes." I want this man to have it. I want him to teach me everything he knows.

"Good. Take a deep breath for me, Abbi."

I do, and he angles his hand, pushing his fingers in. I wince with the sudden pinch. It's not unbearable, but it's certainly uncomfortable.

It finally dawns on me what Henry did.

"You'll thank me for doing that now instead of later." He stills his hand as my body adjusts to having two fingers inside me, but his thumb keeps working small circles around my clit, rubbing with the perfect amount of pressure.

"Does that mean—"

He chuckles. "Don't worry. You're still a virgin. For now." I turn my face to meet his, his chin settled on my shoulder. His mouth kicks up in a sexy smirk, but his eyes don't shift, locked on what his hand is doing between my legs.

I need to feel his mouth pressed against mine, his tongue slipping against mine, so badly. He hasn't made a move to kiss me yet, though. There's no point hesitating anymore. I lean in and coast my lips over the corner of his mouth. His eyes snap to mine and then my mouth, his hand stilling, and I'm afraid I've done something wrong.

"Please?" I whisper.

With his free hand, he seizes the back of my head, fisting my hair and angling my head back to give his mouth full access. He takes it aggressively, his tongue invading my mouth, the taste of him overwhelming my senses.

Kissing is one thing I've had a lot of practice at, and yet this kiss...

I can't handle the expertise with which he so quickly and so completely consumes me, thrusting his tongue into my mouth with abandon. It's nearly more erotic than what he's doing with his hand down below, and both things happening simultaneously is more than I can handle at once. I pull back from him slightly, sliding my tongue over the seam of his lips in a teasing manner as well as a silent plea that he guide me rather than dominate me.

It seems to work.

"Fuck, your mouth tastes sweet," he whispers, and suddenly I'm shifting in his powerful arms. My back hits the mattress and his hard, fully clothed body is pressed against my side, my head resting on one of his arms, his hand roaming my naked flesh. "I can't wait to taste the rest of you."

My heart jumps in my chest at the thought of his lips down *there*. But that's not happening now, I guess, because his mouth is back on mine and his hand begins its rhythmic motion, his fingers pumping in and out of me once again now that the pain has abated.

"Have you ever come before?"

I hesitate and it makes him growl.

"I'm going to know every square inch of your body *very*

soon, Abbi. There's no point hiding anything from me anymore. So tell me, have you orgasmed before?"

"Yes." It comes out as a squeak.

He leaves my lips to peer down at me. "By touching yourself?"

I flush, but I can't truly be ashamed right now, not with his hand inside me. "Obviously."

He smirks. "Thinking of me?"

I nod. "That night that I saw Katie and Rachel... you know."

"You enjoyed watching that, didn't you?"

I purse my lips to hide my embarrassed smile. "I don't know, honestly. It's nothing like being with you."

His fingers curl to find a sensitive spot deep inside and against my belly. He begins rubbing it, all while his thumb keeps working against my clit.

A strange mewling sound escapes my throat as pressure quickly builds inside me. I can feel the strange tingling in my spine that tells me my orgasm isn't far behind. "What are you doing?" I pant and writhe against his hand, feeling drips of moisture running out of my body and down along my skin. I didn't think it was possible to be this wet.

"I'm making you come."

I've been hesitant to touch him, but now I reach up to grasp the back of his head and pull him in to my mouth, my fingers weaving through that thick mane of hair that I dreamed about doing this to. It's even more exquisite than I imagined. My other hand grips his arms, my fingers stretching over the strain in his triceps. I tease inside his lips with the tip of my tongue, earning a deep growl and his mouth pressed hard against mine, his tongue slipping over mine, our saliva pooling and mixing together.

When I finally orgasm, it's from a depth I never knew

possible, my entire body convulsing, my screams neither quiet nor shy. Henry's skilled hand doesn't still, dragging every last muscle spasm out in waves until I'm left boneless, my legs splayed to either side, my energy drained. "I've never come like that before," I whisper.

He slips his fingers out of me and stands. I watch him peel off his dress shirt and t-shirt, and toss them to the dresser. I don't think I could ever get enough of his hard, muscular chest, his skin smooth and tan, his nipples tight.

"Sit up," he commands, unbuckling his belt and unfastening his pants. His knuckles skate across my lips "I can't meet people with a raging hard-on."

*He wants a blow job.* I shyly reach up to push the wool material of his pants away, my palm grazing against the prominent erection beneath his cotton briefs. It jumps in response. I don't know how to do this.

"I have complete faith in you," he whispers, as if he can read my mind. "Start by pulling it out."

I gingerly push his pants down to his knees and then gently curl my fingertips around the elastic of his boxer briefs, tugging them down, stretching them around his front. His cock emerges, a long, thick rod, angled perfectly toward me.

I never expected to think of a cock as a beautiful thing, but Henry's can only be described as such. It's a healthy pinkish-purple, and smooth, the tip soft. I don't know how my body will ever stretch to fit it inside me, but the pulsing sensation in my belly—only minutes after that mind-blowing orgasm—tells me I'm desperate to find out.

"It's so big." I sound like a silly girl when I say that, but it's true. It was sizeable when I saw him in the shower, across the room. Now it's literally staring me right in the face.

He smirks, waiting, his eyes blazing with heat and anticipation.

I wrap my hand around the bottom of it, my fingertips barely meeting. I imitate what I watched Henry do to himself, sliding my fist up and down along its length, enthralled with how silky and impossibly hard it feels.

"Exactly like that. Tighter." I squeeze him and then look up to find him staring at me through hooded eyes, his lips parted. I lean forward and trace the tip of him with my tongue, where the bead of moisture sits on the end, tasting the saltiness.

"Do that again, but look up at me this time," he demands, his voice turning husky.

I lean in and lick him again, my eyes never leaving his, earning his appreciative smile. He mouths "again," and I do it again, only this time I take my time, twirling my tongue around his tip. I open my mouth wider and run it along the entire underside.

"Fuck," he hisses. He curls his large hand around the back of my head and pulls me to him. I open wide to give him access to my mouth, hoping I'm doing it right as I close my lips over it. "Suck," he commands and I do, feeling a gentle pull against my hair, his silent instruction for me to mimic my hand earlier. I grip his base tightly and slide my mouth up and down as far as I can go, which is surprisingly farther than I thought.

His grasp of my hair tightens and his hips begin to thrust.

"You have a pretty little mouth, Abbi. It's so warm and wet and tight. Perfect for fucking."

His words are so filthy and his cock is in my mouth and I can't believe I'm doing this. And enjoying it immensely.

My mouth strains to fit him all over and over again, bits

of drool escaping around the rim, but I don't stop sucking on him. Sometimes my teeth scrape, but he only moans when that happens, so I think he's okay with it.

Sitting on the edge of his bed, naked and with Henry's cock pumping in and out of my mouth, my lips swollen, heady desire is building in my body again. While a little sore, I'm already desperate to spread my legs for his fingers —and more—to plunge inside me again.

"I'm close," he whispers. "I need to come in your mouth. I need you to take it all in, Abbi. Swallow all of me." His voice is pleading and desperate as if me not swallowing would ruin something monumental.

Of course I will. Right now, I'd do anything for this man.

His dick swells even more and his thrusts come harder and faster, until my eyes are watering from the strain. Then suddenly he cries out, and holds my head down, and a flood of warm salty liquid hits the back of my throat in burst after burst. So much cum.

He stills and then pulls out of my mouth, allowing me to swallow every last drop of it as he strokes the hair back off my face slowly, affectionately. I peer up at him in awe.

I just made Henry Wolf come with my mouth.

Now what?

The feel of his dark, hooded gaze drifting over my heavy breasts coaxes me to lie back and give him a better view. And, hopefully, to entice him. I'm still afraid this is some marathon dirty dream and I'm going to wake up before I feel him inside me.

"Oh, babe." He chuckles as he steps forward to grip my bent knees, pushing against them until my legs are back and my pussy is spread wide, his eyes on it. "We need to give that beautiful, tight little hole a rest before I fuck it raw."

I clench in anticipation, that deep throb intensifying

again. He inhales deeply, and I know he can smell the muskiness in the air. Of me, ready for him. His words, coupled with his eyes, could make me come.

Releasing my legs, he takes several measured steps back, his cock still erect and bobbing. "I'm going to the gym before dinner. You can call it a day." Just like that, the steely calm is back.

I watch his superb backside as he disappears behind the pocket door of the bathroom, pulling it closed all the way.

I slip on my panties and skirt, grab my pantyhose, and duck out, keeping my head down all the way to my cabin, my mind in a whirlwind over what I just did.

# twenty-one

Katie's perfume announces her presence behind me. "Did you know they were going to fire her?" Her tone is accusatory, but her eyes bleed sadness.

"I just heard about it today, I swear." I force myself to swallow a mouthful of sweet potatoes that I'd normally devour, but now can barely taste. All evidence of Rachel was already packed up and gone when I arrived at the cabin. She was shipped off on the first ferry out, apparently, as Henry had demanded.

"They're a bag of dicks," Katie grumbles.

That has been the general consensus around the staff lounge, the murmurs carrying to my ears. Everyone knows that Rachel is gone, and everyone knows exactly why. Rachel broke rules. Wolf Hotel is strict on following rules, and Mr. Wolf is a hard-ass who waltzes around with all his money, looking down on everyone, and not giving anyone a break.

"I'm so sorry. I know, it sucks."

"I don't see why it's such a big deal. Come on, it was the

lead singer of Death Jam! Wolf *wants* him telling everyone about how awesome this place is. And thanks to Rachel, he will. How can you have a rule about sleeping with guests, anyway? What she does off-shift is her business. Seriously! I get having rules about fucking your boss, but..."

*Just keeping chewing your food, Abbi.* Hopefully that will keep the guilty panic from showing on my face. Not that Henry and I have had sex but, if what he said today is true, it's only a matter of time before we do.

The thought of it gives me heart palpitations.

"Did you try talking to him? Reasoning with him? He knew she was your roommate, right?"

"I'm not sure. But I know she gave that guy a bunch of high-end alcohol for free without getting permission."

She rolls her eyes. "A few drinks and that's stupid. They could have written it off, easily. You don't fire someone over a few drinks."

The way she looks at me, I feel like I've failed her. "I'm sorry. There wasn't anything I could do. Plus, I was too busy begging him not to fire us." That may not be completely true but it's close. "Wolf found out about us using the spa room. A guest complained to Belinda."

"Shit," Katie mumbles. "What happened?"

"I got written up, but I told them that I made you do it, so hopefully nothing will land on you."

"Damn. I heard Wolf was strict on employee conduct, but I didn't realize exactly how strict until now." She pauses. "How do you work with him day in, day out? I mean, is he always so rigid and law-abiding?"

I stifle the snort that wants to escape. A part of me wants to defend him, tell her that he did what he thought was right, that he has thousands of employees to keep in line, beyond the hundred or so here. But I'm afraid she'll see through my defensive words to what hides beneath. Lies, to protect a hypocrite.

I don't know what else to call him. By his words, I should be fired. And, technically, so should he, if it's possible to fire the owner. According to his father, it is.

And yet I wasn't about to stop what happened between us today. Nor will I do anything to stop it from happening again.

"He's all right when you get used to him," is all I manage to say, struggling to keep my face from going red. I'm still reeling from the sudden change in course. It's mind-boggling, how quickly I went from quietly pining for Henry to being naked and on his lap. I guess there were signs; things that, were I not such an insecure, inexperienced person, I would have seen.

Who am I kidding? Never in a million years should I expect a man like that to be interested in a girl like me. But it appears he is. I can still feel how much he is every time I shift in my seat, where he stretched me with his fingers, and every time I press my fingertips to my lips to test the swelling there.

So what now?

Do I let this happen, knowing it's wrong? That it's against the rules? *His* rules? That it's against everything that I've been raised to believe in? If we go any further than we have, it will change everything for me. And what about Jed? I'm thousands of miles away from him, making it easier to forget the hurt that he caused me, to assume I'll be able to turn him away. But this thing—whatever this thing is between Henry and me—isn't going to last past the summer. So then what? I go back to Chicago for my last year of college, sexually educated by the hotel billionaire himself, and I'm no longer hurt? A lifetime of memories with Jed no longer affect me?

What if Jed does come back to me?

What if I can get past the hurt he has caused, only to lose him because I slept with another man?

Katie sighs, eying the food line. "This really sucks."

"It does." My work phone beeps with an incoming message. It takes everything in me to not dive for it in my pocket, knowing it's Henry.

She heard it and now glares at my pocket through narrow eyes. "I'll let you get your message from the devil. I'm going to get dinner."

She heads for the line and I pull my phone out.

**Henry:** *How are you?*

Before I can chicken out, I type:

**Abbi:** *I'm confused.*

I want to rescind the text as soon as it's gone. He's at Lux now. Even though he asked, I'm sure the last thing he wants to get is an emotional "confused" text. What if it makes him regret what happened?

I sit there, biting my thumbnail. Trying not to wait for a response.

Ten long minutes later, as Katie's heading back with her tray, the three telltale dots appear, showing me that he's typing. My heart flutters with a mixture of excitement and nervousness.

**Henry:** *I'll clear up things in the morning. See you at seven.*

Always so cryptic. I set my phone on vibrate and stick it into my pocket, restraining myself from messaging back because what the hell does that mean?

Is every day here going to leave me reeling?

~

I STEP through the service entry door to the sound of Henry's angry voice. "I don't care what their focus groups have told them. This is not what my family's business stands for!"

He leans back in his chair, rolling a pen between his fingers as he listens to the man give reasons for the strategy —demographics, the future, a successful Sandals campaign —over the speaker phone, the morning sun streaming in through the window, highlighting the streaks of golden brown in his hair.

Henry's face is stony, his jaw taut. And yet he's still oh so beautiful, dressed in a simple charcoal suit, white shirt and silver tie that coordinates well. "I don't give a fuck what worked for Sandals. This is Wolf! We're not a bunch of copycats and we're not going ahead with this campaign, Blake." That's his six thirty call with Wolf's vice president of marketing. At least he's on schedule today. "Tell them to scrap it and start over and if they can't do that, we'll find an agency who can. Got it?" Without even acknowledging me with a glance, he gestures me over with that infamous two-fingered waggle.

I approach, unsure of how this morning is going to go. I'm guessing it's not a good idea to bring up last night until I've tested the waters.

Blake grumbles an unhappy, "Yeah."

"I'd like to see a new concept in a week for approval, since I can't rely on my VP to get it right." Henry slams his finger on the orange button to hang up. The finger that was deep inside me last night, bringing me to a quivering mess in mere minutes. I squeeze my thighs together with the memory.

"Morning," I offer softly.

Finally, Henry turns to me, stress and anger painted across his face. "I have a meeting right now?"

"Yes. A conference call with Wolf Shanghai."

He punches a couple of keys on his laptop and sends a meeting cancellation through Outlook.

Spinning his chair to face me, his legs splayed on either side of my body, he reaches beneath my skirt, his hands running up my outer thighs. His touch makes me wet almost instantly, the dull, needy throb between my legs appearing out of thin air as if it's been simmering there for days without relief.

"Don't wear these anymore," he mutters, grabbing the top of my nylons and unceremoniously tugging at them until they slip to my feet. He reaches back up to grab the sides of my panties and pulls them all the way down my legs. "Or these." I let out a small yelp as he grabs me by the hips and hoists me onto the smooth wood as if I weigh nothing at all. Peeling my shoes, nylons, and panties off completely, he demands, "lie back." The soft, sensual Henry from yesterday afternoon is absent.

I'm not sure what's going to happen, but I stretch out across the hard wood surface. It's not exactly comfortable. The sun is streaming down over me, forcing me to close my eyes and shield my face with my arm. It's warm, at least.

Henry pushes my skirt up until it's pooling at my waist and I'm bare. With hands gripping the backs of my thighs, he pushes my legs up and apart.

"What are you doing?" I ask with a shaky voice, acutely aware that I'm exposed in broad daylight and Henry is at eye level with the space between my legs.

"You said you were confused."

I gasp at the first swipe of his tongue along my cleft, my legs closing of their own accord.

"No," he growls, his firm hands denying me the moment of modesty, pushing them even farther apart, until the sides of my knees are grazing the desk's cool surface and my pelvis is completely open to him.

"People will see!" I hiss, and yet I feel myself growing wetter with excitement.

His low chuckle vibrates against my sensitive pink flesh, only amplifying his tongue's intoxicating strokes. "Don't worry. No one's going to see."

His tongue dives deep inside me and swirls, eliciting a moan from deep within my chest.

"I was wrong," he whispers, his breath skating across my most private spot. "Your pussy tastes even sweeter than your mouth." He licks me again, this time flattening his tongue against me.

I've never had anyone speak to me like Henry does. It makes me uncomfortable and yet I crave hearing him say those words. I'm arousing him, and that makes me more aroused, more confident, more comfortable with what he's doing to me.

I try to relax. With Henry Wolf's face between my legs at 7:00 a.m.

It feels a thousand times better than I ever imagined it would.

His tongue leaves my core to give my clit some attention, twirling around it like Katie did for Rachel that night before he clamps down to suck and toy with it mercilessly until I whimper.

"Are you sore?"

"No," I lie, reaching down to weave my fingers through his mop of waves. I *am* sore, but I forgot the discomfort the second I stepped into the cabin, longing for more of this.

He releases one of my thighs, but I no longer feel the

urge to close my legs. I gasp as his finger slides into me, followed by a second.

"I've never felt a pussy this tight before." He pushes a third finger in slowly and stills his hand, waiting for my body to adjust.

"Is that a problem?" I moan softly as his fingers find that same magical spot and he puts pressure on it again. I can't help bucking into him, wanting to get closer, his tongue working my clit harder.

"No. It's perfect. You're perfect."

I smile and close my eyes with his words, my inhibitions quickly melting away. I no longer care that I'm half naked on Henry's desk or that his face is in my crotch. All I want is to revel in the feel of his tongue against me, knowing that he enjoys it, and that it will end with a mind-blowing release from this pressure lower in my belly.

Henry slides his fingers out and reaches around to grip my thighs again, making my skin slick as he slides my body toward the edge of the desk and seals his mouth over my clit, sucking with punishing pressure.

"Oh!" I cry out, curling my fist through his hair as that tingle builds deep inside me, rolling my hips upwards, on the brink of another monstrous orgasm. I can't get his mouth and tongue close enough. I grab the back of his head and pull him to me as I grind my hips against his face shamelessly.

My orgasm comes on fast and strong, making me arch my back and gasp aloud as the blood pulses between my legs.

I'm faintly aware of him kissing the insides of my thighs, his freshly shaven jaw leaving a slick trail of *me* along my skin. Strong arms pull me into a sitting position, and then

I'm pressed against Henry's chest in a cradle hold and he's carrying me toward his bedroom.

I giggle, taking in his glistening mouth. "I'm all over you."

"You are," he whispers, no longer agitated as he was when I first arrived. He leans down to press his lips against mine until I can taste the odd muskiness. "You thoroughly fucked my face." Setting me down on the bed, he adds in a low growl, "Now I'm going to thoroughly fuck that pretty, tight pink hole of yours."

Flutters erupt in my stomach.

"Take your clothes off."

He simply stands there and watches with hungry, impatient eyes as I unzip and slip off my rumpled skirt, letting it pool on the floor by my ankles. With shaky fingers, I unbutton my blouse and slip it off, then unhook my bra and cast it to the side.

And I'm naked in front of Henry once again.

"Watch me. Don't be shy." He takes his time, working at the knot in his tie, unbuttoning his shirt, shedding every article of clothing until he's naked in front of me, stroking that intimidating, swollen cock of his.

I move to take him in my mouth again, to devour his delicious, salty cream, but he demands, "Lie down."

As gracefully as possible, I scoot back and lie down. With only a moment's hesitation, I pull my knees up and spread my legs for him.

"You don't need to be nervous," he murmurs, strolling over to open his nightstand drawer and pull out a condom.

How can I not be, when I look at that engorged thing in his hand, when I'm worried that I'll be terrible, that he won't enjoy this. I want to remind him that I've never done this before, that I hope he enjoys himself anyway, but I bite my bottom lip and keep those fears to myself.

Henry isn't attracted to insecurity and, soon enough, I'll no longer be a virgin.

I watch with fascination as he tears open the silver foil pack with his teeth and rolls on the clear rubber ring, his demeanor calm and confident. Not a single shake in his hands.

As small as the condom is, it stretches over his entire shaft.

He smirks. "You have a very curious look on your face."

"I've never seen a real condom before," I admit sheepishly.

He frowns. "Not even in Sex Ed?"

"You don't teach with condoms when you're promoting abstinence."

He shakes his head and grumbles something incoherent as he kneels between my legs, his sheathed cock jutting toward the ceiling, his hand immediately going for my core. He pushes two fingers in and sighs, pumping in and out, stirring that potent musky smell in the air once again. "Fuck, you get so wet for me, don't you?"

"Yes," I whisper shamelessly.

"You have a beautiful pussy," he murmurs, his heated gaze on me as his hand works against me, sending tingles directly to my clit. "Spread a little wider for me."

I pull my legs apart, my embarrassment over his words or his perusal of my most private area no longer enough to keep me from tempting him.

"I'll go as slow as I can. At the beginning, anyway. After that, I can't promise anything." Lustful blue eyes settle on mine, and I feel him assessing me, silently asking me if I'm ready for this.

I simply nod.

And then suddenly he's hovering above me, resting his weight on his elbows to keep from crushing me beneath his massive body. The head of his cock nudges at my opening.

In this moment, I sense a part of me slipping away. Jed's sweet, innocent Abbi... She will be irrevocably lost after I let this man inside me, after I give him a piece of me that I can never get back.

I rope my hands around Henry's head and pull his mouth down to mine, my tongue sliding against his in an erotic dance, kissing him with all the passion and emotion that I feel in this very moment.

His hard cock pushes into me.

I gasp as my body begins to stretch around it.

"Relax." He stops pushing, letting me become accustomed to his girth. This feels nothing like one or two or even three fingers.

But I take shallow, calming breaths, trying to relax, to simply enjoy this moment, and the feel of his weight pressed against my body. My hands explore, to slide over his triceps, his bulging shoulders, and that delicious collarbone.

He pushes deeper inside.

"Fuck, you are so goddamn tight," he growls, his jaw clenching.

"It doesn't hurt you, does it?"

He starts to laugh. "No, babe. It's just taking all my willpower not to shove my cock straight into you. But I need you to relax."

"I'm trying."

He leans down to kiss me, his mouth softer and more pliable, less animalistic and hungry. It's an affectionate kiss between lovers. I feel myself responding, growing wetter, the tension beginning to slip from my limbs.

He edges his cock a little deeper as he keeps kissing me, coaxing my body into submission.

He's so hard. I wonder if all men are this hard when they're inside a woman.

His lips leave mine to skim across my jaw and along my neck, sending shivers down my torso. Instinctively, I arch my back as his mouth approaches my breast and he captures my nipple, sucking on it like he sucked on my clit earlier. I sigh with the wet, hot sensation, ticklish and yet erotic, stirring the blood between my legs more.

Opening me up even wider.

He puts all of his weight on one elbow, allowing him to fill his hand with my breast, massaging it gently as he toys with my nipple.

And he pushes deeper inside.

I'm so completely, utterly full with him, I don't know how much deeper he can get. I'm afraid to ask, but I trust that he knows what he's doing and he won't hurt me. Not intentionally anyway. Not physically.

I don't want to think about the future emotional downfall of this, even though my subconscious is already preparing for the inevitable.

He repositions himself above me, one arm hooking beneath my knee and lifting my leg up to curl around his back so he can push in. Oh God, he's so deep. It's so intense and though not painful, not entirely enjoyable.

"Breathe," he whispers against my mouth. "I'm there."

"You are?"

He smiles, slipping one hand beneath my neck while the other one reaches down between us to rub circles against my clit.

And then he slowly pulls his hips back, dragging his

long, hard cock out of me, leaving me feeling suddenly empty.

But only for a second, and then he's back, pushing in, that intense, almost unbearable fullness forcing a cry from my lips.

Over and over again, so slowly, Henry pulls out and thrusts back in, each time becoming a little easier, my body accommodating his size more easily, then more greedily, until I feel the urge to move my hips with him.

He moans, as if he's been waiting for that moment and his body begins plunging harder into me, lifting my pelvis with each thrust. His hips slap against my thighs, the rhythmic sound competing with the creak in the bed.

My breasts bounce violently and I know they're going to be sore later, but right now I don't care, reveling in the growing slickness between my legs as my body accepts all of Henry. I wonder if all sex feels this incredible, or if it's just sex with Henry that makes me feel euphoric and free.

My hands slip over his skin, now coated with a thin sheen of sweat as his hips pump into me again and again, mercilessly, his hooded gaze locked on my face, smiling every time a gasp or moan escapes my lips.

"Henry..." I moan, trailing my tongue along the salty edge of his collarbone.

"I want to fuck you harder."

"Yes," I hear myself whisper, because instinctively I know I want him to, though I have no idea what that may feel like, and whether I can handle it. But I know I want it.

His eyes are full of amazement as he pushes up and back to rest on his knees, hooking arms behind my legs to lift my hips, his cock never slipping out. He slips his thumb over my clit again, applying pressure and rubbing circles around it. "You're going to come with me." It sounds like a demand.

One that I think I can meet, my entire body blushed and humming with uninhibited desire, that same sensation I've felt twice with him already hovering in the recesses.

His powerful body thrusts into me and I cry out, his cock so deep inside that it's borderline painful, and yet the idea of him being that deep turns me on, makes me want him to do it again.

And he does, hard and fast, slamming into me relentlessly, lifting my body off the bed, pulling a gasp each time.

It's when my body welcomes the almost violent intrusion, giving itself completely over to Henry, that the warmth begins to spread through my middle, the tingle creeps along my spine, the urge to spread my legs and open myself up as much as humanly possible as my muscles tighten hits me.

I cry out as my orgasm rips through my spent body.

A guttural sound tears from Henry's mouth, his face contorting, the last few slams against me coming so fast I can't catch my breath, and then I feel him swelling inside me, his cock pumping out streams of cum.

And I can't help but fantasize that he was shooting into me, instead of the condom, the primitive core of me craving his seed.

Henry slides out of me. I'm too spent to miss him in me yet, but I'm sure I will. My body sinks into the fluffy, soft bedding, now damp from our sweat and bodily fluids, and I listen to Henry's shallow pants. He still looks as glorious as ever, resting on his haunches with his eyes closed, his lips parted, and his head tilted back, that lickable Adam's apple jutting out.

"So, that's what sex is like," I mumble, earning his laugh.

He rubs his hand along my leg casually. "That's just the beginning, Abbi."

I meet his eyes and see the promise in them as they rake

over my naked, boneless body. He's still erect. I'm beginning to wonder if this guy ever isn't. "You look like an angel that accidently fell into my bed," he murmurs. "If I could keep you here and fuck you all day, I would."

As sore and used and exhausted as my body is, I feel his words between my legs like a teasing caress.

With a sigh, he climbs off the bed, pulling the condom off and depositing it into a tissue. He glances at the clock. "I have a breakfast meeting in fifteen minutes, don't I?"

"At eight. Yes."

He heads for the shower. If I could find it in me to move, I'd like to get in there with him. But he's on a timeline and I've noticed he doesn't like being late.

It's a quick shower, and then he's out, toweling off and redressing quickly.

"I need you to call Rich Rowley and ask him to contact Shanghai today for a status update, and then send me a full recap."

Just like yesterday, the moment it's over, the seductive, attentive Henry is gone, replaced by business.

"Okay." I pull myself up, swinging my legs over the end. I'm not entirely sure I'm capable of standing.

He slips his arms through his dress shirt sleeves. "About your text to me last night. Are you still confused?"

"Honestly? I don't know what I am right now."

"Besides no longer a little virgin farm girl?"

My cheeks burn with embarrassment, making him chuckle as he buttons his shirt with expertly fast hands. He holds out his silver tie.

I stand and take it. "Seriously? You tied your own tie this morning! Unless you had someone else do it," I joke, slipping it around his thick neck. But my face falls as that thought settles. Maybe he did.

"I know how to tie a tie." He smiles, easing my paranoia. "But I like having you do it. Is it such an unpleasant job?"

"No. I enjoy it actually," I admit. I feel his gaze on my face as I loop the ends and pull them through, adjusting the knot with my fingers. "There."

"You know, you're very good at it."

"It's not hard." I slide the silky material through my fingers. "Especially when they're such high quality."

The pad of his thumb slides over my bottom lip. "I wasn't talking about the tie."

"Oh," I sigh, and then my cheeks begin to burn. I've just had sex with this man and I'm still blushing over sexual suggestions. Will that ever go away?

"Remember," he leans down to tease my lips with his own, "I'm Mr. Wolf outside these walls. Just another rich tyrant. You have no idea how good my cock feels driving into you. Right?"

"Right," I whisper, shakily. "But you're not a tyrant."

"If anyone calls me a tyrant or an asshole, don't defend me. In fact, if you want to agree with them, I'm okay with that."

The staff gossip from last night rings in my ear. "Because what we're doing is wrong?"

"Is it against Wolf corporate rules? Yes. Is it wrong?" He sighs. "Every time I think about you, every time I'm near you, I don't give a shit about what anyone else thinks."

His frank words make my chest swell. "You think about me?"

He chuckles. "Yes, too much, which is why this happened in the first place. I have a hotel to get off the ground so I had to either fire you or fuck you." His hand slips behind my neck, rubbing it affectionately. "I didn't want to fire you."

"So, what now? What are we doing here, exactly?"

He grazes my cheek with his knuckles. "You're getting over an idiot ex and fucking your boss for the next four months. I'm running a hotel and fucking my assistant for the next four months. That's all."

That's all. There's no mention of a relationship or exclusivity and now is not the time to bring it up. Perhaps before I spread my legs would have been a good time, but I already know that had he come out and said that he can't give me either, I likely still would have allowed this to happen.

Because I feel happy and wanted and desirable for the first time in a long time. And that pain in my chest over Jed's rejection?

It's been buried under a heap of lust for Henry. The idea of spending the next four months working and sleeping with this man is enough for me right now, as shocking as that is for me to admit to myself.

"Will you get into trouble?"

His smile slips off. "Once the Wolf chain is officially handed over to me, no one is going to tell me that I can't fuck you."

"When is that supposed to happen?"

"June 30 is the official date. Just around the corner. Until then, no one can know." He reaches up to cup my left breast, full and overflowing in his grasp, a "goddamn" slipping out under his breath.

He glances at his watch and then silences any possible next words with a peck on my cheek. Grabbing his suit jacket from a nearby chair, he heads for the door. "I'll text you later." His feet slow. "Don't take anything I say or do while we're outside these walls personally. Okay? I don't mean any of it."

I nod.

# twenty-two

"We'll have the photo ops done here. It should be good lighting at that time of day, with the view." Belinda waves her manicured fingers toward the right side of the ballroom's wall of windows. "That should happen between four and five, before people get too far into the open bar."

The room is half set up with cocktail tables and clusters of lounge chairs, and a small stage for an orchestra on the left of the photography stage. It sounds like a ferry's worth of flowers is being brought in to fill every empty space of this grand room within two days' time.

"Abbi, you're getting all of this, right?" Henry snaps. He doesn't even glance in my direction.

"Yes, Mr. Wolf," I mumble, my head bowed and my focus on my iPad, reminding myself of his words this morning before he left. This is what he meant about not taking anything personally. His tone with me has been sharp and his words clipped, since I met him for the staff meeting earlier. They've carried through to the grand opening planning checkpoints that have followed.

It must be working, because Belinda has barely given me a glance today. She must be convinced that Henry would rather fire me than sleep with me.

But everything has changed.

"We have everything under control. The Wolf men just need to show up, smile, and look sharp, and everything will go smoothly," she purrs.

I'm going to meet Henry's father. I wonder what he's like in person.

"Great," Henry murmurs, checking his watch.

"What time is the photography session this afternoon, again?" Belinda asks Henry, though her raised brow is directed at me.

"Uh..." I frown, pulling out my calendar. Photography session?

"You got my message, didn't you? I sent it at *seven* this morning."

At seven this morning I was splayed out on Henry's desk with his face between my legs. I swallow, struggling to keep my cheeks from flaming. "I don't know how I missed it."

"*World Hotel* is here to do a spread on Mr. Wolf *this* afternoon and you missed my message?" She glances at her watch. "It's already noon!"

"Enough. What is this about?" Henry asks irritably.

"They want three hours of your time to take some pictures around the hotel and out in the Alaskan wild at one o'clock this afternoon," I explain, reading out the top line of Belinda's e-mail for the first time. Somehow I skipped over it. "For a feature as one of the most eligible bachelors in the world." I keep my expression smooth, hiding my disdain.

"Three hours?" he mutters, and I know this isn't an act; he's truly annoyed. "I don't have three hours."

"You'll have to make it. It's important for business," Belinda admonishes.

"How is me being a bachelor important for the hotel?"

"Because *everyone* reads those kinds of articles."

"Why is this so last-minute?"

"Because an opportunity came up and I made the executive decision as the hotel manager to take it!" I can't believe she has the nerve to speak to him like that.

He shakes his head. "Wardrobe changes and all, I'm guessing?"

"They asked for three, including a suit. We have an hour. It's okay, we can make this work," I pipe in. I feel like such an ass for missing this email.

"Fuck, I hate these things." He begins to pace. "I never know what to wear."

"Don't worry. I know how to dress you," Belinda offers, and jealousy spikes deep within me.

He's punching something into his phone as he talks. "You're my hotel manager. You need to be here. That's why I have Abbi."

"Abbi." Belinda gives him an "are you serious" glare.

"She's done a good enough job so far."

I'd like to shoot Belinda a snooty glare, but I settle on keeping my head down and hiding my smug smile of satisfaction.

She heaves a frustrated sigh. "Fine. I need you for a few more minutes and then you should go..."

Belinda's words drift into the background as my phone vibrates in my hand. I check it to see a text from Henry.

**Henry:** *You wouldn't mind undressing me and helping me choose a few things to wear, right?*

My heart begins to race. I press my lips together to keep from smiling, as I type in:

**Abbi:** *If I must, though it is a chore.*

Are we already at the playful texting stage? This is moving fast. But I guess that's what happens when you're confined to a remote hotel in the Alaskan wilderness and acting out on primitive needs. That's all we're doing, I remind myself. I can't let my dreams get painted with jet-setting and a trip down the aisle. Or even a real relationship.

Henry is responding to something else Belinda asked as he types, his tone all business.

Another message comes through.

**Henry:** *I can still taste you coming in my mouth.*

My notebook and iPad slip from my suddenly shaky grasp and land on the floor, earning Belinda's annoyed glare. Mouthing an "I'm sorry," I dare a glance Henry's way.

His steely mask is firmly in place, as usual. "Is there anything else, Belinda? Because I have to go smile for three hours in front of a camera, thanks to you."

She clears her throat. "That's all for now. Abbi, I hope you at least remembered to have his tux ready?"

There's that tone again. I could let it bother me, but I don't because I'm the one who gets to dress—and undress—Henry. "Yup." I let my gaze skate over his strong stature. That man in a tux...

Belinda leads the way and I follow, sensing the ghost of warm fingertips at the small of my back.

~

"THE TOM FORD."

I grab the suit off the hook and lay it out on the bed, hollering, "How about the gold tie?"

"Sure."

Glancing over my shoulder, I watch him drag the razor

over the curve of his jaw. He's fresh from yet another shower and wrapped in a towel, and the sight is making my pulse pump hard in my veins. But the playful text from earlier seems to have slipped from his mind. He's all business now.

"Where else do they want to go?"

I scan the forwarded e-mail. "It says 'maybe a few on the docks with the planes, a quick trip around the cove on his private boat, and, if possible, some wilderness'."

"No wardrobe requirements?"

"'More casual' is all it says. So..." My mouth twists with thought as my fingers push through the various items hanging in his closet. All expensive, designer, high-thread-count clothing. He looked hot that day in the woods, cutting wood. And the day I watched him get off the plane. He could make a pair of sweatpants look sexy, to be honest.

I pull out a pair of dark blue jeans and black crew-neck sweater, along with a yellow-and-black checkered coat, similar to the red one he normally wears. I finish it off with his beanie.

He sidles up beside me with a smirk. "You want me to dress as a lumberjack?"

"I don't know." I giggle nervously, collecting the jacket to put it back on the hook. "You should have had Belinda do this for you. I don't know what I'm doing."

He seizes my wrist before I can take two steps. "Don't do that."

"Do what?"

"Discount yourself so easily." He pulls the coat from my grasp and tosses it onto the bed. "I like confident women, and I think that beneath all this insecurity, there is a strong, self-assured woman." Leaning in to plant a soft kiss on the side of my neck, he adds in a murmur, "And I can't wait until you let me see her."

A few orgasms and mind-blowing sex has definitely helped us get more comfortable around each other quickly.

I reach for his chest, my fingers gliding over still-damp but hot skin, memorizing the grooves and curves and ripples, all the way down to his towel. My hand just manages to cover the hard outline of his cock when he seizes it in his. His fingers squeeze and mold over himself, wrapping my hand over his girth.

"We don't have enough time for what I want to do to you." His whisper is pained.

I honestly don't think I could handle any more sex right now; my body still feels thoroughly used from this morning. It's a wonderful feeling though, knowing that Henry was there. Going about my day still *feeling* him there.

"We have fifteen minutes. Let me do what *I* want to do to you." My fingers dip into the fold of the towel, pulling it apart until it falls to the ground and I have Henry standing naked in front of me again. I haven't stopped thinking about the blow job I gave him yesterday. How much I enjoyed it, how much I wanted to do it again. Do it better.

His eyes burn as he watches me sit on the edge of the bed. I pull him toward me with my hands on his hips, face-to-face with his cock, swollen and glistening at the tip. My mouth waters. Just knowing that I've caused that reaction is enough to make me grow wet. I'm never not wet around Henry anymore, though.

"Who knew you'd be so greedy," he murmurs. I look up to see the smirk on his lips before his hand comes around to the back of my head. Fingers weave through my hair and then he pulls me forward.

I lick him more confidently than I did yesterday, now that I know what he likes, flattening my tongue as I run it along the underside, leaving a glistening trail from root to tip. I do it again, only this time I let my small pink tongue dart out to tickle the ball sac hanging beneath, so heavy and full.

"Fuck," he groans, his head falling back in pleasure as I keep licking him, teasing him. "Suck me, *please*," he finally begs.

I open my mouth wide and wrap my lips around his soft skin, taking in as much of him in as I can. He hits the back of my throat each time, and I'm so glad for my nearly non-existent gag reflex, something I never appreciated until now.

He tastes so good, like nothing I can describe, but I can't get enough of it and the feel of him gently tugging my hair and the motion of his hips as he occasionally thrusts himself in.

Suddenly, he whispers, "Let me pull out. I want to come on you." I release him and he slips his cock out of my mouth and pushes back against my shoulder. "Lean back, onto your elbows."

I follow instructions, while watching him intently. With two strong, frantic hands, he grabs hold of either side of my blouse and tears. Buttons pop as the blouse rips open, all the way down to where it's tucked into my skirt. He yanks against my bra cups until my breasts spill out the top.

And then he grabs hold of his heavy cock, still wet from my mouth and swollen, and he begins pumping it hard and fast and shamelessly.

It's such an erotic sight to take in his beautiful, powerful body as he so confidently jerks off in front of me, that my legs begin spreading, my thighs opening up to him. It's my body's involuntary urge to feel him inside me.

"Push up your skirt."

I do, letting it bunch around my hips. He hooks a finger around the crotch of my panties and he yanks until they slide down, past my knees, down to my ankles, exposing my sore sex to him. "What I would do to have that again right now," he pushes out through gritted teeth. His hand suddenly shoots out, gently pushing me down until I'm lying on the bed.

With his loud cry, cum spurts out in hot streams all over my bare breasts and stomach and thighs. One stream lands right on my clit. His hand slows with the last spray, his pants hard and fast. "Christ, woman."

"We need to have a discussion about your use of the Lord's name."

His head falls back with his deep laugh. I smile, watching this magnificent man in front of me, naked, laugh about something I've said while still recovering from orgasming with me. It's just so intimate.

When his laughter dies down, he strolls to the vanity, dampening a washcloth. I can't keep my eyes off his still semi-hard cock bobbing up and down on his way back. I want it in me again. I already miss that full feeling.

His hand is gentle as he wipes himself off my body, paying extra attention to the cum dripping off my nipples. When he gets to my lower half, he slides a finger across my sore clit and brings it to my lips. "Taste me."

I open my mouth. He dips his finger in and I suck off the salty cream watching his eyes light up with excitement. "I like that you're so eager." He keeps wiping away until my skin is clean.

"I never thought that would be something a man would want to do, coming on a woman's body."

He grins darkly. "I can't wait to show you all the things I like to do."

My stomach spasms at the promise.

"You should work naked for me."

"I may have to if you do that to my uniform again." The buttons are torn and scattered, my skirt covered in his semen.

"Yeah, I went a little bit overboard. Run to your cabin and get changed and let me get dressed, or I'll be late for this session. I'm already going to be late."

I glance at the clock. That took all of eight minutes, giving him seven minutes to dress. Not enough time.

Taking me by the hand, he pulls me off the bed. I yelp at his swat against my ass. "I can't have your naked tits in my face anymore or the outline of my cock will be on the cover of *World Hotel*." Just before I duck out of his bedroom, he adds, "Toss the blouse. There's no way to explain why it was ripped open."

*Shit.* "My other one's at the cleaners."

"Don't bother with the uniform today. Wear something casual."

Casual. Okay. I fix myself as best I can, thankful for the sweater and vest I wore this morning, and then head for my cabin.

# twenty-three

"Can you turn your head to the left, just a touch. Yes. Perfect," Hachiro croons, aiming his giant lens. "Fuck, these are going to be hot."

I say nothing about the pint-sized photographer's lack of professionalism, instead focusing on his subject, a sharp-looking Henry in the Tom Ford suit and gold tie that I laid out for him, leaning against a stack of armor stones outside the main lodge. I have to agree with him, though, and it's not just because of the man he's capturing. The entire vista is dreamlike. Most Americans will never venture this far north to see the foreign part of their own country.

"It must be something, working so closely with a man like that. He's like steel. You can see the power he wields in his steady jaw," Hachiro murmurs, glancing over at me, his narrow eyes drifting over my black leggings and hiking boots. They look decent enough with the vest and sweater that Henry bought me and, all in all, are the most stylish thing I own besides jeans. And, being next to Henry, I'm wishing I had an entire new wardrobe and someone to dress me.

I don't take the overview personally. I noticed right away that he assesses everything and everybody within his line of sight. I guess it's the photographer in him.

"Yes. He wields a lot of power." I fight to roll my eyes.

Henry stands tall, calm and collected, seemingly unbothered by the guests who linger, watching as the handsome billionaire gets photographed.

Nothing like the version I saw only thirty minutes ago, his face contorted with ecstasy, his hand grasping himself so aggressively, his cries escaping from a deep and vulnerable place.

I hide my smile behind a sip of water. My intimate memories of him are mine and mine alone.

"Okay, now give me your back, and slide your hands into your pockets casually. Look into the distance, but give me your right profile," Hachiro directs, nodding emphatically when Henry does as asked. I can already see this picture as being one I want to stare at for hours.

"When will the magazine be published?" I ask.

"Next month," he confirms, then in a lower voice, "Hey, so do you think he'd agree to some nudes?"

I press my lips together to keep from bursting out with laughter. "I'll have to get back to you on that one."

"You were fine on the ferry trip over, weren't you?" Henry peers at me with worried eyes as he steers the boat. Behind him, Hachiro's face watches with a mix of annoyance and disgust. I am taking up valuable time with his steely muse, after all.

"Yes. But that boat was bigger and it wasn't so rocky." As

if in answer, a gust of wind sweeps past, swaying Henry's boat. And my stomach.

"We're going back." Henry begins turning the wheel.

"No! Don't. You do what you need to do, and I'm just going to lie down in the cabin and wait for the Antivert to kick in. I'll be fine."

That doesn't seem to appease Henry, but at least he doesn't argue with me, allowing me to duck past him and through the small door to the cabin below. It's cramped and yet quaint, reminding me of my aunt May's small travel trailer, with a narrow couch on one side, a dinette table on the other, and a compact kitchen area behind me. Ahead, in the bow of the boat, I see a bed.

I head for that now, diving onto the wool blanket, inhaling the scent of Henry's cologne. When did he lie here last?

Was he alone?

The thought of him with another woman twists my gut in an unpleasant way. A way that reminds me of catching Jed with that girl. I don't think I can survive that again.

I push all of those thoughts aside and close my eyes, focusing on my breathing, hoping that the medication will work and that I don't have to use the plastic bag I stuffed into my purse before boarding.

The sea sickness has almost subsided fifteen minutes later when my personal phone beeps with a text. I seldom get texts. Really, only one person texts me.

**Jed:** *How is Alaska? I hear you're working for some rich guy?*

I haven't talked to Jed since March, and *this* is the first message he sends me? I'm annoyed, and angry, and yet I can't stop myself from responding.

**Abbi:** *Alaska is incredible. Yup. SUPER rich.*

The old me would have responded with a "how are

things?" question. But I let the phone fall to the mattress as I wait for his response, the deeply hidden vindictive part of me thinking of a hundred other highly inappropriate, hopefully hurtful things that I could respond with.

*Yes, his name is Henry and he made me orgasm with his mouth.*

*You should see the size of his dick.*

*Cum is warmer than I expected.*

My phone beeps with another incoming text. I'm surprised I'm even getting them out here.

**Jed:** *What do you do for him?*

I can't help it. I burst out laughing.

"Abbi?" I hear Henry holler from outside the cabin. The boat's engine has quieted, the motion slowed. I heard some commotion out there a moment ago. Maybe we've anchored.

"I'm fine," I call back, smiling up at the ceiling. I'm more than fine. A week in Alaska and I'm doing exactly what I wanted to do: forgetting the past and encountering things I've never experienced before.

Like sex with a gorgeous, powerful man.

The cabin door pops open and Henry's massive body squeezes through. "Are you feeling better?"

"Yes, except please tell me that Hachiro isn't driving the boat."

He chuckles, sliding into bed next to me. This is the first time we've lain together like this and the small, cramped space makes it all the more cozy in here with him. "Hell, no. I wanted to give you a chance to get better so I docked us. He's up taking some pictures of my grandparents' old place and finding a shoot location. I told him I'd be up soon." He sighs. "The guy's a little bit weird."

I smile. "Yes, he is."

"What were you laughing about?"

"I don't want to talk about it." He waits for me with a raised brow, and I know he's not going to let it go. "Jed texted me. I mentioned my new job to an old friend in an e-mail a few days ago and I guess it got back to him. You know, small town."

"What'd he say?" His tone is less than amused, and I expected as much. He has never hidden how he feels about Jed.

I pull up the text and show it to him. When he scrolls through and reads the last line, he starts to chuckle. "What are you going to tell him?"

I shrug.

"May I?" His fingers start tapping out an answer before I can respond.

"What are you doing?"

He hands the phone back to me and I watch in horror as the green message lights up, having been received. "Oh my God! I would never say this!" I cry, reading over the entire thing.

**Abbi:** *I wash his dirty clothes, scrub his toilets, and tie his ties. I'm his personal Cinderella. TBH, the guy's a fucking prick. But at least he's something to look at and, I swear, I keep catching him staring at my tits.*

"Maybe you've changed."

"Not *that* much." I laugh, picturing the confused look on Jed's face as he reads that. Will it worry him, to have some rich, hot "prick" eying me like this?

I don't know if I even care anymore. Henry said that I'm doing this to get over him and for a while, it was easy to accept that. But I actually *like* Henry. I like being around him, and talking to him. I like taking care of him, even if he's paying me to do it.

He pushes a strand of hair off my face. "How are you

feeling? You're still pale."

"But not green, right?"

"No. Not green."

"That's good, because my hair doesn't suit green." I smile. "Give me another few minutes and I'll be fine. And thanks for docking. That was nice of you." I don't know why I'm surprised that he'd be that considerate, but I am.

His hand slips beneath my shoulder to begin prodding me. "Roll over." I do as asked and am pleasantly surprised when his strong fingers run down the length of my back, testing grooves and muscles with a touch of pressure, before circling back and doing it again. He's giving me a back rub. It's a very non-boss, non-fuck-buddy, boyfriend-y thing to do. But I push that thought out of my head and moan with appreciation.

"I wouldn't be making noises like that, if I were you," he warns, his voice turning gravelly.

"I can't help it. This feels *so* nice." I sigh and turn my head to face him, appreciating the way the crew-neck sweater that I picked settles around his thick, sinewy neck. "Black looks good on you."

"Is that what color I'm wearing?" he asks mockingly, but then smiles.

"Hachiro seemed to like the casual woodsman look."

"Yeah, he asked me if he could get a picture of me cutting firewood after this."

I snort, and then giggle. "He asked me if you'd consider posing nude."

"What?" Henry shakes his head, but he's smiling. "What'd you say?"

"That you'd definitely be into that." I keep a straight face for all of three seconds before I start to laugh and the gig is up.

"What a ballsy little guy."

"You should do it. *I'd* buy that magazine."

His hand makes its way down my back, only this time it keeps going, caressing the soft mounds of my ass, first one cheek, then the other. "You don't work out, do you?"

"No, I've never felt that I needed to. Why?" An inkling of trepidation stirs. Is this his way of telling me that I *should* be sweating on a treadmill?

"Because my farm girl has one hell of a nice ass." His fingers grip tightly—almost to the point of pain, but not quite. Enough to stir desire in me, to feel the telltale start of what will be soaked panties. Again.

But his words strike a chord within me. My farm girl. I'm his.

"I thought you were a boob guy," I murmur, as his finger runs down my center, along my crack, and farther down.

He probes between my legs. "You're warm here. And wet."

"I don't think I ever dried out."

"Are you sore?"

"Yes," I admit shyly. "But it's a good sore."

Easing up off his elbow, Henry disappears from view, but I can sense him there, behind me, his knees sinking into the bed on either side of my thighs. His fingers curl around the elastic of my leggings and he begins pulling them down.

"Henry! What about Hachiro!" I hiss, straining to turn my body and look out the cabin door, half-expecting to find a giant black lens aimed at my backside.

"Don't worry, I locked it. And we'll hear him if he jumps on. But he won't, trust me. He wanted nothing to do with a seasick woman. He's in heaven up there." He adds in a low murmur, "And I'm in heaven down here."

"This is..." I bite my lip nervously as the cool air skates over my bare backside, now exposed to him.

"Don't worry. I'll be gentle. And you won't take long." He speaks so confidently as he slides my leggings all the way down past my knees. Then again, he's probably right. I'm already panting for this man in anticipation of what he's going to do. When he seizes me by the pelvis and hoists me to my knees, I let out a shaky laugh.

"Relax."

I try to, closing my eyes and focusing on the feel of his warm, large hands as they seize either side of my ass, massaging each meaty cheek with skilled hands. And not on the fact that he has an unobstructed view of my entire behind, and stretching my body like that lets him see the part of me that only one other person has seen—Katie.

It's almost exactly the same view that I had of Rachel that night, and so I know firsthand exactly how explicit that view is. My breathing grows ragged as his thumbs reach closer to my core, stretching out my folds to expose me. His mouth lands on the soft pink flesh moments later and I gasp as he begins probing me with his tongue, plunging it in and out, taking long swipes of my clit.

He's right. I won't take long at all.

"In answer to your question about being a boob man..."

His warm breath skates across that most private spot and I clench instinctively, but I can't hide it from him. He's hooked his arms around my thighs, holding my hips tightly and my legs spread, keeping me from squirming away.

I gasp as his wet tongue slides over my puckered skin.

"Relax," he says again, his voice soft. "I wouldn't do it if I didn't enjoy it. And this ass of yours..." His finger traces around the rim in a circle. "I can't wait to fuck it."

My mouth drops open. I don't know how I feel about

that idea. Or this, right now. I'm still getting used to having this man's face between my legs, let alone back there. But there's just no saying no to him, not that I'd want to. He doesn't seem to hesitate, taking what he wants.

And he wants me. Every square inch of me, it would seem.

His hands smooth over my cheeks, and then he presses his erection against my hip. The tiny cabin fills with the sound of his heavy, heady pants. "I wish I had brought a condom," he whispers.

He wants sex. Again. My body responds instantly.

"We need to get you on birth control."

"I'm on it," I blurt without thinking.

Dead silence. "You are?"

"Yes."

"For your cycles," he murmurs, as if suddenly understanding. He exhales, and I can feel it deep inside my chest. His hands grip either side of my hips. "I need in you. Now." He pushes first one finger, then another, then a third one into me. I'm sore but wet, and the intrusion is welcome. "Let me come inside you."

It sounds like a demand but I know it's a question.

"I know you're clean, and I'm clean—"

"Are you sure? I mean, when were you last with someone?" Am I allowed to ask that?

"I'm clean, I promise you." He sounds so confident, so resolute.

And I want him inside me again. I want him to come inside me.

His hand must be waiting on his zipper because the second I say, "Okay," I hear it unfasten. "Put your face in that pillow. This is going to be hard and fast and you can't cry out," he warns, positioning himself behind me.

I do as asked, his words alone making my pussy clench with anticipation.

His hands push against the inside of my thighs, guiding my legs farther apart, and then he presses his cock against me, into me. "Oh fuck, you feel like heaven."

I'm sore, but I ignore the ache because I have Henry inside me again. This angle feels different than being on my back. Less intimate, dirtier, sexier.

He reaches around to touch my clit with two fingers, rubbing in circles while he pulls his cock in and out several times, letting my body get accustomed to him.

"We don't have a lot of time. Are you ready?" Both of his hands grip my hips again, so tightly that I'm afraid I'll have bruises there.

"Yes."

This time when he pulls out, he slams back into me. I muffle my cry with the pillow.

"That's it, baby. Take it." He slams into me again, his pelvis hitting my ass.

And then his thrusts come hard and fast and punishing until, ten thrusts later, he's gritting his teeth as his cock pulses inside me.

As he fills me with his seed.

"I'm sorry you didn't come," he whispers, pulling out. A trail of wet drips out and down my thigh. His cum, spilling out of my pleasantly abused pussy. "Hold on a sec." Grabbing a tissue from a nearby box, he cleans me up and then slides my leggings back over my hips. "Feeling better now?" he asks, leaving a kiss on each ass cheek before climbing off the bed and opening a door to a tiny restroom. A tap turns on and I listen to him wash his hands.

I sigh with a smile. "Yes, I'm feeling better."

He smirks. "I'll meet you out on the dock."

I watch him leave, wondering for the thousandth time what I did to deserve that man's affections.

My phone dings with an incoming text from Jed. I take a quick glance.

**Jed:** *I've been thinking about you a lot lately.*

*Sure you have.* I toss my phone back into my purse and leave it there.

Unanswered.

~

"THIS PLACE IS..." My words trail off as I stare in awe at the giant log beams that run the length of the ceiling in awe.

"Rustic?"

"Yes," I agree, inhaling the scent of stale air and old cedar, pungent from lack of air circulation. "But stunning. I guess, because of the gold mines, I expected your grandparents to have something more like Wolf Cove."

"It's ironic, isn't it? My grandfather started a luxury hotel chain and yet he preferred the simple life. He built this himself, nearly sixty years ago." Henry palms the front of a massive stone fireplace that stretches two stories. "He built this whole place by himself."

It's not a huge, complicated cabin. If I had to guess, I'd say it's about two thousand square feet, with a great room overlooking the water, a loft with three small bedrooms, and a kitchen and dining area in the back. Everything is made of cedar and hemlock, from the cupboards down to the floors.

"This is where you spent your summers?"

Henry nods, pointing toward the antique kitchen stove. "My grandmother loved to bake and cook. She'd be in there every afternoon, making something for my brother and me." His hand runs across the rough wood mantel and a nostalgic smile touches his lips as he checks his hand for the thick layer of dust. "Some of the best days of my life were up here."

"Where are your grandparents now?"

"They both passed. Now this place sits here, like a tomb of my childhood memories." His gaze reaches the rafters. "I stayed here once, a few years ago. It wasn't the same."

"You need to make new memories here."

He seems to ponder that for a moment. "Yeah, maybe."

Hachiro pokes his head in from the porch. "Okay, I have the perfect setup. Can I get you out here?" He glances at me. "You look a lot better. More color in your cheeks."

"Yes. A lot rosier. Those drugs you have work well." Henry says mockingly.

I hide my embarrassed blush behind his broad back as I trail him out, giving him a playful jab in the side. "Yes, they definitely help."

"Okay, I want something casual and hip, but manly. Take the coat off for this one and throw that beanie on. Yeah, yeah... perfect," Hachiro murmurs, as Henry follows directions. I can almost feel the eye roll he's stifling. "Okay, now lean over the railing. Wait." He grabs the deck rail and shakes it. "This isn't going to break is it? I don't want you plummeting to your death."

"I'll be fine." Henry smirks, resting his forearms over the wood, his eyes catching mine for a brief second—flashing amusement—before refocusing on the camera. Hachiro has already started snapping.

I find my spot behind the spunky little photographer, mimicking Henry with my pose. The view of the cove here is much more quiet and peaceful. I can't even see the hotel from here, hidden by trees.

Below is a rocky shoreline. I picture a young, brown-haired Henry standing on the edge with a fishing rod, or splashing in the water. What must he have been like growing up? And what was his childhood like? So different from mine, I have to assume. Were his parents here with him? Did he get along with his brother as a boy?

I would love to spend time up here, just us. No Mr. Wolf and assistant. No worries of inappropriateness. Not that we've been acting at all worried. Maybe we should be more cautious. For a guy who could lose so much, he sure seems driven by his dick lately. Maybe the threat from his father is empty. Wolf Cove is doing exceptionally well, after all. How can his father begrudge him that?

If the last few days tell me anything, it's that a weekend alone here would be all-consuming lust. All Henry.

He is a surprisingly soft and passionate man.

But how long can this last?

And what will it be like to say good-bye to him at the end of summer?

These aren't thoughts I want to or should be having right now. We just only started this *thing.* And I just ended a lifelong relationship; I shouldn't be in a rush to find another one. I need to take step back and relax and enjoy him. Thrive on what he's giving me, which is incredible sex.

I don't even realize that Hachiro has turned the camera to point at me until I catch the lens from the corner of my eye. "What are you doing?"

He shrugs. "I saw a moment, and had to capture it. I'm a photographer, that's what I do. Okay, Mr. Wolf, one more of these and then we're golden."

My tall, beautiful man resumes his pose.

"Eyes over here."

He turns to look at Hachiro. Past Hachiro, locking gazes with me. In them is something unreadable.

# *twenty-four*

Mama must have ESP.

I swear that's the case, because the moment we step through the door of Penthouse Cabin One, my personal phone rings.

"You going to get that?" Henry tosses his jacket onto the chair and then, as if thinking better of it, he hangs it up on the entranceway hook.

"It's just home calling. And I have a pile of things I have to do for you."

"Go ahead and answer." He strolls past me, tossing his wallet and room keys on a side table and heading for his bedroom.

I heave a sigh. May as well get this over with, I guess. "Hi, Mama."

"Oh, you're there! I thought I'd be leaving *another* message."

"I know, I'm sorry. It's been a zoo around here with the hotel opening."

"You can make ten minutes for your mama, Abigail," she scolds in that stern voice.

"Yes. I know." And I could have, easily. She doesn't get that she's as much the reason I needed to get away as Jed is, and I don't have the heart to tell her.

"And why am I just hearing about this new job of yours? What happened to landscaping?"

I roll my eyes, playing through various degrees of separation between Mama and Lucy. Mama doesn't usually go to the feed mill and she doesn't like my childhood friend enough to strike up a conversation. Who am I kidding? She probably heard it from Jed. "It was a sudden change, but it's good. I'm making *a lot* more money." And enjoying it immensely.

"And this *man* that you're working for?" She spits the word out like it tastes bad.

"What about him?"

"I don't like the looks of him."

"You don't like good-looking men?" I laugh.

"That's exactly what I mean, Abigail," she snaps. "Men who look like that only want one thing from women."

I'm used to Mama's unfair judgment, but hearing it directed at Henry irritates me. "He's my boss, Mama. I'm here to schedule his meetings and keep him organized, that's all." Unease slips into my shoulders. I didn't hesitate to lie to her. I don't know that I've ever lied to her before. But she's overbearing, and I've had enough.

"Until he starts lookin' for more. 'Wolf.' What a name." She lets out a derisive snort.

"He's been nice to me."

"I'm sure he has. That's because he hasn't shown you his teeth yet. You be careful around him, you hear me? I'll bet he'd love to take advantage of a girl like you. I knew this was a bad idea, you going up there," she grumbles. "You should be back here, where you belong."

"He would never take advantage of me." I glance over my shoulder to make sure Henry isn't standing behind me.

"Like I said. You can't be trusting men like that. They lie and cheat until they get what they want. Mark my words: if you give him what he wants, he'll have you on the first plane back to Pennsylvania. You and him are from different worlds."

"He doesn't want *that* from me, Mama!" I say this with as much conviction in my voice as I can, even as I stare at my reflection in the mirror, my cheeks still flushed, and my body sore in all the best ways. I feel like a different person.

"I know how the world works."

*"How?* You've only ever been with Dad. You've never left Greenbank!" How worldly can she possibly be? I struggle to hide the growing frustration as that little voice in my head, the fearful one, asks if she could be right. What if she's right? Do I really think this is going to continue for four months? Only days after he hired me, I've already given my virginity to this man. *Days.* Will this last four days, let alone four months? Will he keep me around for that long? What if he gets bored with me?

I have to give Mama one thing: we certainly are from different worlds.

I'm scowling at my reflection. Leave it to her to introduce worrisome thoughts into my consciousness after a day of bliss.

"You already don't sound like yourself. Don't you be losing your way up there."

*Losing my way.* Since this whole turmoil with Jed, she has been afraid that I'll "lose my way."

I need her off this topic before she weasels the truth out of me, like only Mama can do. "How's everything at home? How's Dad? Managing the farm all right without me?" Dad will be turning forty-one this November and, while his health is leaps and bounds better than hers, he's not nearly as spry as he once was.

"Oh, you know your father. He's complaining about a sore back but won't leave the grain for the workers. Says they work hard enough. Jean's daughter had her baby. Eight pound girl. They named her Rosalina."

"Please pass on my congratulations." Jean has been working on our farm for as long as I can remember. His daughter, Jennifer, went to school with Jed and me.

"And Roger, over at the mill, his son's wife is expecting their second."

I tune my mama out. Three years ago when I told her I wanted to go to college, she pushed back and it was as much to do with me leaving home and getting an expensive education just to come back and run the farm, as it was because it would delay her goal for grandbabies. Now she makes sure to point out every person having babies. At least she's not talking about Jed, I guess.

"You wouldn't believe who came to Sunday service with that girl."

*Spoken too soon.*

"They sat right up in the front, holding hands, in church!" She tsks. "You've made yourself too easy to forget for that boy."

Will she ever let up? "He forgot about me when I was right in front of him."

"Maybe you didn't give him enough attention."

"You mean a blow job?" I snap.

"Abigail Mitchell! What on God's green earth has gotten into you?"

I hear the sound of the tap running in the en suite.

Henry. That's what's gotten into me. Well, that's *who's* gotten into me.

I take a deep, calming breath. "I don't want to hear about or talk about or think about Jed anymore, Mama. *He* left me. *He* screwed up. She can have him." I sound more confident than I feel.

Silence hangs over the receiver. "You *will* have to come back to reality, and that reality is your family, your church, this farm and, yes, Jed. Don't be coming back with regrets, Abigail."

Five minutes on the phone with her and I'm emotionally exhausted. "Call you in a few days."

We hang up and I simply stare at my reflection for a moment. As much as I want to push her words aside, I can't help but weigh her warning. Today has been incredible. Magical. Like nothing I could ever have predicted. It's happened fast and unexpectedly. But did I just flip an hourglass on my time here at Wolf Cove?

I'm still pondering that worry when Henry emerges.

"Is she still pushing for the big reconciliation?"

I turn to find him filling the doorframe, his dress pants already fastened, his button-down hanging open over a simple V-neck t-shirt. He wet and combed his hair back, and it's settling into a sexy mane of waves. I simply stare, mesmerized. How someone was placed on Earth looking that perfect, I'll never comprehend.

There are a lot of things I won't ever comprehend as they relate to Henry.

Mainly, why he wants me.

A frown creases his forehead. "What's going on?"

"Nothing."

"You're a terrible liar." He sighs and I don't miss the hint of irritation. "Remember what I said before? The only way this will work is if we trust each other."

"My mama doesn't like the look of you."

"The look of me?" He holds his hands to his chest in mock horror, his lack of concern almost comical. "That's odd. I don't think I've met a woman yet who didn't like the look of me."

"You ass." I giggle at his cockiness. "You're too handsome. She's convinced that you're going to try to sway me with your good looks and charm and lure me away from my Christian values."

"Your mama sounds smart." He pauses. "You denied that, of course."

"Of course."

He watches me for a moment, his perceptive gaze picking up my unease. "What else?"

I hesitate. "She warned me that if I 'lose my way' and commit the ungodly sin of premarital sex, you'll only fire me after."

"And do you believe that?"

I know I don't *want* to believe that. "I'm still here," I answer halfheartedly, not convincing at all.

He heaves a sigh, and that steely hard jaw takes over. It reminds me of the first night when he carried me drunk from the dock. "Follow me, please." An edge has crept into his tone, and I'm afraid that it's disappointment in me.

I perch on the edge of the bed to watch him dress. Another last minute-surprise a la Belinda, who caught us on the way up from the docks to tell us that the governor of Alaska was here and she'd arranged a dinner meeting on Henry's behalf.

He fastens the buttons on his shirt and I pout as his collarbone disappears from view. It's possibly one of the sexiest parts on him. No... who am I kidding. Every part of him is sexy as hell, down to his toes.

"I have a luxury hotel to see succeed, and an entire corporation to run from this remote spot in the world. I have a lot more on my plate than most men do. My stress levels are high. You'd agree, yes?"

"Yes, of course."

"I also like to fuck." The blunt, crass statement makes me blush. If he notices, he doesn't let on, his expression and tone serious. "It's one of my favorite things to do, especially when I'm stressed. I don't see myself *not* being stressed while I'm up here. And you—" He throws a black tie around his neck and wanders over to me. He doesn't need to ask anymore; I stand and gladly reach for the ends automatically. "—are my *very* capable personal assistant who I hired to take care of my needs while I'm here for the season." He reaches up to gently squeeze my bottom lip between his thumb and index finger. "You have these pouty, pink lips and big, beautiful tits that bounce and the sweetest, tightest pink hole that I've ever slid my cock into." The muscles inside it clench automatically. His grin is devilish. "And I don't care what you or your mama or anyone else may say. You also like to fuck. Don't you?"

I swallow hard, the feel of his hands on my skin, of his weight pressing me into the mattress, of him stretching and filling me so completely, still firmly emblazoned in my mind.

And nod.

"I enjoy fucking you." He pushes his index finger against my teeth and I open, allowing him access, sealing my lips over him to suck. "And I don't see that changing anytime soon. Okay?" His gaze drops to my lips and for a moment I think—I hope—that he's going to lean in and kiss me. "I have to go now. I can't keep the Governor waiting, or I'll never hear the end of it from Belinda."

*Belinda.* "You and her... Was it serious?"

He heaves a sigh. "I don't discuss my past relationships, Abbi."

I nod, feeling chastised.

After a long moment, and perhaps because of the look on my face, he offers, "It was one night, two years ago. I was drunk and under a great deal of stress and she made herself available. I've regretted it every day since. But I didn't fire her after. So hopefully that puts your mind at ease."

"It does. Thank you." It also strikes me with a moment of insane jealousy, knowing those lips that have devoured me have also devoured someone else. Someone for whom I have a face and name. But I have to push that aside because I'm sure Henry has been with *many* women. That's the reality of a man as powerful and beautiful and seductive as him.

"What time do you want me to get here in the morning?"

"I don't want you here in the morning." He says it so coolly.

I frown, confused.

"I want you waiting for me when I get back."

Tonight? My heart skips three beats. I get more time with Henry. "I guess I have enough work to keep me busy."

He pushes strands of my hair off my forehead, tucking them behind my ear. "Do whatever you want. Order dinner, watch a movie, take a long, hot bath."

I moan at the sound of that last option, my poor body sore from overuse.

Henry slides his hand down the front of my leggings and into my panties, to push a single finger inside me again.

"Make sure you spend a lot of time thinking about what I'm going to do to you tonight when I get home."

I instantly grow slick around his finger and it slips in and out of me easily.

I stifle my whimper as he pulls his hand away and sticks the finger into his mouth, sucking it clean. The sight is so intimate, so depraved. So erotic.

He smirks. "What's that look?"

"Is this how all men are?"

He considers that for a moment, and then takes a step forward, his hand finding purchase on my ass and pulling me in to him until his erection presses hard against my stomach. "I don't know other men. I know me, and I want to violate every square inch of this tight little body when I get back."

He plants a contradictory peck on my nose, and then releases me. With a casual wave over his head, he heads out the door to meet the governor of Alaska. With an erection.

Leaving me with hours to kill.

My eyes crack open to take in the low glow of the fire. It was burning bright when I made myself comfortable on the living room's lush shag rug with a bowl of squash soup and a raspberry mousse, courtesy of room service. How long ago was that?

Turning to check the clock on the wall, I gasp at the sight of Henry sitting in the armchair a few feet away, his tie undone, his shirt unbuttoned, his shoes kicked off, a crystal glass of amber liquid—alcohol, I'm assuming—balanced between his fingertips.

Simply watching me.

I move to rub my eyes, and then remember my contacts. That's why my eyes are so blurry. Crap. I never planned on falling asleep. The rug was so soft, the fire so warm. "What time is it?" Darkness looms beyond the windows.

"Almost midnight."

I allow a yawn to escape and then wince as I adjust my body. Every square inch of me is sore. "When did you get home?"

"An hour ago."

I frown. "Why didn't you wake me?"

"Because I like watching you sleep. And because I needed time to think."

Something in his tone sounds ominous. Is he second-guessing us? Or maybe that's just my paranoia infiltrating my mind, creating issues where there aren't any. That this is going to end eventually is not so much paranoia as fact, though.

I just don't want that ending to be now.

Swallowing my panic, I make to crawl for his chair.

He holds up a hand, staying me.

I don't know what to do or say, so I say nothing and sit quietly, watching him stare first at me, then at his phone.

Finally, he turns it around and shows me the screen.

It's my profile shot, with the weak gust of wind blowing a few strands of my vibrant red hair. I'm peering off into the distance below, a faint smile touching my lips. I've never seen myself look like that. "That's from today?"

"Hachiro sent me the shots he wants to put forward for the magazine, for approval. He included this one as a gift to you."

"That was nice of him." I feel bad for rolling my eyes at the little photographer now.

"I know. Maybe I should have agreed to those nudes after all."

We share a laugh, but the silence that hangs in the air afterward is deafening.

"Is something the matter?"

His lips purse, but he doesn't answer.

So I throw his own words back at him. "If this is going to work, we have to trust and be honest with each other."

"My father says I make too many selfish, reckless decisions. Sometimes I wonder if maybe he's right." He carefully sets his phone on the end table. "You are such a wholesome, innocent girl. You're a people pleaser. And you came here highly vulnerable. I saw that the moment I watched that video of you. I've exploited it."

I struggle to keep my composure, to not jump to conclusions. But this is quite the turn of events. He left here at dinnertime promising to violate me when he got home. Now it sounds like he's regretting the last couple of days. My stomach tightens at the thought of him regretting it. *I* certainly don't regret it.

"Did you know that you wanted *this* then?"

"To fuck you? No." He pauses a beat. "I fuck supermodels and CEOs. Women who tell me they want my cock five minutes into a conversation, and who don't give a shit whether others approve. You can't even get through a five-minute conversation with your mother without feeling guilty. You took me by complete surprise. I shouldn't have acted on it, and yet I was too weak to control myself."

"I'm glad you were." I can't help the tremble in my voice. None of this is what I want to hear.

He opens his mouth but falters. Instead of answering, he reaches for his drink. How much has he had tonight? Is that what this is about? Is he drunk and pensive? He's not slurring, but I don't know him well enough to judge that.

"I don't know if this is fair to you. I'm afraid of how I might taint you," he says, adding softly, "more than I already have."

"You haven't tainted me." I plead for him to see it in my eyes, if he can't believe it from my words.

He settles his forehead against his fingertips, and closes his eyes. "I'm not so sure."

I don't want this to happen. I don't want him to take away the intimacy that he *just* gave me. "Well, then maybe I want to be tainted." I can't believe I'm speaking so brazenly, but if that's what I need to do to get this afternoon's Henry back, I'll say and do anything.

Nearly a minute passes where we face each other but say nothing, where he struggles with his internal conflict. I can see it in his eyes. He hasn't veiled it behind his usual mask. Finally he sighs, his jaw tensing with his hard swallow. "Fine. Take off your clothes." The demand is made in a soft voice, and yet his gaze is hard as he simply sits there, watching.

I inhale deeply, steeling myself for what I want—to give Henry *everything* he wants. Pinching the hem of my shirt between my fingers, I slowly peel it off and toss it to the floor next to me. Henry watches with dark, hungry eyes as I reach back and unfasten my bra, letting it fall to my lap. My breasts spill out, my nipples already tight with anticipation. My chest heaves with my breaths. Climbing to my knees, I hook my thumbs under the waistband of my leggings and slide them down all the way to my knees, taking my panties with them, until I can take a seat on the floor and wriggle out of them semi-gracefully.

Leaving me naked on Henry's rug by the fire, my heart

racing. Waiting quietly for him. Still, he makes no move, simply assessing me from his vantage point.

It reminds me of a television program I once saw, of a lone wolf that sat quietly at the edge of a meadow, watching a doe graze. It looked as passive as Henry does now, sitting in that chair.

The doe's tail and ears twitched; she knew the wolf was there, waiting, calculating. She knew she was in danger. And she also knew that there was truly no running from that wolf; that run or not, the wolf would end up devouring her. So she simply tried to enjoy the last few peaceful moments of her life, grazing in that field.

"Lie back."

I do, resting on my elbows so I can still see him, flutters stirring in my stomach as I spread my legs, hoping to entice him over. His gaze over my slit is searing, and I feel myself growing wet.

"Touch yourself."

"What?" *In front of him?* Unease slips down my back.

There is no hint of a smile touching his lips. "You heard me. Touch yourself like you did that night you made yourself come in your room, thinking of me." When I still don't move, he adds a softer, "please."

I don't know why I'm so shy about this after what we've already done, and how much Henry turns me on. I shouldn't be. He wants this and he's asking me for it. Swallowing my nerves, I lie back until my head rests against the rug and drag tentative fingers over my navel, stalling at the small strip of pubic hair left.

Closing my eyes, my cheeks flaming, I finally let my index finger slip down to brush first my clit and then lower down to my slick opening. As nervous as I am right now,

Henry's eyes alone make me wet. Or maybe it's the depravity of this act.

Like a stealthy animal, he slides off the chair to land on the floor in front of me on his knees, his eyes raking over my naked body beneath him on the rug. "Don't stop," he commands, when my hand pulls away to reach for him.

He watches me as I draw slow circles around my clit. I desperately want him to undress but he doesn't; he simply kneels before me, his lips parted, his steely gaze on my hand.

"You look sore. Are you?"

"Yes," I admit in a whisper, because, as wet and turned on as I am, there's no avoiding the aftereffects of today.

Finally...

Finally, Henry grabs hold of my slender hips and pulls me off the ground and up high, until my legs are slung over his shoulders and I'm staring down at him, his soft breaths skimming across my sore pussy. His tongue snakes out to take a swipe along my slit. "I should never have been so rough with you today. That's what I mean about being selfish. I knew it was too much and I did it anyway." He licks again, this time with a flat tongue, the warmth from it soothing enough to pull a soft moan from me.

My arms are splayed out on either side of me, his fingers digging in to my hips to hold me up, my back resting along his body, his hard cock pressed against my spine. It's not the most comfortable of positions but I don't care.

"Watch what I'm doing to you," he demands, and I do, watching with fascination as his mouth opens and his tongue curls around and around my clit.

The moment I start to feel the build in my pelvis, Henry's eyes flash with satisfaction. He somehow knows I'm close to orgasm. He guides my body down and, in with a few quick tugs and pulls, his pants are undone, his cock is out, and he's pushing into me.

I cry out at the sudden pressure and the deep angle, with him still on his knees and my hips pulled up to meet him, but he doesn't slow down, hooking his arms around the backs of my thighs and driving into me over and over again until I'm so wet that his thrusts become noisy with slick slaps. There's something different about this time—the look in his eyes, the lack of words, the steely gritted tension in his jaw—that sets off an alarm somewhere in the back of my mind.

But I ignore it, unable to focus on anything right now but my euphoric high.

My orgasm comes on so suddenly that I'm not ready for it, and Henry is pounding against me so hard and fast that it's paralyzing in its ferocity.

He follows only moments later, grunting rather than crying out, his muscular body straining beneath his shirt. The moment I feel the last jerking pulse of his cock, he pulls out and releases my body to slide down to the ground like a floppy rag doll, fully spent.

"Get dressed. I'll walk you home." He stands and heads immediately for the bathroom.

Leaving me lying naked on the white rug.

Feeling truly used for the first time, and not in a good way.

I struggle with my confusion as I pull my clothes on.

We walk in complete silence all the way to the staff village, two feet between us at all times and, when we reach cabin seven, all Henry says is, "See you at seven tomorrow morning."

I stare after him until he disappears into trees and darkness, bewildered.

# twenty-five

The morning sun is streaming through the window when I arrive at seven. Henry's already dressed in his suit and at the desk, typing furiously.

"Good morning," I offer, helping myself to a cup of coffee. Despite going to bed with tangled thoughts, my body shut down and did not want to restart this morning when my alarm went off at six. While I hoped I'd wake up having come up with some logical explanation for Henry and his severe swings in mood and intentions, all I woke up accepting is that I have no idea which version of Henry I'm going to get when I walk in today.

He finishes up what he's doing and hits Send before offering a "good morning" back. His eyes settle on me through a sip of his coffee. "How are you feeling today?"

*Because you abused my body yesterday?* "Fine."

"Good." He nods more to himself, a thought skittering behind those blue eyes. "I have a meeting with some people this morning, and my father and brother are arriving in the afternoon, along with droves of media flying in for tomorrow's grand opening event. There will be a lot going on, and a lot of people will want my attention. It's going to be a stressful time for me."

"How do you plan on handling that stress?" I keep my tone neutral, though the implication is thick.

He offers only a tight smile. "Things will be different around here for a few days."

I get his meaning. *Around here* means between us. I can't blame him for that. "Just let me know how I can best help with the circus."

"I will. Thank you." His eyes finally lift to meet mine. I see worry in there. And something else. A touch of fear. "I can trust you to remain discreet, right? What we had—have—will stay between the two of us?"

"Of course." My heart tightens at the past tense slip, but I blame it on his nerves. His mind is clearly wrapped up in something. I'm sure it has to do with his father, and all the media attention.

Finishing the last of his coffee, he stands to leave. Taking a few steps away, he stalls, then turns and walks back to plant a soft kiss on my lips.

"Everything will be okay."

He gives me a tight smile and then heads out the door.

I guess I need to get used to this, with a guy as successful and important as Henry.

It'll certainly keep things interesting around here.

With a sigh, I take the seat he just vacated and open his e-mail inbox. One of those "Confidential—Legal" e-mails sits on top. It must have come in last night, while I was passed out on the carpet. It's no longer bolded so I know he has seen it.

I make to drag it into the Legal folder but I accidently click on it instead. I'm aiming the mouse for the "x" to close it when a name catches my eyes.

Kiera.

That name that both Belinda and those men that day around the table mentioned.

I can't help myself.

*Henry,*

*Kiera's lawyer has informed me that she has decided not to sign and accept the settlement we're offering. Her husband has persuaded her to file a civil suit against Wolf Hotels. She is also pressing criminal charges against you for forced sexual intercourse. We need to get PR involved for damage control ASAP, and discuss what the prosecutors may be able to dig up on similar indiscretions, etc. The media will eat this up. I haven't informed your father yet. Would you prefer to do it?*

*Call me.*

*D.C.*

I FEEL the blood drain from my face. Forced sexual intercourse? Damage control? Criminal charges? Similar indiscretions, etc.?

This can't be about Henry. But it is. It says the charges are going to be against him.

With shaky fingers over the mouse, I scan the e-mails in the folder marked "confidential." They're all correspondence between Henry and some guy named Dyson, a Wolf attorney based on his signature. E-mails about paperwork for a settlement being delivered, and such. I scroll further back, to an e-mail from a month ago with an attachment for review.

I click on the attachment.

It's a sixteen-page settlement offer to Mrs. Kiera Clayton, former Wolf Hotel employee, whose position was terminated three months ago.

Her position as Henry's personal assistant.

And she's being offered several hundred thousand dollars in exchange for her agreement for complete confidentiality, including discussion of any sexual relationship she may have had with her boss.

Henry M. Wolf.

I curl my arm around my stomach as it begins to churn, threatening to kick its contents out. "Oh God."

What kind of man did I just get involved with?

~

Did you enjoy Tempt Me? If so, please leave a review.

~

Abbi and Henry's story continues in Break Me, The Wolf Hotel #2, available now.

# sneak peek: break me (the wolf hotel, #2)

"Crap, crap, crap..." I pace around the dining table, my arms hugging my stomach in attempt to quell the nauseating churn as I dwell on the contents of those e-mails.

The confidential ones that Henry told me under no circumstances to read.

Now I know why.

Henry's a... what, a rapist? Is that what that lawyer, Dyson, meant when he said Kiera is pressing criminal charges for forced sexual intercourse? What on earth did Henry do to his last assistant? His *married* assistant.

Whatever it was, it was enough to try and buy her off with a couple hundred thousand dollars and a gag order. That's what Henry and his dad were talking about, that day I overheard them talking on the phone. Kiera is the "unfortunate situation" that Henry was sure was resolved, which means Henry's father knows all about this.

Is it true? Is it possible that this beautiful, complicated man who made sure I didn't end up at the bottom of the bay that first night, who didn't so much as kiss me back when I drunkenly threw myself at him the first night, is the type of man to force himself on a woman?

I don't know Henry at all. I can *think* I know him. I can pine over those intimate moments—about him carrying my inebriated butt home, about him in the woods that day, with his protective arm around me to calm me about the grizzly, about the worried look on his face when I was sick on the boat—and I can convince myself that he would never force himself on a woman. I can picture his handsome face and perfect masculine form, and tell myself that he'd *never have* to force himself on anyone because no woman would ever *not* willingly give herself to him.

But I don't really know him. I've known him for a hot minute. I'd be an idiot to convince myself otherwise. I'd be the silly farm girl everyone believes me to be.

I groan. My exciting summer of escape, my chance to shed the pain that Jed caused and the control my mother holds over me, this intoxicating cloud that has consumed me since the moment I met Henry, it's all over. Everything has changed with the accidental stroke of a key.

Why did I have to read that e-mail? Why couldn't I have remained ignorant?

Then again, if what that lawyer says is true, I'll be hearing about it soon enough anyway. Around the same time that everyone else does. And then they'll all be looking at me, his new assistant. Wondering, questioning. Has the billionaire heir to Wolf Hotels forced himself on his latest assistant, too? Am I one of those "similar indiscretions" that Henry and his lawyer will want to discuss? How many are there?

What if everyone figures out that we've slept together?

What if they call me to testify at Henry's trial? I'll be under oath. I'll have to admit that we've slept together but that it wasn't rape, that it was consensual—*very* consensual—and then the media will hear about it and report it. It'll be all over the newspapers, and Mama and everyone in Greenbank will be talking about how I willingly had a sexual relationship with Henry Wolf, the rapist, and Reverend Enderbey will preach at Sunday service about how I was tempted by the devil.

"Crap, crap, crap!" I can barely breathe, my chest is so tight with panic.

I just don't get it! Henry is aggressive and mercurial and he can be an outright ass in public, but he's never actually done anything to harm me, or that I didn't want, or enjoy. So what exactly happened between him and this Kiera? Does he have a thing for sleeping with his assistants? Did she say no and did he not accept it?

A squeal escapes me as the shrill ring of my work phone cuts into the silence of Penthouse Cabin One, temporarily paralyzing me.

There's only one person who could be calling me on that line.

I let it ring once... twice... three times, and if I don't get it soon, he's going to know I read those e-mails that I wasn't supposed to read. Should I even care? Do I have a right to be 100 percent appalled with him and not feel guilty? Hell, yes, I do!

Unless there's been some big misunderstanding. Unless that tiny voice in the back of my head that tells me this can't be true is right.

Either way, I'm not going to find out by avoiding his calls.

"Get it together, Abbi," I mutter as I round the table and head for the desk where my phone sits. Where he had me naked and spread out only yesterday morning. God, it was only yesterday! I've only been working for him for a week! For all the time we've spent together, it feels like an eternity ago. It's like the moment Henry touched me, I fell through this strange rabbit hole into an alternate reality, where time and intelligence don't matter.

All that has mattered is hot inappropriate sex with my boss.

But now I've been kicked out of that rabbit hole, and into a swirl of confusion, panic, and overwhelming disappointment.

"Hello? Hi. Hey." I purse my lips together to stop myself from babbling, as I tend to do when I get nervous.

"I need you in the lobby right now." Henry's deep melodic voice fills my ear, only now it's the abrupt version I get whenever we're in public, not the husky one he reserves for sending shivers through my body.

I know what I'm supposed to say. *Yes, Mr. Wolf, I'll be right there.* I'm supposed to grab my things and run to him. But when I open my mouth, I'm hit with the overwhelming urge to demand the truth. I let this man inside me, after all. I gave him something personal and private and cherished. I gave him *me*. I have a right to know if my life is about to be thrown into a mixer and set to high speed because of something horrible that he did.

"Abbi!"

I jump at the bark in my ear. "Yes?"

"Did you hear me?"

This isn't a conversation for the phone. "I'll see you in a few minutes."

"No, I won't be there. I need you to greet the reporter from *Luxury Travel* magazine."

I frown. "Roshana Mafi?" The one who is receiving

flowers with a personally written card from Henry? I thought he was meeting all the key media contacts himself.

"Yeah. Sure," he mutters dismissively. I can hear his dress shoes click against the floor. He's likely in one of the lower-level staff areas. Wherever he is, it's quiet and he's walking quickly.

"What time will she be there?"

"How the fuck would I know?" he snaps, but then heaves a sigh. "Ask Belinda. I have some important calls I need to make."

Not any I scheduled because his calendar is clear for greeting key guests. I'm guessing one of those calls is to his attorney. Henry's stressed, that much is obvious.

"Should I have Belinda greet her instead?"

"No. There was an incident between them years ago. She hates Belinda."

I roll my eyes. I'm not going to ask for details. "Okay. Is there anything specific you want me to tell her?"

"That I'll see her later. Actually, send Michael to her for an in-room massage. She'll like that and it'll keep her occupied."

"Okay." I hold my breath, waiting to hear the line go dead so I know I can hang up.

There's a long pause. "What took you so long to answer?" Suspicion laces his tone.

"Peeing. I mean, restroom," I blurt out, because it's the first thing that comes to mind. I cringe, waiting for him to call me a liar, to confront me.

"Make sure she gets settled in." The line goes dead.

~

"Who did he say he's meeting with?" Belinda's black patent heel taps impatiently on the marble.

"He has a few important calls to make."

"More important than *this*? Show me his calendar." Glossy crimson claws stretch for my iPad, but I hug it tight to my chest, earning her sigh of frustration. "Well, doesn't he have you trained well already."

I say nothing and stare out at the dark blue waters and, beyond that, an endless sea of evergreens reaching all the way to the mountain range, still capped with white in mid-May. Alaska is still as breathtakingly beautiful as the first time I took it in.

Only, the magic of Wolf Cove has been sullied.

"Does this have to do with his father coming in? Because I swear, every time William Wolf is within a mile radius, Henry starts acting all reckless."

"Maybe. I don't know. He didn't say." That e-mail from the lawyer makes me think that telling Henry's father about the pending charges and the lawsuit is not going to be easy. I wonder how his father is going to react. It sounds like he holds Wolf Hotels' reputation on a pedestal.

The ferry rounding the corner distracts Belinda from pressing me for more information about Henry's whereabouts. "Okay, ten minutes and counting. Here's her room key." She thrusts the card toward me. "She's staying in Penthouse Cabin Two."

"Beside Henr—I mean, Mr. Wolf?" Henry was adamant that he is *always* Mr. Wolf outside the privacy of his cabin walls.

"Yes. As requested by Mr. Wolf, himself. Call Housekeeping and ask them to deliver her welcome package in exactly five minutes; we don't want the ice bucket melting. And have her liaison ready. She needs to be fully entertained until Mr. Wolf frees himself from whatever it is that he's doing."

"Already taken care of. Michael will be coming shortly."

"Massage?"

I nod. "Mr. Wolf's request."

She gives a small nod of satisfaction, adjusting her heavy black-rimmed glasses and smoothing her movie-star blonde waves. "Roshana Mafi needs to be impressed. We need nothing short of an exemplary review from her. Can you handle all of this?"

"Yes."

"Really? Because your breasts are practically hanging out."

My eyes drop to my gaping shirt in a panic, where the top button has slipped out of the slightly too-large buttonhole again. It's a replacement blouse, after Henry tore the buttons off my other one. "This button won't hold," I mutter, fumbling with it as my cheeks heat.

"The cleaners should have a safety pin for you to use until we can get you another shirt. Button your blazer. That might help." At least Belinda doesn't sound mad about it. As the hotel manager, she's next in charge below Henry. She also wears low-cut tops that intentionally flaunt her breasts, so this is a pot and kettle moment if there ever was one.

I fasten the single oversized button at my waist. I don't know how much that really helps though. It's more for fashion than function.

"Okay. Do you remember everything I told you?" She's never hidden the fact that she thinks I'm dimwitted.

I make sure my head is turned away when I roll my eyes. "Yes. I'll be fine." In truth, I'm so preoccupied with the e-mail bomb I opened this morning, I've barely listened to a word Belinda has said. But I'm not too worried, because if what Henry's attorney wrote is true, then no exemplary review will save Henry or Wolf Hotels from the coming shit storm.

"Oh, and one more thing... Roshana's a viper. Don't take anything she says personally."

I heave a sigh. *Great. Can't wait.*

~

**Continue with Henry Wolf**

# *also by k.a. tucker*

*The Wolf Hotel Series*:

Tempt Me (#1)

Break Me (#2)

Teach Me (#3)

Surrender To Me (#4)

Own Me (#5)

*Empire Nightclub Series:*

Sweet Mercy (#1)

Gabriel Fallen (#2)

Dirty Empire (#3)

Fallen Empire (#4)

For K.A. Tucker's entire backlist, visit katuckerbooks.com

# about the author

K.A. Tucker writes captivating stories with an edge.

She is the internationally bestselling author of the Ten Tiny Breaths and Burying Water series, He Will Be My Ruin, Until It Fades, Keep Her Safe, The Simple Wild, Be the Girl, and Say You Still Love Me. Her books have been featured in national publications including USA Today, Globe & Mail, Suspense Magazine, Publisher's Weekly, Oprah Mag, and First for Women.

K.A. Tucker resides outside of Toronto. Learn more about K.A. Tucker and her books at katuckerbooks.com

Milton Keynes UK
Ingram Content Group UK Ltd.
UKHW020643300924
449049UK00010B/79